**Other Mysteries by
Martha Kemm Landes**

Upcycled To Death

FRAMED FUR MURDER

By

Martha Kemm Landes

Elemar Publishing

This is a work of fiction.
All identities, locations and situations
have been greatly embellished.

www.marthalandes.com

Pitymystery@gmail.com

Print ISBN: 978-1-956912-25-8
e-Book ISBN: 978-1-956912-26-5

Cover design by Tahomina Mitu

First Edition

Dedication

This book is dedicated to my husband, Dan,
who introduced me to South Dakota and
spent many hours editing Framed Fur Murder.

I would also like to honor the state of South Dakota.
I was quickly charmed by its rolling prairies,
dramatic Black Hills, and friendly midwestern people.
During my five years there, I experienced cold and snow
like never before and even got to see sun dogs!
Living by a lake, I saw pheasants and waterfowl daily.
I was introduced to hot dish, bars, lefse,
wild game feeds (yum), and lutefisk (not my favorite).
Because of my awesome community development
position with SDSU Extension, I traversed the state
and met incredible people from rural South Dakota.

Special thanks to all those friends and community
members who welcomed me and shared their lovely northern
way of life. Because of my buddies, Dot, and the Kratochvils,
I even learned to cross-country ski and ice fish!

Framed Fur Murder

Martha Kemm Landes

CHAPTER 1

When a voice squawked, "Say cheese!" the toddler, dressed in yards of frilly pink lace, giggled and answered in an unnaturally high voice, "Cheese!"

I couldn't imagine a better expression and took my chance. Click. I studied the camera's LCD screen. There it was; the perfect shot of the curly-haired, dimpled three-year-old.

Little Emma looked more like she was sitting in a cloud of cotton candy than wearing an Easter dress. Her clear blue eyes sparkled as she squeezed her pet bunny with her mouth open in delight. What family member could resist a copy of that photo?

Emma beamed and pointed as she squealed, "Funny birdy!"

I turned my head cautiously to the right, hoping my eye would miss the beak of my spunky parrot perched on my right shoulder. He replied in his somewhat harsh voice, "Pretty girl."

When the little girl giggled in delight I said, "His name is Flash." I pulled a peanut from my pocket and paid my associate.

Emma shouted, "Hi Fas," in the cutest voice ever. As much as I don't love kids, I had to admit she was precious.

A different voice screeched in my left ear without warning, "Oh, look at that! It's perfect!" I whipped my head around and my mouth filled with the mother's mousy brown hair.

I jerked my head to the right so Emma's mom could see the camera screen, but mainly so I could spit out her hair. Gross.

Trying to be polite, I said, "Anna, I'm glad you like it, but we're not finished yet. I'll show you all the images soon. So, if you don't mind standing...over there." I pointed again to the place near my coffeemaker where I had asked her to wait several times before.

Anna had been a year behind me in school and even though I didn't know her well, I remembered she was annoying. Still oblivious to her invasion of space, she ran to her daughter and repositioned the squirmy rabbit.

In a babyish voice, similar to her toddler's, Anna squeaked, "Emma, do what Miss Ande says. She's an expert. She took that pretty picture of your friend, Skye. We want one like that."

Emma ignored her mom, clearly mesmerized by my secret photography weapon. Who could blame her? I adopted Flash almost a year ago and he still enthralled me. When I discovered my parrot could be an asset to my photography studio, I taught the very talkative bird a few choice phrases. He was incredibly gifted at getting the attention of kids and loved his new job. Since Flash started working for me, he stopped pulling out his feathers. I just hoped my secret never got out because I, Andrea Nilsen, of "Picture This on Main" wanted to have the only photography studio in South Dakota with a feathered employee.

I pulled down the backdrop of a Blue Spruce and positioned Emma in front of the life-sized tree. When the bunny wiggled more, I worried he was getting stressed and said, "Let's take this picture without Snowball." I reluctantly handed the incredibly soft rabbit to Anna and imagined the amazing shots I could get of the sweet black and white furball by itself. After all, I prefer taking photos of animals to humans.

Back at my tripod, just as I prepared to take a photo, Anna spoke in her irritating voice. "The tree looks so real, Ande. Where did you find that backdrop?"

I concentrated on Emma, not wanting to miss a good shot, and snapped a few pictures before answering. "My brother is an art major. He painted it."

Anna squealed, "Are you talking about Jon? Wow. He's really good!"

It made sense that Anna would know Jon since he had been a top basketball player, star baseball player, and prom king at Brookings High School. I answered, "Yes, he's the one."

She continued with rapid-fire questions. "He's really good. Does he go to SDSU?"

"Yes. Jon's a junior."

She wrinkled her nose. "I thought he would be graduating this year. He's my sister's age, right?"

I didn't want to get too personal with this woman whom I barely knew, so I told a partial truth. "Jon changed his major and is taking a little more time than he expected to finish."

In reality, Jon had planned to graduate this spring, but after some problems with alcohol and minor scrapes with the law, he got behind in his studies. Not only that, but he lost his job and subsequently couldn't pay rent, so he moved in with me. Now, I share my tiny one-bedroom apartment with him and he paints my backdrops to earn his keep. But, this woman didn't need to know all the details of Jon's life.

I shook off thoughts of my sweet, talented brother and told myself to focus – literally.

Eye to the viewfinder, I said, "Flash, I need your help."

In response, Flash shifted his feet on my shoulder and squawked, "Smile at the birdy!"

Emma laughed and I clicked. After several more backdrops and props, Emma climbed off the stool and said with a voice that could have been helium induced, "Can I pet Fas?"

I gulped. "Um…I'm not sure that's a good idea." I pictured how he easily cracked hard walnut shells with his beak. Just imagining what he could do to her tiny fingers made me shudder.

Anna waved me off. "Oh, I'm sure he's fine. Emma, just be gentle, like with Michael's hamster."

Giving in, I straightened my left forefinger and held it to my shoulder as a perch for Flash. The parrot stepped up one foot at a time, his claws gripping my finger firmly. With his head twisted to the side, he studied the child with one eye. My finger (and the bird) slowly lowered towards the girl. When he neared Emma,

Flash tucked his beak into his chest, which I knew meant, "Pet my head."

As her tiny fingers inched toward the bird, I held my breath, praying Flash would be nice. Emma gently ruffled the soft green feathers of his head back and forth. I sighed heavily, then quickly lifted him back up to safety, whispering "Good boy" into his feathers.

With Flash safely back on his tall perch next to his cage, I gave him another peanut. He cracked it and tossed the shell across the room causing Emma to shriek with laughter.

Once Anna had chosen her images and paid for the sitting fee and photos, I opened the door and said, "Nice to see you again. Watch your step. Goodbye Emma and Snowball."

Emma cried out, "Happy Meal!" as she exited.

I frowned to see a crumpled bag and cup from the famous fast food joint laying by my door. Disgusted, I explained, "Sorry. That must have been left by one of the construction workers."

I picked up the trash, which was not from a Happy Meal but rather a Quarter Pounder, and looked down the street. There, stood members of the construction crew smoking and laughing. What a waste of taxpayers' money.

Anna said, "No darling, we can't go to McDonald's today." This caused Emma to erupt into a full-on tantrum." Jeez. Just when I thought I'd finally met a decent child.

I threw the trash away and smiled at the huge order Anna had placed. Most of the prints would be of the first winning shot. In that one session, I had made almost enough to pay my studio rent for a month.

With only thirty minutes to set up for the next photo shoot, I tried to make things perfect. I was nervous about photographing the family of Brookings' new mayor, Carter Fox. I'd never met him, but his picture was always in The Register and his wife was a known socialite in town. A good recommendation from this couple could bring in more customers.

The family arrived promptly at 2 o'clock, looking as though they had come to pose for a fashion magazine. The parents were dressed impeccably. The mayor wore a sleek dark gray suit with a blue tie that matched her blue flowered dress. A boy and girl who looked to be the same age followed. They too wore coordinating outfits of blue.

"Hi, Mr. Fox. I'm Ande." I held my hand out to the mayor, who took it. His hand was surprisingly warm considering the cold temperature outside.

"This is my wife, Debra, and our twins, Simon and Simone."

Seriously? Could they have chosen more hoity-toity names?

I nodded to Debra and leaned down to the kids. "Let me guess...you two are in the third grade?" I figured they were younger than that, but nothing makes kids happier than people thinking they are older. I wish the same were true with adults.

Instead of the smiles and giggles I had expected, Simon twitched his mouth and rolled his eyes with an air of superiority. "No. I am six and she's six too. We're in the first grade."

The girl looked me up and down and spat, "You're short."

Well, that was blunt. But I had to admit at only five-foot-one, I felt like a fellow first-grader, especially when standing by their mother with mile-long legs.

Before I could reply, Simone yelled, "Is that a bird?" She ran over to the cage and jumped up, trying to grab Flash. I flew across the room to shield my parrot from the child.

Mr. Fox calmly walked over to us, took the girl's hand, and led her back. When she screamed like a toddler, I began to dread the photoshoot. Why, oh why couldn't I make enough money to only do pet photos? I really couldn't stand bratty kids.

I sighed at the near-miss with Flash and picked up my portfolio saying cheerfully to the couple, "So, what kind of portraits are you hoping for today? Here are examples of the backdrops and lighting available."

The woman blatantly turned her head away as if she had no interest in being there, so I handed the book to Mr. Fox.

After flipping through the photo options, he handed the book back to me with a smile, "Nice! You're clearly the expert. We trust you to decide."

As I set up a black backdrop I kept my eyes on the unpredictable children, then positioned the family for their first pose.

Although Flash did his job and said the perfect things at just the right time, it was difficult to capture good photos of the unruly twins. One or the other seemed to always have eyes closed or a head turned. The parents, however, posed like professional models. The stoic, handsome Carter had dark eyes that pierced through my lens and Debra's luxurious honey-colored hair could easily promote Pantene. It was uncanny how she turned her grimace into a beaming smile the moment the shutter closed.

At one point the wife crinkled her forehead and said, "What is that ungodly noise?"

The mayor said, "It's just the construction on Main Street, Debra. Nothing to worry about."

"Well, it's giving me a horrific headache."

I had to agree with the woman. The pounding was awful.

After numerous attempts and very little help from the parents in corralling the children, I finally managed to get some decent shots.

While I was busy changing backdrops, Simon screamed, "I want to see my picture!" I turned in horror to see the boy try to grab my camera from the tripod. Thankfully, Mr. Fox took charge just before the whole thing toppled over. Oh my gosh! Bring Emma and Snowball back, please!

When we finally finished, Mr. Fox approached me to pay the sitting fee and place their order. I couldn't help but stare up at the dark-haired hunk standing only inches from me. Dang, he had it all: wealth, looks, and he smelled so good I almost leaned in to get a better whiff.

Even though the Fox family was fairly new to town, Carter was already famous for his philanthropic endeavors. I should have addressed him as 'Your Highness' or at least 'Mayor Fox' while placing him for photos. But instead, I had just blurted, "Mom and Dad, you sit here."

Debra stood impatiently by the door looking at her fingernails while the kids wrestled around my studio. I was torn between grabbing the twins by the ears and staying in the comfort of the handsome man's aura. With no imminent danger I chose Zen mode. I watched Mr. Fox study the images on my computer and mark his choices for prints.

"These are amazing, Ande."

After calculating the order, I handed the mayor my iPad, hoping he wouldn't balk at the price. But he gave me his credit card without blinking, and I slid it through my Square.

In a deep sexy voice, Carter said, "My mother is turning 70 and we'd like to have a group photo with the extended family to surprise her. Can you do that?"

I said, "Of course! I don't mind large groups." I waited for the card to go through.

He looked at my small studio. "We wouldn't all fit in here. Can you do photos outside?"

I gave a nervous laugh. "Have camera will travel! I'll go anywhere – a park or…your house."

In truth, I was dying to see where they lived. I heard it was a mansion on Lake Campbell. To emphasize my flexibility I said, "I've taken photos on campus, at the Sioux Falls falls, and even at a color run, where people threw colored powder at sweaty runners." I realized I was rambling and stopped there.

He curled his lip up and said, "That sounds really messy."

I nodded and handed him his credit card and the iPad to sign. With his long index finger, he signed his name.

"Mr. Fox, here is a card with ideas of what I do." I traded the iPad for a cute postcard Jon had designed for me. It read,

'Come to Picture This on Main or we'll travel to you.'
We specialize in:

- Pet photography
- Senior pictures
- Engagement and wedding photos

- Maternity and newborn photos
- Travel photos
- Family portraits
- Sports photos
- School photos
- Party pics
- Holiday photos
- Christmas cards and gifts

Schedule your 'Picture This' appointment today.
Call Ande at 605-555-1212.

He read the card and said, "You spell your name with an e?"

I glanced at his wife who seemed extremely bored and shrugged. "It's a long story."

When he noticed Debra's apathy he nodded. "So, you do travel photos?"

I blinked. Except for family trips with my parents, I hadn't actually done any. I just added travel photos to my list since I was very willing to get paid to travel. I considered how to answer and shrugged as if I'd done a dozen trips. "Sure. I'll go anywhere." I considered using that as my slogan.

The mother of the year who was still ignoring her kids said in a snippy voice, "Carter, is this going to be an all-day event? I have an afternoon tea, you know."

He showed a glimmer of annoyance. "Just a second, dear." He turned back to me and smiled. "We're taking the family down the Amazon next year. We'll consider taking you along."

My heartbeat quickened in anticipation of the possible lucrative and exciting job. Just then, Flash fluttered up to the top of the backdrop bracket. The monster twins jumped up and tried to grab him.

I shouted impatiently, "Please leave my bird alone!" Their faces dropped in shock as if I was the first person ever to correct them.

Jeez, would I really want to be on vacation with these holy terrors, taking pictures as they chased monkeys and macaws, or terrorized sloths? Two weeks of that and I'd want to push them overboard into the Amazon River. And that wife…ugh.

But, for some reason, I said with a smile, "Great!" What was my problem? I added, "In the meantime, do let me know about scheduling the group photo session for your mother's gift."

Mr. Fox tried to wrangle his kids, who had abandoned Flash to make silly poses in front of my prairie backdrop. I worried they would yank on the fabric and pull the heavy apparatus down on their heads. But eventually, the mayor got them out safe and sound.

Before the door closed, Debra said, "This street is a filthy mess, Carter. I nearly broke the heel of my Jimmy Choo in that crack. Can't you do something about it?"

The door shut and I fell back into my chair. Ahhh…silence. If children weren't my bread and butter, I'd ban them from my studio altogether.

I looked down at the app on my iPad and almost choked. Mr. Fox had added a $50 tip. I'd never gotten any tip before. Even though I should consider the bonus hazard pay, it was sweet!

My four o'clock client with the infant called to cancel. The new mother had seen the holes in the sidewalk and decided it wasn't worth the risk. I told her I would be happy to reschedule once construction was finished, or I could even go to her house. But she said she would just go to Northern Exposure in Watertown. The danged construction mess was now sending people to my rival!

The rest of the afternoon, I worked on photo orders and payments alongside Flash. I jumped when my door opened and a man wearing a bright orange vest barged inside my studio.

I studied the man. He wasn't a typical customer, but the weathered lines on his face could make for an interesting subject if I cropped out the neon vest. "Can I help you?"

His voice was gruff. "Where's your plug? My phone's dying."

I laughed. "Are you serious? You're gonna just walk in here and tell me you're going to use my electrical outlet?"

"Boss lady said we had to keep charged up. She said ya'll wouldn't care."

"Well, she's wrong." I have little patience for bratty kids, but even less for bratty adults.

He looked dumbfounded or maybe just dumb, and sputtered, "But…"

I plastered on a smile and pointed to an outlet. "On second thought, plug it in. I'm closing the studio for the day, but you can pick your phone up tomorrow. It should be fully charged by then."

He cocked his head. "But… then I couldn't use my phone all night."

I shrugged. "Oh yeah. I guess you're right. Well, just a hint, the next time you need something, you might want to ask instead of making a demand."

Apparently, he changed his mind for he backed out of my studio with his phone in hand an angry glare on his face.

I grumbled to Flash as I put him in his cage, "Had the man asked nicely or at all, I would have been happy to let him plug in his phone for a bit." I locked my door, turned my sign from open to closed, and went upstairs to my apartment to relax on the couch.

I must have fallen asleep because I woke up at six o'clock. Nothing like a nap to escape real-life drama. I went downstairs and stopped by the birdcage. "Hold down the fort, buddy. I'll be back in a bit. If you're a good boy, I'll bring you some pizza crust."

Flash said, "Pizza Pizza!"

I laughed. "That's right." I grabbed my coat and left to go to Spinners Pub for Thursday night pizza and beer.

When I exited my shop, I had to leap over a huge chunk of cracked concrete in the middle of the sidewalk – just part of the Main Street mess left by construction workers. Every day it got worse. My head still pounded from the morning's din of jackhammers. Whether beer would help with the headache or make it worse was a risk I was willing to take.

I smiled when the vintage streetlights flickered as they lit up at dusk. Hopefully, the developers would preserve the charm of the historic Brookings Main Street through all the changes, but so far it wasn't looking good. Rumors swirled that they were taking out the brick streets and upgrading them to concrete. I really hoped the streetlights would survive the changes.

A few doors down, I tapped on the window of Antique Alley and stepped inside, calling softly to my furry friend, "Memory! Come here, Memory." I heard a soft thump and my sweet tiger-striped buddy wove herself between the legs of an old player piano and then through mine. I reached down and lifted the fluffball and scratched behind her ears, just the way she liked.

The owner, Peggy, walked up from her bargain basement carrying a box full of vases. "Hey, Ande! I'll make it down to Spinners in a minute. Gotta lock up first. Oh, Mike and Leo are coming too, so count them in for pizza." She walked around the corner to the other side of the store.

I smiled. Of course, they were coming. The Krebs brothers would never miss a Thursday night at the pub. I put the cat back on the floor and headed down the street dodging a few uncovered holes in the sidewalk. A group of college kids came out of Pizza Prince carrying the familiar square boxes with the prince logo. We would be doing the same thing in just a few minutes.

The weather was so nice tonight – in the high 40's. We had an unusually cold and wet winter even for South Dakota. Now that it was March, I was ready for longer days and sunshine.

CHAPTER 2

Spinners Pub stands on the corner of Main and Oak. Like most structures lining Main Street, the two-story brick building was built in the late 1800s. When I opened the massive door to the old taproom, a strong scent of beer and popcorn hit me, which makes sense since that is all they serve.

Before I made it through the door, I heard Leo's booming voice. "Ande! It's about time!"

I wasn't surprised the boys had beaten me there. Nor was I surprised to see the gang sitting in our regular corner. Mike pulled up an extra small table to add to the three already filled by the friendly group of Main Street merchants. I grabbed two chairs and dragged them up to the table and sat next to Leo. I explained, "I had a big day and took a much-needed nap."

"Well, we're glad you made it." He patted my back.

Spinners was noisy as usual with college students taking a break from studies to have a brew and play pool. The cool old pub was a destination for people all over the eastern side of South Dakota. As usual, our table was the rowdiest. I could never meet this clan at a quiet venue since they were so loud, especially Leo and Mike. And don't get me started on their earsplitting laughter. But here at Spinners, nobody cared.

Leo is short of stature but has an enormous personality. The outgoing widower shines even more when single women are around. He jokingly refers to his lady friends as his 'harem' because he frequently goes with more than one woman to concerts. Leo hopes to find someone special to settle down with someday. On this night he was with a new lady who gave me a little wave.

He barked, "Ande, this is Jean. She lives in Mitchell. I said she had to experience Spinners." He turned to Jean and said, "Ande is our local photographer. She can make anyone look good in a picture – even my brother." As expected, Mike rolled his eyes.

I had to shout to be heard above the pub noise, "Welcome to our crazy crew, Jean!"

Jean, who looked to be in her 50s, smiled and asked, "Do you have a studio?"

"Yes. I own 'Picture This on Main' a few doors down. My passion is pet photos, but in order to pay the rent, I photograph everyone - even children and weddings – I made a sour face.

She opened her mouth but before she could speak, Jenny, our regular waitress asked me, "Pitcher of Nordeast, Ande?"

It is kind of sad that the servers know my order, but since we are regulars and usually only drink versions of Minnesota's Grainbelt beer, it was an easy guess.

I held up a finger for her to wait and asked the group, "Nordeast Anyone?"

"Duh", "Of course," and "Don't forget the olives."

I turned back to her with a shrug, "Guess the answer is yes. And green olives please."

Someone tapped my shoulder. I looked up as Stan walked by in his bike jersey and helmet. Stan is a professor at SDSU and is an animal on a bicycle. The rest of our gang ride occasionally, but this guy bikes daily except when the snow is too deep. He asked a couple at a neighboring table if he could have their empty chairs and pulled them over to our group.

Leo yelled to our server who had just walked away, "Jenny! Get Dr. Stan a Dr. Pepper!"

Before I could recover from his obnoxious eruption, Leo shouted to the door, loud enough this time to hurt my eardrum, "Get your butt over here and have a beer!"

I held my hand over my damaged ear and berated myself for sitting by Leo. Then, I turned to see my best friend, Doc, enter. I moved over a chair so he could be a buffer to protect my ears.

Doc is the owner of the hardware store on the north side of Main. He wore dirty jeans, a red plaid flannel shirt, and a black Grainbelt Beer stocking cap. Doc sat next to me and took off his hat, making his sandy-colored hair stand up on end. Doc never cared how he looked or what people thought of him. I liked that about him.

He gave me a little punch on the arm and I nudged him back.

Jean leaned forward and said, "Is this your dad?"

We faced each other and laughed. Doc said, "We can't help it if she looks 16 and I look 70."

In reality, I was 28 and he was my dad's age, 50, so it wasn't that big of a stretch.

Jean's face turned pink. "Oh, I'm sorry. Are you dating?"

We laughed even harder. Leo said with a snort, "Ande couldn't date Doc. He's too opinionated and sloppy."

Doc smirked. "I could never date her. She's too opinionated and organized."

None of that changed the fact that we hung out together most weekends. I felt bad for laughing at Jean's innocent questions and turned to her. "Don't worry. We get that all the time too. We're just good friends."

Leo changed the subject by yelling, "Who's in for pizza?" All hands went up and he counted. "OK, that's eight."

I added, "Don't forget your sister-in-law."

"Oh yeah, Peggy. How about a large sausage, salami and onion, large sauerkraut and bacon, and a large double pepperoni?"

We nodded. Mike calculated the bill and said the usual, "Six bucks, six bucks, six bucks!"

We each threw $6 in bills to the center of the sticky table while Leo called Prince's Pizza to place the order. Since Spinners doesn't serve food, we bring in our own. This group of business owners and friends has been getting together every Thursday for at least five years. Although I only joined the gang a year ago, I already feel like part of the family and wouldn't go anywhere else on a Thursday night.

Doc leaned over to me. "How was work today?"

Before I could answer, Jenny brought the pitcher of Nordeast, a tumbler full of olives, and extra mugs. Doc poured himself a beer, spilling it over the side of the mug. I gave Jenny $15. "Keep the change."

Doc said, "I'll get the next pitcher." He poured one for me and I cringed when he put his dirty fingers into the cup of olives and dropped a couple in my mug before adding some to his own.

When Mike lifted his beer above his head we rolled our eyes and groaned, pretending to be aggravated. He belted out his usual, "May the road rise up to meet you. May the wind be always at your back. May the sun shine warm upon your face, the rains fall soft upon your fields, and until we meet again may God hold you in the palm of his hand."

We clinked our mugs as we did every week after he recited the sweet Irish blessing. I took a sip and smiled as I took in the familiar old pub. Besides hanging out with the friendly gang, I was comfortable in the rustic place with eclectic furnishings. The Formica tables and torn vinyl-covered chairs contrasted greatly with the cool century-old tin ceiling tiles and stately walnut bar.

I turned to Doc and told him about my photoshoot with Mayor Fox and then about my frustration with the construction mess. "It's as if they're trying to be loud and trashy on purpose!"

He nodded. "Get this. Today, that project manager ordered me to loan her a jackhammer."

I snorted, thinking about how that must have gone over. "And?"

Doc smirked. "Well, I told her no, but that I had one she could rent. Then, she got all huffy and snarled, 'It would behoove you to support the project and you should be careful parking that car on Main Street - it could get damaged in the construction.' She pointed right at my BMW."

My eyes widened. "Was that a threat?"

Doc shrugged. "Don't know, but if anything happens to my car…Well, that'll be the end of it." He pounded the table in mock fury which caused the spilled beer to splash me.

He was joking but Doc did have a temper. I heard he was fired from his last job for punching someone. He never did like working for "the man" so owning his own store was perfect for him. I wiped the splattered beer from my shirt.

Having overheard our conversation, others in our group joined in complaining about the disaster that once was our sweet street.

Our ever so timid florist, Davis, spoke so quietly I could barely hear him, "Today, on the first nice day of the year, I finally got to open my doors to get some fresh air. One of those workers smoked a cigarette right outside my door all day so my customers couldn't even smell the flowers. It was disgusting."

I said, "Davis, did you ask him to move?"

He sighed. "No."

Poor Davis was a pushover. Once, when a snooty customer found an ant in her flowers, he gave her a full refund. Another time, some sorority girls bullied him into making a flower arrangement for free because they needed to cheer up a friend who flunked her big exam. He explained, saying, "But, they had tears."

This time I told him, "I can give you a lesson on how to be firm, buddy. Just let me know when."

Marla, the coffee shop owner, rolled her eyes and said, "That is nothing. You should hear what I have to put up with. That Fiona Pratt is driving me crazy. She…"

The big oak door slammed open and Peggy stormed inside. She stomped over to us, yanked up another chair and plopped down next to her husband. Turning to him she growled, "Mike, you have to help me tomorrow. Fiona just came by and told me I have to move my concrete planters inside my shop because her crew is demolishing that sidewalk tomorrow."

Mike shook his head but said in a calm voice, "It's no problem, Peggy. I'll do it before I go to work."

Mike is a lawyer with an office just a few blocks off Main. He spends most of his free time helping Peggy at her antique store and loves it. No wonder they've been married 30 years.

Leo raised his palms. "What's the big deal, Peggy? You're on a corner and have another entrance."

I too wondered why she was so upset.

"You haven't seen my other door." Her face turned red. "Today, a worker let go of his jackhammer and it skidded across the pavement and broke the glass in my door. They patched the glass with cardboard, but I can't use that entrance until they fix it on Monday."

My eyes met Doc's. So that was the reason Fiona needed another jackhammer.

Jean furrowed her brow. "Who is this Fiona person anyway?"

Peggy noticed the stranger for the first time and pushed a piece of her prematurely gray hair behind her ear. "She's the project manager. Came in from Rapid City and thinks she's all that in her fancy suit. Like there aren't any qualified engineers here or in Sioux Falls that the city could have hired."

Marla raised her hand and said, "Okay. That's bad, but I've got all of you beat." She took a shaky breath. "Fiona moved her stuff into a booth in Viking Coffee last week and she hasn't left! She set it up like it's her very own office. And she orders me around like I'm her personal barista. I have to boil sassafras root to make her special tea and keep a pitcher of it in the refrigerator at all times."

A new barmaid handed Stan another glass of Dr. Pepper as he said, "Can't you just tell her to leave?"

"No. The City Council determined she needs a place to work during the project." Marla sniffed, grabbed a napkin off the table, and blew her nose before continuing. "Someone on the City Council suggested she use a table in the back of my coffee shop. I figured she might stop by every now and then, so I agreed to host her. But the witch took a booth right in the front and is there all the time talking loudly on her phone. It's affecting my business. I hate her!"

I was surprised by Marla's outburst since is usually easygoing. My shoulders dropped in empathy for the poor lady. She probably didn't want to ruffle the feathers of the City Council since she's the newest member.

Peggy raised her hands in question. "How can she keep an eye on the workers if she's inside your shop all the time?"

We all took in the information.

Leo shrugged and said, "Well, Marla...are you at least making good money by selling her drinks?"

Marla burst out a loud, "Ha! She hasn't paid me a penny. She just tells me to put it on her tab. I'll bet she wants the town of Brookings to pay for it, but that is definitely not in the budget."

We sat in silence, mulling this over when the door banged open again. In walked the purported devil herself, Fiona Pratt.

The tall, 40-something woman wore a dark pantsuit and carried a briefcase. Her black hair came to her shoulders in a perfect blunt cut, but she held her stylish head high in a haughty manner. Although I hadn't met Fiona Pratt, I recognized her immediately from photos in the *Brookings Register*.

She scanned the pub then marched over to our group of tables and stopped right beside me. Hands-on-hips and nose in the air she said, "I'm looking for the manager of the post office...a Mr. Krebs?"

We glanced at Leo, wondering why in the world she needed to see him on a Thursday night.

Leo raised a finger. "That would be me. But you do know the post office is closed now."

"I understand that." She rolled her eyes. "I'm expecting an important package addressed to me, Fiona Pratt, to arrive tomorrow. You need to deliver it to the coffee shop as soon as it arrives."

Leo leaned forward and put his elbows on the table. "Well Ms. Pratt, we don't actually deliver. But I'll hold it just like we do for any other package with no address. Feel free to pick it up at your convenience. Oh and make sure to bring a photo I.D. so we can confirm you are the addressee."

It sounded funny to hear that the Post Office didn't deliver, but I guess it wasn't the manager's job to deliver a package with no address, even in a small town like Brookings.

Fiona must not have liked his response for she pinched the bridge of her nose.

I raised a hand. "Now that we have that problem solved, some of us have concerns."

Fiona looked at me as if she smelled something acrid. "And who are you?"

"I'm Ande Nilsen, of "Picture This on Main.""

She sniffed. "What is that?"

I sighed. "My photography studio."

She laughed and said, "This is not the time nor place for an interrogation by a photographer or any retailers for that matter." Her words were said in disdain.

Mike, the only one of us wearing a suit, cleared his throat and sat up straight. "Ms. Pratt, this small group of Main Street merchants would like to discuss the construction progress. Would you prefer we schedule a formal meeting with all of the Main Street business owners present? Or perhaps the few members here could represent the rest and voice some concerns now?"

She pondered the suggestion. The prospect of meeting with a larger crowd must not have appealed to her because she said with a slight shake of the head, "Well? What is it you want to say?"

I took a breath and began, "For one thing, I'm concerned with the mess your construction workers are leaving behind each day. Chunks of concrete litter the sidewalks and there are large holes everywhere with hardly any barriers. It was like navigating an obstacle course just to get here tonight. Can you explain this?"

She raised an eyebrow and said smoothly, "As far as I know, my men have been diligent in removing excess materials. Just where is it you are talking about?"

The group gave a collective scoff. Doc couldn't control himself. "Have you even walked down Main Street? Or do you just hide away in the coffee shop all day?"

We nodded in solidarity, but Marla lowered her head. Fiona squirmed then straightened up and responded with confidence, "Perhaps the City Council should look into hiring a clean-up crew. Is that all?"

Baffled at her response but worried she would bolt, I said, "No. It's not. These fine Brookings businessmen and women..." I waved my hand around the room as if I was a lawyer giving my opening argument, "have never even seen the plans for the new Main Street." I was on a roll and kept going, "And we would like to know the projected date of completion?"

Peggy added, "We hope it's soon. The obvious lack of safety standards is an accident waiting to happen. And sales for all merchants have slowed dramatically during the construction. The bookstore already closed down for fear they wouldn't sell anything during the roadwork."

Fiona flicked her hair and said defensively, "Well, some people just can't handle change. Those with a vision woud be patient and understand that business will be much better once the project is complete. We're doing just what the City Council members asked. Blame her..." She pointed a manicured finger at Marla "...if you haven't seen the written plans. It's certainly not my job to show them to you."

Marla's face turned pink and her eyes squeezed tight as though she wanted to disappear. Davis, who has had a crush on Marla since she moved to town, patted her shoulder.

Fiona glowered at each one of us in turn as she spoke. "The Main Street renovation is projected to be finished at the end of June. Now if that's all, I have a real meeting to attend." She grabbed her bag and left before anyone could object.

I stared at the door thinking if it weren't for her horrible personality, Fiona would be very pretty. I said, "Wow. What a spectacular disappearing act."

Leo's eyes were wide. "Now isn't she a sweetheart?"

Jean blew out a puff of air. "I'm glad I'm not involved in this thing."

Stan shook his head. "Me too."

"Imagine what it's like to deal with that up close and personal every single day," Marla said with her head in her hands.

We sat silently sipping our beer as a server brought another pitcher. My incident with the cell phone dude was nothing compared to her ordeal. The more I thought about it, the more steamed I got. I pounded the table ala Doc and announced, "I vow to make Ms. Pratt fix this die trying." I tend to get overly dramatic at times.

We were still discussing Fiona's rude behavior when a group of six workers wearing orange vests barged through the door whooping and hollering. A few men stumbled, apparently already inebriated. When one of them let out an obnoxious belch, I made a face at Peggy who frowned back.

I watched, stunned, as the tallest man slapped Jenny on the rear and another made catcalls to a student. So, this was the lovely crew working on our street.

Leo started to stand up, but his brother put his hand on his arm. Mike knew it was a bad idea to let any of us get involved with drunken guys full of machismo. I considered interfering, but even I wasn't ready to tackle a group of strangers twice my size.

Doc silently stared at the unruly clan while biting the inside of his cheek obviously agitated. I had heard that when he was younger, he had gotten into a few bar fights. I could see that now.

Our group was unusually hushed as we watched the disruptive men make their way across the pub.

Stan asked quietly, "Anyone know those guys?"

We all shook our heads. I said, "None look familiar to me."

Davis whispered, "That last guy was the one smoking outside my shop. I overheard him make a phone call. He complained about how small Brookings is and that there is nothing to do here. Sounded like they're all from Rapid City."

Doc nodded. "So, Brookings is paying people from the other side of the state to do inferior workmanship? You've got to be kidding."

This sunk in. I said, "Jon just started working for Matthews Construction, but there isn't much work yet with the ground still frozen. They could have been doing this job."

My buddies nodded in agreement. Leo looked at his watch. "I hate to leave this happy party, but I should go get the pizzas while they're hot. Let me know if I miss anything." He stood, stuffing the wad of bills in his pocket. He helped Jean into her coat and held out his arm to her. She giggled and went with him.

Doc lightened the mood by yelling to Leo, "Don't forget the barf dust."

What a disgusting name for parmesan cheese. I said, "Gross, Doc."

When the workers found a table on the other side of the pub, we went back to discussing the matters at hand. Before the pizza arrived, I made a trip to the bathroom and had to pass the table of construction workers. One of them, a big guy with a porn star mustache, growled at me and winked. "Hey Baby, come sit with us. We'll give you a night to remember."

I shuddered at his audacity. Then I stopped, turned around, and walked back to them. I leaned down, put my elbows on their dirty table, and said sweetly, "Oh, but you already have. I will always remember your foul-mouthed, rude behavior." As I stood, I added, "Why don't you grow up and act like real men?" I turned and walked on, knowing my face was beet red.

The men laughed and made lewd remarks as I pushed the bathroom door open. I wanted so much to go back and sock that Mustache Man in the nose but I reminded myself he wasn't worth it. Don't get yourself worked up over a bunch of idiots, Ande.

Four girls who may have just left a sorority house, primped in the mirror. One blonde with a pixie face turned to me and yelled with wide eyes, "Ande! Hi!" She grew quiet when she noticed my face. She said softly, "Are you OK?"

I was still breathing hard and probably looked like a mess. I squinted at her. How did I know this girl? Was she a friend of Jon's? Had I taken her photos? As I struggled to remember, I had time to calm down from my run-in with the workers. Finally, I composed myself enough to shrug and say, "Just some jerks." I nodded to the door.

The girls nodded and the mystery girl said, "Oh, we already encountered them."

A brunette spoke in a southern drawl, which is unusual for South Dakota, "One of those guys actually grabbed my hand as I walked by. So gross."

The blonde turned to her gaggle and explained, "Ande took my family's portrait last month and she has this hilarious parrot who says, 'Say cheese!' It was so adorbs. You guys should go get your photos done there. Her studio is on Main Street. And she takes pet photos too! She's great!"

Aha! Mystery solved. A tall girl scrunched up her face and said, "You own your own business? How old are you?"

I was a little tired of hearing this question but chuckled. "Yup. I do. I'm 28 and actually have a Bachelor of Arts in Photography."

The girls were dumbstruck. The one who asked the question said, "You're so cute and you look 15."

Another held her hands to her face. "I'd love to have a portrait of Pom Pom. Do you have any openings next week?"

It could picture this preppy girl holding a Pomeranian wearing a tutu. I said, "I'm sure I can fit you in." I dug in my purse for a card and handed one to her. "Just give me a call."

The girls' excitement grew to an unacceptable level as they discussed plans to have their pets' pictures taken. I wondered if I could invite just their dogs and not the noisy girls.

I said, "Look, I'd better get going. Have fun and stay away from those creeps."

I studied my reflection in the mirror while washing my hands. I frowned at the new blotches on my face caused by the encounter and wondered how I could make myself look older. I have blue eyes and what most people call a baby face. I could easily change my hair. My blonde ponytail probably didn't help matters, but it did keep hair out of my face while working. Maybe I should dye it darker? I'd have to make a hair appointment soon.

On my way back from the bathroom, I felt Mustache Man's creepy stare. Uneasiness crept over me as I made my way back to my merry band of overgrown kids.

I started to tell Doc about my escapade but changed my mind. He might go over and punch them out, and he really didn't need to get arrested.

Leo and Jean arrived with the pizzas and we passed the boxes around, taking as many of the 3-inch squares as we wanted. It's a wonder I don't weigh 200 pounds from eating this way every week.

We talked, chowed down, and joked for another hour, occasionally bringing up Fiona.

After cleaning up our pizza mess and thanking Jenny, I noticed the orange vested men were even noisier. For once, we weren't the loudest table in the bar.

Doc walked me back to my studio and I handed him a napkin full of crust. He shrugged. "I'm pretty full."

"Wanna give Flash his pizza crust?"

Flash immediately said, "Pizza pizza", which cracked Doc up.

He held out a piece. "Here ya go, buddy." The bird grabbed it, nearly taking his finger along with the crust. Doc said, "Okay, okay, I'll just put the rest in your cup." He did so, then leaned in and said, "Flash, repeat after me, 'Help! I've been turned into a parrot!'"

I laughed at his silly statement. "Good luck, Doc. I've tried to teach him to say, 'I love you,' for months, but he just says whatever he wants."

Doc lifted his shoulder. "It's worth a try." On his way out, he stopped and frowned at my ceiling. I followed his gaze but didn't see anything out of the ordinary. He pointed. "The screws are coming out of your bracket. I'll fix that tomorrow when you don't have any customers."

He was right. A few strong pulls and my backdrop brace might fall along with the heavy rolls of fabric. I figured the Fox twins had something to do with it. "That would be great."

Doc can and will fix anything for anybody, but he seemed to always be helping me. I said, "But just because you have every tool ever made doesn't mean you are obliged to fix my stuff."

He winked and said, "I have my reasons. Mostly that I don't have anything else to do."

"Well then, I'll make dinner as a thank you."

He nodded with a smile. "And that's the other reason."

When Doc left, I locked the door behind him and turned to Flash. "Ready for bed?"

He walked the length of his perch, then up the side of the cage before swinging himself inside. I was happy Flash liked the studio so much that he wanted to sleep downstairs. When he lived up in my apartment, he talked whenever the light was on. If I went to the bathroom in the middle of the night, he blabbered or imitated the flushing sounds and I couldn't go back to sleep. It was so annoying. Now, with him downstairs, I sleep in peace.

I said, "Night, night, Flashman. See you tomorrow. I love you."

I waited to see if he would mimic me but he just said his, "Night night!" in a sing-song voice full of fake vibrato. Oh well, that still made me smile.

At the top of the stairs, I opened my door to find my brother, Jon, sitting on the couch with a dazed expression on his face. His light-colored hair looked greasy. My heart leapt into my throat. Was he drunk? Was he high? Oh please no. Not again.

CHAPTER 3

I spoke quietly so as not to startle my brother, "You okay?"

He looked up at me with clear eyes which was a good sign. "Yeah. I'm just really tired." He took a breath. "We started building that house in Wolf Run addition. It was hard work, but it sure felt good to be outdoors and sweat a little."

"That's great, Jon." I sighed, realizing I'd been holding my breath. Despite the news that he'd gone to work today, I hoped he had also gone to class. Even though I was deemed responsible for Jon while our parents were snowbirding in Alabama, I didn't want to be a nag. I had to tread lightly with this guy.

He said, "And before you ask, yes, I went to class too."

I chuckled. "Wasn't even going to ask."

I put my purse down on the kitchen counter. "If you're tired, why don't you go to sleep?"

He cocked his head at me. "Well, my bed is in the middle of your living room. What if you wanted to watch TV?"

He said this with an edge to his voice. I knew he was appreciative of my hospitality, but the frustration of not having his own place made him bitter at times.

I shrugged. "Don't worry about that. I have another TV in my room. I'm not in the mood to watch anyway. I'll just read." I sat on the chair next to him and changed the subject. "You should have come down to Spinners for some pizza."

As soon as the words came out, I regretted saying them. Jon has stayed clear of pubs for several months for fear he'd be tempted to start drinking again.

Before he could reply, I jumped in with, "There were these disgusting construction guys who showed up - the crew from the Main Street widening project. Anyway, they were drunk and super rude. One even tried to hit on me."

Instead of getting protective as one might expect from a brother, Jon's lip curled into a half-smile and his eyes sparkled. "I'll bet he found out you weren't one to mess with."

I winked. "You know me too well. But Jon, you would have been so proud. I didn't throw a single punch." I stood and went to the sink for a glass of water.

He shook his head. "I am surprised, but we all have to grow up sometime – even you, Ande."

Our parents raised us to be strong individuals but I always took it a step further. Recently, Mom said, "Andrea, you need to back off and stop getting so riled up. No man wants a girlfriend who is so opinionated and strong-willed."

I didn't tell her that finding a boyfriend was not at the top of my list, nor did I tell her that if I did meet someone, he would just have to deal with my impulsiveness. I had no plans to change.

For some odd reason, the handsome Carter Fox came to mind. I turned to Jon. "Oh, and guess what else happened today?" I told him about meeting the handsome man, his awful kids, and his cold-hearted wife. Then came the punch line. "He gave me a $50 tip!"

Jon perked up and said, "That's cool. So, now you can buy me that Harley I've always wanted?"

"Haha! Always the jokester. Are you hungry? I can whip something up."

"Nah. I just had those leftover ribs in the fridge. I'm gonna hit the couch."

"OK." I smiled and leaned down to give him a hug. I was happy to find that his hair was wet rather than greasy. His fresh shampoo scent brought back memories of us as kids snuggling while we watched TV after our evening baths.

The next morning, I awoke to a surprise. A few inches of fresh snow covered the ground. I knew it wouldn't last long because it was supposed to warm up to 60 today.

I prepared for my morning Easter session with my favorite Golden Retriever, Shakira. Her owner, Jamal, brought her in for every holiday and she was the perfect model. Without being told, Shakira hopped right up on my low table and gave me an open-mouthed smile. Seriously, the dog could smile. I got a few good shots. When I put an Easter basket in her mouth, she held it. I almost cried at the cuteness. For the third pose, I directed Shakira to lay her head on a huge plastic Easter egg. I shouldn't even charge Jamal for the sessions since I enjoyed them so much. As they left, I said, "See you two in a few months for the 4th of July."

My only other scheduled shoot was an outdoor kid's birthday party in the afternoon. I dreaded it, but the pay was great.

I still had several hours free and since my photography job didn't involve much physical activity, a walk sounded like a perfect idea. I gathered my coat, turned the hands of my cardboard clock to 'Be Back At clock at 11:30,' and left the studio.

As I neared the corner of my building, a workman stood smoking. I said, "Perhaps you could smoke farther away from this door. The beauty shop customers would prefer not to get lung cancer due to second-hand smoke."

He threw the cigarette on the sidewalk, ground it out with his boot, and said something under his breath. Mustache Man watched from across the street and a chill went down my spine.

I walked briskly past Mike and Peggy's blue, 2-story house and was surprised to see they were adding a second story to their free-standing garage. That's cool. How had I missed that? Doc's big yellow house loomed at the end of the next block. I just loved his big front porch.

It would be a long while before I could afford a house of my own, especially with the recent rise in housing prices. I was shocked last week when I flipped through a real estate leaflet and saw the inflated prices. Oh, stop the pity party. I am 25 years younger than Mike and Peggy. At my age, I should be proud to own a business and have housing at all. My appointments should increase if the construction ever ended.

By thinking positive thoughts, my pace picked up. I approached a beautiful Victorian house where a white-haired woman with a walker tried to sweep snow from the walkway. She wasn't having much success.

I walked across her snow-covered lawn and said, "Can I help you?"

Her voice was gravelly with age. "Oh, yes, please. The steps are shaded and the snow never seems to melt here. I don't want to fall. At my age, it's a big deal."

She moved back and I took the broom and swept the dry snow away in big easy strokes. "There you go."

"Thank you so much, dear. I'm glad you came along. Do you live near here?"

"I do. I live in an apartment above my photography shop on Main Street."

Her hand went to her mouth. "Oh, you poor thing."

That was an odd thing for her to say. Most people thought it was cool to live downtown.

She continued, "It looks like a tornado went through there. I tried to go to the Post Office yesterday but the street was such a mess I ended up driving over to the one in the Hy-Vee store."

I nodded, acknowledging her all-too-common story. "I'm as upset as you are about the mess, but we spoke with the project manager last night and hope she'll sort it out. So sorry for your bad experience."

I worried people would avoid downtown altogether and start driving to the new shopping mall in Watertown. Personally, I was most worried about my danged rival studio, Northern Exposure. I made a silent vow to do my part to keep customers happy.

The woman watched me sweep off her steps and asked, "What kind of photos do you take?"

I gave my pat answer. "Oh, anybody and anything, including pets. We'll even travel to you."

Her hazy eyes perked up. "Could you take some pictures of my goldfish?"

My lips twisted thinking, a goldfish? How long did they live, like a month?

I said, "Um...I love taking photos of pets, so of course, I could..." My voice trailed off. I hated to tell her the price for a photo session at her house, but logistically I couldn't see the old woman carrying a goldfish bowl to my shop. I asked, "Is it a special goldfish?"

She raised her eyebrows and smiled. "I've had Bubbles for seven years."

I spat, "Seven years? What in the world do you feed Bubbles?"

The lady chuckled. "Do you want to see her?" She led the way to her front steps, but was so wobbly I worried she would topple over even with the aid of her walker, so I steadied her elbow.

She said, "My name is Mabel. What's yours?"

"I'm Ande Nilsen."

I said no more because when I followed her into a bright sunroom where an aquarium stood on an antique table, I became speechless. Inside the tank, an orange fish about nine inches long swam around. Amazed, I said, "Bubbles is lovely and huge!"

Mabel sighed and smiled lovingly at her pet fish. "I've always wanted to have a photograph of my baby, but I don't have a camera anymore. My grandson cleans the aquarium for me, but he isn't interested in taking a picture."

My eyes grew large as I looked past her to the room filled with beautiful antiques. I realized I was standing what could be my dream house. I longed to climb the gorgeous oak staircase to discover what beauties lay above. "Your house and furnishings are so beautiful I don't want to leave."

When she gave an adorable giggle, I snapped out of my dream and focused on the aquarium. The lace curtains behind the aquarium would be a perfect backdrop. I wrote a very low quote on a business card and handed it to her. "I would be happy to photograph Bubbles. Call and we'll set up a time for a session."

"I will if I can figure out this mobile telephone." She patted my shoulder. "Now you be careful, Ande. A cute little thing like you could get hurt walking on that unsteady sidewalk downtown."

Cute little thing? The tiny woman was even smaller than me. That was just more proof I must do something about my looks.

I apparently didn't heed Mabel's warning because as soon as I stepped on Main Street, I tripped over a loose brick on the sidewalk that was partially covered by snow. Thankfully, I righted myself before I landed flat on my face.

I heard laughing and looked across the street to find some orange vested guys pointing at me. In the middle of the group stood Mustache Man, giving a smug nod. I couldn't contain myself and started toward them, skirting around a crack the shape and size of Minnesota where the stamped bricks had been violently removed.

By the time I reached the men I had acquired quite a chip on my shoulder and my words came out louder than I planned. "I had hoped Ms. Pratt would talk to you, but apparently she hasn't, so I will do her job for her."

I took a breath and told myself to be civil. As nice as I could, I said, "I realize you are busy working all day but is it possible for you to clean up the site or at least set-out cones or barriers when you leave for the night? Someone is bound to gethurt."

A thin guy wearing a green feed store hat said, "She hasn't told us nothing. And we run this show, not that bitch."

So, besides being slobs, these guys were lying bullies. I nodded sarcastically. "Right. Well, your crew is causing another problem. You need to stop ogling the local females."

Mustache Man flicked his cigarette butt towards me. I watched the red ash land next to my foot but didn't flinch.

He growled, "Honey, we weren't ogling you. You're nothing but a little bee that buzzes around looking for trouble. We swat bees that get in our way."

My heart quickened and I spat, "Are you threatening me?"

He shrugged and took a swig of his coffee while the other men grinned. He swallowed and said, "You best be moving on. We've worked these jobs for years and nobody's died yet."

Furious, but unable to think of a good response, I stormed past them to the coffee shop to check on Marla and confront Fiona. My heartbeat didn't slow as I walked away. In fact, my chest pounded as though one of their jackhammers had moved in.

Chimes jangled as I barged into the cheery shop. Even the cute pictures of the SDSU's cartoon jackrabbit mascot couldn't calm me down. I gasped when I saw Marla standing like a zombie behind the counter. Her hair was a mess and her shirt was buttoned up wrong. The frazzled look was so uncharacteristic of this classy gal that I wondered if she had been attacked or perhaps caught in a windstorm. I stammered, "Are you okay, Marla?"

She shook her head and pointed to a booth stacked with papers and a computer. The table he been transformed into an unorganized office desk. I whispered, "Is that where Fiona lives?"

She grabbed my coat collar and pulled me back to her storeroom, looking behind her frantically as we walked. "Yes."

Once the door shut, Marla sobbed, "Fiona's here all the time and I can't do anything about it. Today she had a conference call and made me leave. I had to lock the front door so nobody would interrupt her. My customers were confused and angry."

I scoffed. "She can't do that. You need to tell her to leave."

Marla actually started to pull on her hair like she was in a cartoon, which explained why it was so messy. Her voice raised an octave. "I can't. She's scary. She just left for the post office, or you would hear her yelling into her phone. I'm so stressed by the end of the day I just go home and cry."

I gave her a hug and took a calmer approach. "Can't you tell the committee that it's not working out? Surely, they can find another place for her." In a softer tone, I said, "Listen, Carter Fox was just in my place yesterday. He seems nice. Have you talked to him about moving her?"

She frowned, looking defeated. "No. I think it was actually his idea for her to come here. I hate to complain, but she's so loud and brash that I'm losing all my customers."

I nodded. "If I get a chance, I'll talk to him. But Marla, can you explain why the City Council hired a manager and crew from Rapid when we have qualified people on this side of the state?"

She closed her eyes. "From what Carter said, he got a solid recommendation for this group after they developed the streets in Deadwood. So he invited Fiona to present her plan at our City Council meeting." Marla became more animated and continued. "Fiona was absolutely charming and did an excellent presentation with before and after shots. Her plans for Brookings's Main Street were beautiful and the price was so good, we voted unanimously for her."

I nodded, realizing I might have done the same thing if I was in her shoes.

Marla shook her head and blew out a big breath. "But Fiona Pratt is not the same person she was when she wanted something from us." When Marla lifted her head, I expected to see tears in her eyes, but instead, they were filled with fury. She spat, "You're right. I'm going to call Carter and tell him we made a mistake in hiring her. I'll be damned if she stays here one more day."

Had I created a monster? I spoke firmly, "Um…Marla, you have every right to be angry, but you need to be in control when you talk to Mr. Fox. Why don't you sleep on it and call him Monday? I find it helps to think things through before acting." Unfortunately, I rarely followed that advice myself.

Marla whined, "But I feel as though it's my fault we're in this situation. I hired her!"

"You're not the only one on Brookings City Council and you're the newbie. Nobody blames you."

Her chest was heaving so much that I thought she might have a panic attack. I had to find a way to calm her down. I said, "Hey Marla, I've always wanted to try Matcha tea. Could you make me one? I promise I'll pay for it." I winked at her.

She took a deep breath and gave me a wary look. "You're trying to change the subject, aren't you?"

I shrugged. "Maybe? But I really do want to try one."

She said, "Fine," then led me back into the shop and took her usual place behind the counter. Her breathing began to slow as she used her tools of the trade. I watched her expertly add the green powder and mix the hot drink into a froth. She finished and handed me a tall Viking Coffee mug. "Here you go, Ande."

I was shocked at the intensely green concoction. I took a sip of the neon mixture and tried not to make a face. It tasted like hot liquid grass, not that I've ever tasted grass. At least it was a little sweet, so it was sort of drinkable.

With nothing else to do, she wrung her hands. I said, "I've got an idea! Now I'll make a drink for you! But you have to give me the step-by-step directions. Here, sit." I pointed to a stool.

She shrugged, but made her way to the stool and put her head in her hands. "OK, for your first time as a barista, how about making me a strawberry lemonade?"

"Oh, come on. That sounds too easy. Let me try an iced frapalini, or a caramel machismo, or a mochalattemoomoo."

She gave a tired chuckle at my nonsensical coffee names and said, "I've had too much caffeine today. Besides, strawberry lemonade isn't that easy. You have to puree the strawberries."

I followed Marla's directions and cleaned strawberries, squeezed lemons, and even made simple syrup. My concoction must have been okay since she didn't choke on it.

Trying to lighten the mood even more I said, "So, I heard Davis asked you out again?"

She rolled her eyes. "He did. I'm not interested in him, but the guy just won't get the message. Did you see him staring at me last night?"

I thought back and remembered him patting her shoulder, but didn't notice much else. Typical for Davis – he always seemed to blend in with the crowd.

I said, "No. I didn't."

"Well, he's a little overbearing." She pointed to a huge bouquet of red roses in a gorgeous vase on her counter. "He brought these today to cheer me up." She read the card with a dramatic flair, "I would do anything for you, Marla. Anything."

Curious about Davis's infatuation, I said, "Okay, I admit that's a little over the top, but at least you got some beautiful flowers out of the deal?"

She shrugged. "I guess."

I noticed the time on her coffee cup wall clock. Eleven. "Look, I'd better head out. Are you feeling better?"

She nodded and I laid down five dollars for my Matcha Tea, even though she tried to refuse my payment. She put the bill in her cash register. While her head was turned, I poured out the rest of the gross concoction, rinsed my cup and set it on the counter.

I said, "I get to go photograph a little boy's outdoor birthday party now. Yay for me!"

"On a Friday afternoon? Oh that's right. It's still spring break."

"That's what I hear." I put my hand on hers. "Try to stand up to Fiona. Then on Monday, talk to Mr. Fox about finding her a new home."

She scoffed. "If I don't kill her before then."

When I walked out her door, I almost ran into Fiona. She was carrying a package, probably the delivery she hounded Leo about last night. I said, "Hello, Ms. Pratt."

Her nose wrinkled up and she gave a curt nod.

I squared my shoulders. "I'm not sure if you have discussed our concerns with the workmen yet, but the street is even worse today than yesterday."

"And exactly what does a photographer know about major street reconstruction?"

When her lip curled in a haughty expression, I couldn't help but get angry. "Well, I know enough that if someone gets hurt, you'll have to deal with a lawsuit."

"Not my problem if people don't heed warning signs."

I scoffed. "What signs?" I had certainly never seen any.

She pointed to a small orange card posted on a light post. A person would have to be within inches of it to read the print. A little deflated by her defense, I took a breath and prepared for round two. "Well, some of your men threatened me today and I have a mind to call the police to report the incident." I nodded behind Fiona at the guys who still stood in a huddle.

I waited for her snippy response and wasn't disappointed. She glanced down the street and laughed. "They threatened you? In what way?"

My face was suddenly hot. It was futile to explain to this woman what had happened. She would probably stick up for them anyway.

She did just that, and even said the phrase I hate most, "Boys will be boys. What do you expect, walking around in your little ponytail? They're trying to get a rise out of you and obviously it worked."

Fiona turned and disappeared through the door without another word. I stood still, baffled at her ridiculous justification, then shut my mouth and crossed the street. My fault? Hmmph. Did the men have something on her?

When I reached my shop, I turned around and stuck my tongue out at the rude woman, knowing full well she couldn't see me. But I got immense satisfaction from it anyway.

However, Mustache Man had witnessed my childish gesture and gave a knowing nod just before entering the coffee shop behind her.

I sat down with Flash and ran my finger down his unbelievably soft feathered back. As usual he urged me to pet his neck. As I did, my breathing slowed considerably. Funny how a little birdbrained pet could calm me down so much. "You're a good boy, Flash"

He took that as a cue to sing the song he'd learned from me, "It's a beautiful day in the neighborhood."

I gave a sharp laugh. "Not this neighborhood. Not today."

Once my breathing returned to normal, I put Flash in his cage and got everything ready for the circus-themed kid's party. It Main Street drama. Just as I stood to leave, shouting came from outside. I looked through my front window to see Fiona standing outside Viking Coffee shaking her finger at Mustache Man. Now that was the kind of drama that interested me. I crept over and opened the door a crack to hear.

I hoped she was telling him to leave me alone but it didn't sound like it when Mustache Man yelled, "Didn't I say it would catch up with you? You play with fire, you're gonna get burned." He stormed away, leaving her shaking her head.

Hm. It sounded like Fiona was up to something and Mustache Man knew it.

Before leaving for the big birthday event, I crossed the street to buy a bouquet at Brookings' Flowers. When I reached the shop, Davis was slumped over his counter, head on his arms.

I flung the door open. "Davis? Are you OK?"

After a long beat, he looked up and sniffed. His face was the color of printer paper, except for his red-rimmed eyes. He had definitely been crying.

I ran to him. "Davis, what's wrong?"

"Everything. Marla still won't date me and I just got a second letter from that Fiona lady saying they are giving the Main Street flower job to someone else this summer because I won't supply the new planters for free. But I can't. If I did I'd go broke."

"Oh my. That's not right." I put my hand on his. "Listen, some out-of-town project manager doesn't decide who maintains the hanging baskets. The City Council does, so don't worry."

He was still too upset to listen. "But, Ande, I've always done the flowers on Main. That's my steady income all summer long." He became animated. "I choose just the right flowers, then water and freshen the pots every week. My business has been horrible since the construction started and Mabry's Flowers in Watertown is booming. What if Fiona has them do it?"

My heart hurt as I watched tears run down his round face. Before I could respond he blurted, "I am so tired of all of them! One of the stupid workmen told me I must be fruity to work in a flower shop. They are awful. I could just shoot that whole crew!"

Whoa. That didn't sound good. I had never seen Davis that angry so I tried to empower him. "Maybe you should write Fiona a letter or give her a call. Tell her it's the City Council who chooses who provides and maintains the Main Street Flowers. She can't bully you."

He shook his head. "I don't know if I can do that."

"Sure you can. You're a smart guy. And as for Marla? Give her some time. You know she's under stress now with Fiona's invasion of Viking Coffee."

He gave a light shrug. "I guess so." He looked up at me for the first time. "Thanks, Ande. I wish I was bold like you."

I scoffed. "Don't wish for that. Sometimes my assertiveness gets me in deep doo doo. But, I have faith in you, Davis."

His tears finally stopped and I felt better leaving him alone. "Look, I need to get to my photo shoot." I turned to leave and stopped short when I saw the bouquet of flowers on the counter.

"Oh, I completely forgot why I stopped by. Can I buy a few sturdy flowers for children to hold as props for my birthday party photo shoot?"

Without waiting, Davis bundled a few brightly colored wildflowers and handed them to me. "Just take them. I appreciate your help."

CHAPTER 4

When I arrived at Seth's 8th birthday celebration I was met by a clown who didn't speak to me but repeatedly honked a horn as he led me to my booth. I pulled my cart full of gear across the massive, muddy lawn. My mouth hung open as I took in the sights. I had expected a party with ten to fifteen kids, a cake, and presents, but this was a social function beyond my imagination. No expense had been spared. We passed men setting up a huge bouncy house on the right. On the left stood a group of four ponies wearing feathered headbands, ready to be ridden. Helium balloons were tied to every chair at eight tables. Had they invited the whole town? The smell of cotton candy and popcorn was so strong my stomach began to growl. I should have had more than half a cup of Matcha Tea.

I thought back to my rather bland birthdays. Times sure have changed. This shebang even had a huge adult tent with wine and cheese. I guess parents must have taken Spring Break off too.

My job was to take photos of the action and also spend an hour taking portraits of the kids. I started setting up my booth, happy that the red and white striped backdrop I brought fit so well with the circus theme. I lay my costumes and props on a table, but the clown wigs, plastic top hats, and stuffed monkeys were cheap and cheesy compared to the live animals, a professional clown, and juggler. Maybe I should have arranged to have a real monkey for the photos.

Seth's mother had asked me to bring Flash, but I politely refused. Last October, he caught a cold from being outside and I wasn't going to risk it this time of year. He is an African parrot and I had to baby my warm climate bird.

I photographed children greeting the birthday boy and stared as people kept adding impeccably wrapped gifts to a huge pile.

Even though I recognized most of the adult guests, I didn't think I should mingle, being a paid worker and all. Seth's mom had asked me to take pictures of everyone, so I stood to the side of the action and started taking photos with my zoom lens, feeling a little like a voyeur. I snapped a picture of a friend I knew from school and was surprised her son was so big. Gee, I must be getting old.

I spotted a former client who shooed her kids away and took a long sip of wine. That reminded me of the torturous session I had with her family. I would drink too if I had those children. As I scanned the area through my viewfinder, my jaw dropped when Mayor Fox filled the screen.

I considered walking over to speak to him, but just then Seth's father made a premature announcement that the photo booth was open. In a panic, I hurried across the lawn trying to beat the rush of kids. They swarmed around me as I tried to set up my new wireless printer.

Never having worked with children without parents overseeing them, I became frustrated. "Hey kids, let's line up over here while I finish setting up." I tried to herd the group, but they were all over the place. I said in a cheerful voice, "The first ones in line can find a costume or prop if you want."

A big boy who was almost as tall as me rushed to the table pushing another boy out of the way. He grabbed the colorful wig, pulled it down over his head, jumped in front of my backdrop and yelled, "Take the picture!" At that moment I realized I could never be a teacher.

Oh, brother, I was in over my head. Why in the world hadn't I hired an assistant? It was impossible to corral the kids, control my props, and print photos all at once. I said to the big boy,

"Hold on, buddy. Not quite ready." I fiddled with the printer as kids fought over the props.

A deep voice said, "Looks like you could use some help?"

An attractive man pushed a little girl in a wheelchair towards me. I closed my eyes and sighed, "Oh, good God, yes."

He gave a sweet laugh and said, "Max, you go back to your place in line. Josh, I think you and Sammy were first." Remarkably, the big boy took the wig off, set it down, and returned to the back of the line without complaining, at least not aloud. The two other boys noisily chose their props and stood on the big dots I had put on the ground, then posed for me.

Who the heck was this magical man sent from heaven who knew the names of the kids? He was tall with medium-length blonde hair and a closely-cropped beard. When I realized I was still gawking at him, I quickly turned to the boys and pressed the shutter. I checked the screen to confirm the image was good, then asked them, "Do you each want a copy?"

"Yes!" They yelled in unison.

While the nice man organized the children, I connected the printer to the wireless settings on my new camera. My shoulders relaxed when the 4x6 prints inched through the machine one at a time. I handed the photos to the boys and said, "You might want to give these to your parents." They ran off, giggling. The pictures were probably crumpled or lost before the ink had even dried. Not my problem.

This procedure continued for a good 45 minutes until a kid shouted, "Bouncy house!" causing the remaining children to leave my line and run towards the giant inflated structure.

I threw my head back and took a few deep breaths. With no chaos at my booth anymore, I had time to notice the olive-skinned girl sitting quietly in her wheelchair. She smiled at me, displaying big dimples and huge green eyes. I didn't know her affliction but assumed she could have a photo taken. I leaned down to her level and said, "Would you like to have a picture taken?" I pointed to the backdrop.

When she nodded, I said, "What would you like to wear? A tiara or a funny hat?"

She looked up at the man, who promptly signed something to her. The girl perked up and signed back to him.

He said, "She wants to hold the monkey."

"Monkey it is." I watched the man, whom I assumed was her father, as he pushed her chair gently to the spot on the grass. She held the monkey so happily that I took several pictures.

I knelt down again. "I'm glad your dad was here to help me."

The girl watched him, but he answered me without signing to her. "I'm not her father, although I wouldn't mind if I was. She's amazing."

My eyebrows shot up. Who was this guy with the engaging smile?

"Katy is one of my students. I'm new at Harlow Elementary. I teach special ed classes, which includes students who are deaf and hard of hearing. Her parents had to work today, so I am her escort."

So, that's how he knew the kids. I sure never had a teacher so handsome. He signed something to Katy who nodded and giggled. I wanted to giggle too. "What did you say?"

He looked at me and said with clear blue eyes, "You're my date today."

Gulp. I understood he was just relaying what he signed to her, but when he looked at me while he said it, my entire body flushed. Embarrassed, I pivoted to my printer. "That's sweet of you…?"

He finished my sentence, "James."

I turned back and handed the photos to Katy, then reached out my hand to him and said, "Nice to meet you, James. I'm Ande Nilsen."

He added, "of 'Picture This on Main', Brookings, South Dakota?"

I was speechless. How did he know that? Then I realized all my information was in plain view on the banner hanging from the table behind me. I smiled and said, "That's right. Thanks again for your help, James." I leaned down to Katy. "And thank you for being so photogenic." I gave her the little bundle of flowers to keep and she giggled.

The charming man mouthed "Thanks", gave me that contagious smile again and wheeled her away. I practically swooned to meet such a gorgeous and clever man with a good heart. I snapped some pictures of him as they left.

I mean, it was my job after all.

When James turned a corner, Carter Fox came into view standing alone by a tent. Since there were no kids waiting for photos, I took my camera and casually snapped a few pics as I made my way to him. In a sly move I accidentally, okay on purpose, bumped into him. I said, "Excuse me," then turned around feigning surprise. "Mayor Fox. What are you doing here?"

He smiled. "It's a kids' birthday party and I have kids. Where else would I be? It's Ande, right?"

"Yes. Bet you know why I'm here." I held up my camera.

He nodded and I swear when his dark eyes twinkled, I melted for the second time today.

"Is your wife here?" Oh, good grief. He's going to think I'm trying to hit on him.

A look of annoyance passed his face and I chastised myself for bothering him. Or was he upset with Debra? But he yelled across the lawn, "Simone, give the toy back to Simon!" When he turned back to me. "Oh, Debra is running errands."

Of course. Why would she have anything to do with her own offspring? I nodded to my camera. "I need to get back to work, but I have a question. Did Marla White call you today?"

He said, "Yes. She left a message, but I haven't had a chance to listen to it."

So much for her waiting to call. "Well," I said, "she's pretty upset about Ms. Pratt putting down roots in her coffee shop. Perhaps you can find another place for her to work?"

His eyebrows closed in together, but I kept going, "In addition to that, several Main Street business owners have concerns about the whole project. The workers are extremely sloppy and very rude."

His eyes grew even darker, then he touched my hand and said, "I'm sorry to hear this."

I was so surprised at his touch that I almost forgot my other question. I took a breath, lowered my hands to my sides, and came to my senses. "Also, would it be possible to see the plans for the Main Street project?"

He smiled. "Of course. Stop by my office tomorrow. No appointment needed."

I was captivated by his warmth but was distracted when his children ran up to him carrying adorable puppies. They shouted in unison, "Look, Dad, Seth got puppies."

Puppies for birthday gifts? Now, that was over the top, but they sure were precious. I quickly snapped a few pictures of the twins clutching the wiggly chocolate labs. The pure joy on their faces made for much better photos than the forced smiles in the studio yesterday. When Simon held a puppy up to his dad, Carter jumped back as if a snake was thrust at him. He put his hands on his chest and spat, "Put them back. Put them back now!"

The twins backed away. Simon lowered his head and mumbled to his sister, "I told you he'd never let us have one."

That just about broke my heart. I looked at the frazzled man. "Not a dog fan?"

He took a breath and cleared his throat. "I don't like animals, especially dogs."

"Ande!" I turned to find Seth's mother waving her hands. "He's opening his presents We need you!"

Dang. Busted on the job. "Oh, of course. I'm coming." I turned back to Carter and shrugged, then scurried off to capture the monumental event.

When I was finally released from all my party pic duties, I packed up my gear. On my way out I stopped to take a few photos of the ponies.

With Flash on my shoulder, I spent a few hours editing the birthday images. I turned my head. "Flash, you're a good boy. Thanks for not being a brat like some of those kids at the party."

He didn't comment but bit my ear lobe gently. Worried he might pierce another hole in it, I set him on the desk and watched him walk around in his funny way with four toes spread flat – two in front and two in back. He picked up a piece of paper and immediately poked holes in it with his beak.

After I emailed the proofs to Seth's mom, I sent the Fox family's large order to the lab across town to be printed. I am super happy to let someone else develop my photos for me even though I have the equipment and should do it myself.

I put Flash back in his cage and stretched my arms up over my head. My eyes were tired from staring so long at the computer screen and I decided to go see Doc.

Doc stood at his counter counting change. He brightened. "Hey, I was just closing up and planned to go over to your place to fix the bracket."

"Oh good! I'm making spaghetti. Does that sound okay?"

"Of course. Free food always sounds good to me."

He locked his door and we stepped into the street but froze when we saw Doc's car. The ragtop on his convertible was slit from the windshield to the back window.

"What the hell?" Doc walked around the car and shook his head slowly as he assessed the damage. "Oh. Fiona is dead now!"

"What should we do? Want me to call the police?"

Doc rubbed his hand across his chin and took a deep breath. Composing himself, he turned to me. "Look, I'll deal with this. Go on home and start your dinner. I'll be there in a while."

I couldn't believe how calm and reasonable he was. If someone had messed with my car, I would scream and cry - and my vehicle isn't an expensive sports car. "Doc, I'm so sorry."

As I crossed to my apartment, I started to get upset for him. Surely Fiona didn't vandalize his car out of spite. After hearing her threat I couldn't think of anyone else to blame, but that just seemed crazy. It had to be someone else – probably a prankster or maybe someone trying to steal something from his car.

While I cooked dinner, Jon came home. He grabbed the slice of bread I was getting ready to butter and stuffed it in his mouth. My adorable little brother wasn't really that little. The blonde 21-year-old stood a foot taller than me. I looked up at him and told him about Doc's car.

"Do you think he needs help?" He started toward the door.

"No. He wants to handle it himself. Go ahead and get cleaned up for dinner."

Jon took off his sweaty shirt, tossed it on the floor, and pulled down his pants exposing his bare bottom. "Jon! Seriously? I don't want to see that!"

He shrugged and finished stripping in the bathroom.

When the food was just about ready and my brother was in the shower, there was a light knock on my apartment door. Assuming it was Doc, I yelled, "Come in!" I was glad he had a key to my photography studio so I didn't have to run downstairs to let him in. It was nice to have someone trustworthy in my life besides Jon. Doc was always fixing something for me anyway.

Doc walked in and acted as if nothing had happened. I watched him calmly sit at the table and take a long drink of water. Why wasn't he furious?

I asked, "Did you call the police?"

"I took care of it." He poured two glasses of wine.

Did that mean he did or didn't call the police? Maybe he wasn't in the mood to talk about it.

Jon walked in and I shook my head at him suggesting he shouldn't bring up the car. I said brightly, "Perfect timing."

While I served plates of pasta with meat sauce, Doc and Jon chatted about Jon's new job.

As Doc slurped his noodles, I relaxed a bit and told them about the outlandish birthday party. "It was unbelievable." I turned to my brother. "Jon, remember our birthdays? My most exciting was when I was 13 and got to invite two girls to go to a movie with me then have a sleepover."

He smirked. "Yeah, not so sure I ever had a real party unless you count the time I got my new sled. A few buddies and I took it out on the pond south of town to play on the ice."

"Oh, I remember that. What a shame it fell through the ice. You never found it, huh?"

"Nope, but Mom felt sorry for me and made us hot chocolate and cookies when we came home without it."

Doc chuckled. "Sounds about like my birthdays. So someone actually gave them puppies? I swear…these kids are so spoiled today and don't get me started about getting prizes just for participation."

I nodded. "Oh, and guess what? I met the sweetest lady who wants me to take photos of her goldfish."

Jon said, "A goldfish? How long do they live? A month?"

I said, "Exactly! But I tell you, Bubbles was huge. But I'll be able to add goldfish photography to my resume."

They chuckled. When I described my visit with Marla and how upset she had been, Doc's mouth twitched. I refrained from telling either of them about Mustache Man's threats or my run-in with Fiona. No point poking these two bears.

The timer rang and I got up to get the garlic bread from the oven. Doc said, "Jon, you know Stan Landry, right?"

He said, "Sure."

Besides being part of the Spinners Thursday night gang, Stan had taught both of us English courses at SDSU and was the one who suggested Jon major in Art. Jon had even gone on a few biking outings with him. Stan was one of us.

"Well, I have some news about him." Doc's expression was grim. I sat down and waited to hear.

He grimaced when he said, "Stan stepped in a hole in front of Mac's Diner this morning and broke his leg in two places. I don't know the details, but he'll be in the hospital a few days."

My hands flew to my mouth. "Not Stan! He's the worst person to break a leg."

Last year the professor bicycled the whole 246-mile span of South Dakota from north to south in one day! He was planning to take on North Dakota when school ended in May. I said, "Stan will be lost if he can't ride his bike. I knew something would happen. Stupid inept construction crew."

Silverware bounced when Jon hit the table. "I'm getting sick of hearing about the lack of safety on this street." He shook his head and turned to me. "This morning, I saw some of the jerks you were talking about. One of the guys tossed a broken brick on the sidewalk. It bounced and hit the side of the bookstore, nearly breaking the window. And then they laughed about it!" Jon shook his head. "I started to go outside and give them a piece of my mind, but this lady in a pantsuit came out of the coffee shop and said something to them. When she turned around, one of the guys gave her the finger."

I was happy to think Fiona had actually reprimanded the guys for something, but too little too late.

Doc said, "Not cool."

Jon nodded. "Oh, and today, I heard our team was supposed to get that job, but at the last minute, the City Council gave it to that whole crew from Rapid."

I shook my head. "Hmpf. You would have been so much better." Because I was riled up and since we were discussing the workers, I blurted out, "Oh, on that subject, remember the rude guy I told you about – Mustache Man?"

Jon nodded, but Doc gave me a curious look. Guess I hadn't told him. I continued. "Well, today he threatened me."

My brother furrowed his brow. "What?"

Doc lifted his chin slowly, "What did he say?"

Oops. I meant to keep this all quiet. I shook my head and tried to diffuse the situation. "I think he was just blowing smoke, but he said something like I was a little bug and that they squash bugs that get in their way. It wasn't that big of a deal, just annoying."

Doc warned, "I don't know about that. You need to be careful, Ande. Those guys aren't from around here and could be trouble."

Jon nodded. "I've worked with a lot of construction workers lately and most of them are fine, but some are pretty sleazy."

I nodded. "I'll be careful." Just thinking about Mustache Man made me angry.

After eating a few more bites, my phone rang. It was my best friend, Sarah, calling all the way from Ghana, Africa. What a perfect way to lift my spirits! I left the boys and my food and ran to my bedroom to talk to Sarah.

I squealed when she said she was finally coming home after a year of working with Doctors Without Borders. She would be here Sunday night and asked if she could stay with me for a few weeks until she found a place.

I said, "Of course, you can! I'm dying to see you, girl. Life hasn't been the same since you left." After we made more plans, I hung up and skipped into the living room.

Jon said, "Did you win the lottery?"

"Or find out they fired Fiona?" Doc tried.

"No." I squeaked, "Sarah's coming home in two days!"

Jon smiled and nodded. "Cool." He always liked my smart, sassy friend.

Then, I realized my mistake. "Um… I told her she could stay here for a few weeks. I'm not sure how that will work with the three of us in this tiny place." (Especially if Jon was apt to strip naked whenever he wanted.)

Jon gave a slow shrug. "I guess I can stay at Mom and Dad's."

This had always been an option, but since we had been keeping his troubles from our parents temporarily, we had both thought it best not to have him stay at their house, at least until they returned and he could talk to them in person.

Doc sized up the situation and without missing a beat said, "Jon, you can stay at my place for a while if you want. I have plenty of room."

He wasn't kidding about that. Doc's house had five bedrooms and four of them were empty. I watched my brother, wondering if he would mind moving down the street temporarily. He smiled and said, "Whatever. That'll work. Thanks."

I said, "Thanks, Doc, but I want him back as soon Sarah finds a place."

After dinner, Doc repaired my bracket while I worried about his state of mind. When he left, I watched him cross the street. His little car was not in its usual place in front of his hardware store. Maybe he took it to his friend who works on foreign automobiles. I hoped he filed a police report and an insurance claim. Poor guy.

Shortly after Doc left, Jon went to the pottery lab to work on a project.

After cleaning up, I studied my tiny apartment. The only place for Sarah to sleep was on the couch, so I lay on it to make sure it was comfortable. It was long enough for Jon and not lumpy so hopefully, it would do. I started emptying drawers of my winter wear into a box so she would have room for her clothes. My phone rang and Marla's name popped up.

"Hey, girl?"

In a frantic voice, Marla's said, "Ande! Come to my shop. It's an emergency!"

Why was Marla acting so dramatic lately? "Okay. I'll be right over." I grabbed my coat and headed down the stairs. Couldn't she just wait until Monday to discuss Fiona? She had always been level-headed, before this week anyway. I locked my studio and crossed the street, shining my flashlight on the ground to avoid stepping in a hole like Stan had.

The coffee shop door was locked but I could see light filtering through the drawn shades. When I knocked, Marla answered the door immediately. She pulled me inside and glanced down both sides of the street as if we were both in a spy movie.

I said, "What in the world, Marla?"

"Look!" She pointed to the booth where Fiona sat slumped over the table. I had a sense of déjà vu after seeing Davis in the same position earlier in the day.

I ran to her. "Fiona, are you OK?" I hoped she was just taking a nap, but she didn't respond to my voice and definitely didn't snore. When I shook her shoulder lightly, her hand slipped from the table and her arm hung loose like a rag doll."

CHAPTER 5

I was stricken dumb. My gaze shot to Marla who stood wide-eyed with her hand over her mouth.

I whispered, "Did you call an ambulance?"

She gulped, "No. I just came in and found her like this. I was so freaked out, that I called you." She squeaked, "I think she may be dead!" Marla's face contorted into an agonized grimace.

I took a shaky breath and spoke as calmly as I could, "Call 9-1-1 while I check for a pulse." I placed my fingers around Fiona's wrist and was shocked by the coolness of her skin. Feeling nothing, I cautiously pressed her neck. I shook my head at Marla while she talked to the dispatcher. Her face turned pale as she spoke. I studied Fiona, but couldn't see any sign of trauma. Maybe it was a heart attack or some other medical episode? Not knowing what to do, I just stood there as my own heart started to race.

Marla had barely hung up when a car screeched to a halt outside the door. I peeked through the shades, relieved to see a police cruiser, but what we really needed was an ambulance.

When Fred Morris stepped out, I cringed. Shoot. We must have caught the annoying officer just before shift change. I sighed as the 50-something veteran policeman carefully placed his hat over his extreme combover and adjusted his gun belt. He patted his gun, threw his shoulders back, and marched to the door.

I have mixed feelings about Fred Morris. On one hand, he was extremely detail-oriented and far more experienced than the other Brookings officers. On the other hand, he was so irritating and nit-picky that he couldn't see the forest for the trees. The peculiar man grated on my nerves. But in this horrible situation, I was happy to have even Fred here.

I unlocked the door and he walked in. His massive set of keys jingled with each step. Morris pointed a finger at me and said in his nasal voice, "Andrea Nilsen," then pointed to Marla. "Marla White," as if he was logging our attendance in his internal database. He spotted Fiona and made a beeline for her. "The emergency medical technicians are on their way." He snapped on a pair of blue medical gloves pulled from his pocket, and checked Fiona's pulse points. "It may be too late."

My heart sank. I had hoped I was just inept at finding a pulse. Maybe the paramedics could do something when they arrived. I stood by Marla and we watched the strange man tiptoe around the area. He pulled a magnifying glass from a retractable clip on his belt and studied the table. He took his phone from a leather clip and snapped photos of every inch. Next came baggies and tweezers. I wasn't sure where they came from, but he meticulously picked up a cup, napkin, and plate and zipped them into individual bags.

What was he doing? No evidence suggested a crime had been committed, but his meticulous investigation got me wondering. Could there have been foul play?

When I heard a siren I ran to the door, happy to distance myself from the scene. Once the EMTs entered, the coffee shop became chaotic with medical procedures.

Marla and I remained to the side as spectators. Morris glided over to us, holding a metal clipboard. His pen was poised, ready to take notes. "Please confirm the name of the injured party."

Marla;s voice was shaky. "Fiona Pratt."

He pursed his lips as he wrote. "Tell me what happened - from the beginning,"

Marla took a deep breath. "I left the shop at two-thirty today to go to Sioux Falls and get supplies. Fiona wanted to stay here, so I closed the shop to let her work. I ended up running some other errands and had dinner in Sioux Falls. When I came back at about 7:30, I found her like this." Marla started to cry.

"What is your relationship with Ms. Pratt?" Morris' flat voice showed no sympathy.

Marla squinted and shook her head. "No relationship. She's the project manager for the construction on Main Street. She's using my shop as her office."

He nodded. "I understand. You are her landlady."

Marla wrinkled her nose, ready to object but Morris turned to me. "And how are you involved?"

Before I could answer, our attention was drawn to the gurney where Fiona lay. I was stunned into silence when the paramedic pulled the sheet over her face. Morris was unaffected by the sight and raised an eyebrow awaiting my response. I turned away from the scene and cleared my throat. "Um…Marla called me when she found her and I came right over."

His face pinched as he moved uncomfortably close to Marla. "You called Ms. Nilsen before dialing 9-1-1?"

Marla's eyes glistened. "I didn't know what to do."

I piped up, "I came immediately. She had no pulse when I got here."

He squeezed his eyes shut. "Miss Nilsen, please tell me you didn't tamper with my investigation."

Oh brother. Here goes. I've had a rocky association with Fred Morris since I can remember. Years ago, he and my father were fishing buddies. Once, Dad took me to Fred's house, where I pulled the feathers off his handmade fishing lures and glued them to my doll's hat. In my defense, I was only four, but he has never forgiven me. To me, the most surprising part of the story was that I didn't get poked with the hooks. But I got no credit at all.

I rolled my eyes. "I assure you, Fred, I didn't touch anything except her wrist and neck."

With irritation, he corrected me, "It's Detective Morris."

That term was debatable. Fred Morris was a self-proclaimed detective. His official rank with Brookings Police is Officer Morris. But in his mind, he is the modern-day Sherlock Holmes and God's gift to our police force. His ego had inflated ten years ago when he solved a burglary case. Of course, he had stumbled upon the theft in progress, but he convinced himself he has a special gift.

Morris moved toward me and lifted his eyebrow. "And did you have a relationship with the deceased?"

I shuddered at the word, deceased, but managed to answer. "I met Ms. Pratt for the first time, last night at Spinners. Then I ran into her here, this morning." I wasn't about to mention the cross words we had on each occasion.

"And what time was that?" His pen hovered over the paper.

I looked at my watch. It was 7:40 pm now. I counted backward through the day. I had run to Doc's at about 5:00. The birthday party was from 1-3. I looked up and saw the coffee cup trying to focus and saw Marla's clock. I clearly remembered seeing th time on it this morning. I stated with confidence, "It was eleven."

Morris snapped his metal clipboard closed and said, "This is a grave situation. There will be an investigation. Do not leave South Dakota. I'll tape off the area until we get a coroner's report. It is not to be disturbed."

I scoffed at the idea of me leaving the state, but Marla said nervously, "How long will that be? I need to open the shop tomorrow morning. Saturday's my busiest day."

He spoke while working. "Ms. White, a death in your establishment is far more serious than catering to the frivolous Millennials who spend five dollars for a cup of coffee that they could make at home for a quarter. But to answer your question, it could take anywhere from a few hours to a few weeks to find the official cause of death. I will be sure to keep you informed."

Her horror was apparent by her open mouth. When the strange officer finally left, I put my arm around her. "You should go home and try to forget this for tonight. Do you have anyone you can call?" I realized how little I knew about Marla's personal life.

She sniffed and said, "My nephew is in town now. I'm sure he'll come over."

Relieved she wouldn't be alone, I said, "Okay, then I'll head home too. Call me if you want."

Marla was already making a phone call as I left the shop. Just outside the door, a silver earring lay on the ground. It might be Marla's but I didn't want to bother her now, so I put it in my pocket to ask her about it tomorrow.

That night I dreamed a group of woodpeckers had a party on my windowsill. They pecked with such vigor they broke the glass. When I awoke and focused on the window, I was reassured to find the glass fully intact. Jackhammers at 7 a.m.? So much for sleeping in on Saturday.

I frowned when I remembered the incident from the night before. It was hard to erase the image of Fiona's body being taken from the coffee shop. A sick feeling filled my stomach.

When I went into the living room, Jon wasn't on the couch. It was a good sign he was up so early. I turned on some music to drown out the insistent pounding outside and sat at my window with my cup of coffee. Today, the street below was closed to traffic so the mess was literally blocking the road to my livelihood. Perhaps Marla wouldn't lose many more customers anyway. A flock of orange vests dotted our block, looking like ladybugs from this distance. I was surprised the workers were up so early if they drank as much last night as they had on Thursday. I sighed. At least they were working.

My only session of the day was at two so I had plenty of time to check out rummage sales before going to see Carter Fox. I messaged Doc and he wrote back immediately with a list of places and times for the sales. I made up my mind to tell him about Fiona in person rather than via text.

After a shower, I put my hair in my signature ponytail, cut some fresh fruit, and snacked as I went downstairs to greet Flash. I opened his cage and gave him some of my breakfast to eat while

I was gone. As I exited the door, an obnoxious sound came from his cage. Oh, no way!

I growled, "Flash, that is not funny. You are not allowed to imitate a jackhammer."

He looked at me like, 'What are you going to do about it?'

At the first sale, Doc greeted me with a cup of "25-cent" coffee straight from his thermos. I followed him around as he perused tools. He had added a healthy dose of Irish Cream. I said, "Yum. So, Doc, I have something to tell you."

When he raised his eyebrows, I pulled him away from the other shoppers and whispered, "After you left, Marla called me to her shop. She found Fiona in her booth...dead!"

He blinked then said, "Really?" Then he puffed out some air and added, "Karma's a bitch."

His comment was insensitive even for Doc, who always spoke his mind. My mouth hung open as I studied him. Wasn't he even curious as to how she died?

He picked up a hammer and finally asked, "How'd she die?"

I shrugged. "Not sure. She was just slumped over the table. Probably some sort of medical episode." Irritated by his ambivalence, I snapped, "All I know is that it was awful to find her like that."

He must have realized my frustration and laid a hand on my shoulder. "I'm sorry you had to see that, Ande."

His friendly touch converted me back to myself. "And of course, Morris had to be on duty. He was being himself as usual."

Doc nodded. "What do you expect from our local Sherlock?" After a brief pause, he changed the topic completely. "You might want to look at the camera over there. It's kinda cool."

I followed him to a Kodak Instamatic with a box of flashcubes for $10. I couldn't resist yet another old camera. Dog costumes and squeaky toys happened to be stacked beside it – a gold mine. I bought the whole lot and tried not to spill my coffee as I carried them.

Doc smirked. "Bet you don't have any cat toys."

I pointed my only free finger at him. "Bet I do. But you would know if you ever brought G and T in for portraits."

"Why do I need pictures of them? Those holy terrors are in my face all day and all night."

I laughed. "I know, but you would be lost without your babies." My grumpy friend had a soft spot for his matching black and white cats, Gin and Tonic. He truly adored them.

We spent another hour touring Brookings's cluttered driveways and garages. I was glad for the distraction. At one sale, we ran into Peggy and Mike hauling treasures to their SUV. It's not surprising that they are regular rummagers since an antique store is a perfect place to resell found treasures.

When I told them about Fiona, Peggy said, "Uffdaa!" She shook her head and added, "Well, it's no secret none of us liked her, but still, that's awful. What happened?"

I shook my head. "Dunno. I didn't see any signs of injury."

Mike wiped his brow. "That's horrible. I wonder who will take over as project manager?"

Doc shrugged, "Whoever it is, can't be worse than she was."

Just then, Leo drove up and rolled down his window. "Did you guys hear about Fiona?"

We nodded then he asked, "Well, did you hear about Stan?"

Doc and I frowned, but since Mike and Peggy hadn't heard, so Leo told the story to his brother and sister-in-law.

When he finished, I said, "I think I'll run over to see Stan now. Anyone wanna go with?"

Leo said, "I already stopped by as soon as I heard this morning. He'll be happy to see you. I gotta git. I have to install a washer at Jean's house." He winked and drove away.

Peggy frowned. "I can't go. I'm opening the shop today even if people have to walk a plank to get inside. Tell Stan hi and let him know how sorry we are. Mike, are you ready?"

Mike said, "Yep." He turned to me. "Tell him we'll stop by tonight." They got in their car and headed to the antique store.

Doc said, "I'll go. Jack is working the store anyway."

"Great. I'll pick you up in a bit. Thanks for the coffee." I handed his mug back and watched him get in his truck. Why hadn't he told the others about the vandalism to his convertible?

Stan lay on a stark white hospital bed wearing his signature ball cap. His leg, wrapped twice its normal size, was elevated. After basic chit-chat, we learned that aside from the pain, he was depressed because he wouldn't be able to bike for months.

I said, "So, tell me what happened."

Stan shifted in his bed and winced in pain. "I rode my bike to the south end of Main, hopped off, and walked it so I could "safely" make my way through the construction maze." He rolled his eyes at the irony and continued. "I avoided the few barriers and cones that were visible. And then it happened! I stepped on a patch of innocent-looking snow. Down I went and here I am."

I cringed. "Can you tell me the size of the hole?"

He studied the ceiling as he calculated. "Maybe 15 inches across and 10 inches deep. Enough to break my tibia and fibula."

My stomach flipped at the thought. I've never been good with injuries. One more profession I need to avoid – medicine.

Doc nodded and with a very serious face said, "But...just tell us the bike is OK. I mean, that is our main concern, right?"

We laughed. Our group always joked that Stan took better care of his bicycles than himself. One of his bikes cost almost as much as my car.

"It's a little scratched up, but I'm not stupid. I don't ride my road bikes this time of year."

"You know," Doc said, "You should sue the construction crew. We warned them this could happen. They owe you a really good hybrid for this."

I nodded. "Right. We should talk to Mike about it. Fiona pointed out some posted caution signs, but they are so tiny, I doubt anyone would notice them."

Stan said, "Well, I sure didn't."

Doc rolled his eyes and said, "I'll bet she put them up after your accident."

All this talk about Fiona and I'd forgotten to tell Stan she had died! I cleared my throat and told him the news.

"Wow. That's bad, but after all I've heard, I wouldn't be surprised if someone did her in." He shook his head. "At least I have a pretty good alibi." He pointed to his leg.

Murder? I sure hoped it wasn't, but just in case, what was my alibi? I had been alone several hours after the party and before going to see Doc. Yikes.

Before we left, I touched Stan's arm and said seriously, "I'm really very sorry this happened."

I took my rummage sale stash home and drove to Brookings Bank and Trust to visit Mayor Fox before the bank closed at noon. Since the Brookings mayor position is only part-time, he kept his job as bank manager when he was elected this year.

The bank is one of two stately buildings on Main Street, the other being the post office. The marble steps out front are so massive that they seem more like the entrance to a national monument than a place to deposit a check.

Once inside the ornate lobby, I asked my teller friend, Marlene, for directions to the mayor's office. She pointed down a hall and I made my way to a huge wooden door with a brass plaque that read, Carter Fox - Bank Manager.

My hand was set to knock when the door opened to reveal Mrs. Fox. She wore a gorgeous lavender coat made of felted wool. It was a striking backdrop for her long golden hair. She scrunched her nose as if she saw something vile. What was her problem? Blocking the door, she hissed, "What are you doing here? Oh God, I know." She sighed. "You probably have a crush on Carter. I caught the way you looked at him the other day. Well, you're not the first and you certainly won't be the last."

My mouth went dry, rendering me speechless. I was glad she hadn't seen me talking to her husband at the birthday party or she would have thought I was stalking him.

Debra peered down her perfect nose at me and scowled. "Stay clear. He's married."

Before I could respond, the tall graceful woman sashayed down the hallway and disappeared into the lobby. I was flustered. Should I leave? Wait! No. The mayor is a public figure and I have every right to talk to him. I will not be bullied by anyone. I took a deep breath and knocked on his door.

His smoky voice said, "Come in."

I pushed the heavy door open and was surprised at the size of his office. It was huge. Mr. Fox sat behind a stately mahogany desk. As soon as he saw me, he stood and flashed a huge smile. He walked around his desk to greet me. The walnut floors must have been recently waxed for they shone like glass. When I took a step, the rug slipped, and I stumbled. He reached out and steadied me with his warm strong hands, making me blush.

"Hi, Ande. I guess you've come to see the plans?" He motioned for me to take a seat.

I nodded and sat in a large leather armchair that squeaked as I settled in.

Mr. Fox sat in his oversized office chair across the desk. "Great. I have them ready for you, But, first, did you hear about Ms. Pratt?"

"Yes." I swallowed. "I was there when the EMT's arrived."

He frowned. "I'm sorry to hear that. That must have been very difficult for you."

I nodded. "It was, but it was even worse for poor Marla who will probably relive the scene every day when she sees the booth. Worse yet, the police taped her place off like it's a crime scene."

His face turned ashen and he asked, "Why?"

I waved the thought away. "Oh, that's the way Officer Morris rolls. I'm no doctor but she must have had some sort of medical episode." I remembered what Mike had said and asked, "I know it's probably too early to ask, but what are you going to do about a project manager? We have excellent engineers in the area."

"I'm considering one of the foremen on the job."

I found that statement to be absurd. None of the workmen I had met seemed fit for the job. I said, "Well whoever it is, I hope they will crack down on the shoddy workmanship."

He cocked his head. "Is that one of your concerns?"

Ready to get down to business, I sat up straight. "Yes. The Mainstreet Merchant's Association is concerned with the lack of safety on Main Street. The crew is not cleaning up after themselves or taking precautions to keep people safe."

Mr. Fox leaned in with his elbows on his desk. "I'm sure it's not as bad as you think."

What? This man's own family had to step over chunks of concrete outside my studio on Thursday. Suddenly the meeting felt more formal, especially with the enormous desk between us. Ready with a comeback I said, "There has already been one accident due to the lack of safety."

He narrowed his eyes as I continued. "A friend who is a professor at SDSU was walking to Mac's Diner yesterday and stepped in a patch of snow that covered a large hole. He broke his leg in two places and is in the hospital." I continued, "What makes the accident especially tragic is that he is an avid bicyclist. You probably saw his picture in the paper last fall for riding across the state in one day. Dr. Stan Landry?"

The recognition in his eyes was instant. "I believe I've met him. Well, that's a real shame. We will send flowers to Dr. Landry on behalf of the City Council." He wrote something on a pad of paper then stood and walked to a table without mentioning the hole. It was as if the whole safety topic had been solved with flowers. He looked back at me as if I should follow, so I did.

The top of a gorgeous oak table was covered in large drawings. Mr. Fox explained the comprehensive plans and quite honestly, the widening project was amazing in this format. The drawings included minute details, from planters to benches and the trees to be planted along a beautiful new median. I was pleased to see the old street lamps would still be used.

I stuttered, "Um…These look very nice." Based on the plans, I could see why they hired Fiona but still had to defend my brother's company. "Did you get bids from businesses on this half of the state? There are many qualified local workers who could have done an excellent job. And the town could have saved the cost of travel and hotels."

He nodded. "We try to hire locally when we can, but this proposal was too good to pass up." He pointed to the plans as if they spoke for themselves. "And Ms. Pratt had her own crew, so we didn't have to worry about hiring the workers."

He paused and put his hand over his heart in reverence, then widened his eyes. "I hope Fiona didn't take your complaints too personally. Even though she seemed strong, you never know what would cause someone to take their own life.

I whipped my head up in disbelief. Was he suggesting she died by suicide? No way. Not Fiona. And was he insinuating that we contributed to it by asking her to clean up the street? I refused to give credence to that idea. The handsome mayor wasn't looking so handsome anymore.

He said, "But you're right, it was probably a medical issue."

As much as I wanted to debate his earlier logic, I shouldn't anger the mayor. I put on a pleasant face and played to his ego. "So, what new philanthropic endeavor are you working on now?"

His mesmerizing smile reappeared. "Oh, not much, but I am sponsoring a health fair next Saturday. You should stop by and get checked out... to make sure you are in tiptop shape."

I studied him. He really did a lot for the community. "Good for you, Mayor Fox. I'll try to stop by." I cleared my throat. "I'd better go. Thank you for showing me the plans. I'll share your information with the other shop owners, but I do hope you will talk to the new project manager about our safety concern."

Carter followed me to the door. When I turned to say goodbye, he clasped both of my hands and pulled me towards him looking deep into my eyes. "Don't be a stranger, Ande."

I unlocked from his gaze and looked at our hands, confused. Moments ago he suggested Fiona might have killed herself because of me, and he flirted? I pulled my hands back. His wife may have good reason to be jealous.

After faking a smile, I exited with a nervous, "See you later."

CHAPTER 6

I spent an hour Saturday afternoon photographing five adorable puppies: beagles in a red wooden bucket, beagles in a giant Easter basket, and beagles surrounded by silk daisies. The images were so precious, that I decided to make a canvas print for my studio wall. Before she left I said to the owner, "So...you wouldn't notice if just one puppy was missing, would you?"

The beagle mom laughed at the speckled nose poking out from my vest. "Actually, only two of them have been claimed, so the others are available."

Frowning, I relinquished the wiggly pup with velvety soft ears and handed it to her. "I wish I could. My landlord won't allow dogs or cats in my apartment. But when I have a place of my own, you I'll probably have a whole menagerie."

She said, "Well for now, at least you have Flash."

"Yeah, but he's not very cuddly. His beak always gets in the way."

I drove to Mom and Dad's house across town to do my laundry and I was surprised to find Jon finishing up a load of his own. While our folks wintered on the Alabama coast, we promised them we would stop by to check on things. Funny how we timed our visits when our clothes got dirty.

When he saw my laundry basket he said, "Great minds think alike." He sighed. "Man, I can't wait for Mom and Dad to come back. I miss her pot roast."

"And you miss her doing your wash."

He smirked. "Maybe? So Sarah comes back tomorrow night. Are you excited to have the dynamic duo together again?"

"Yes. I'm trying to focus on that instead of Fiona's dead body. I put my sheets in the washer and looked up when he didn't respond. His eyes were huge, apparently in the dark. I explained what I knew about Fiona's death and about my visit to the mayor.

"And I thought life on campus was wild."

"I would have told you earlier, but I haven't seen you since dinner last night."

Jon picked up his laundry bag and said, "Yeah, it was so late when I finished at the pottery lab I stayed at Jason's apartment. Look, I've gotta go play in an intramural soccer game. Promise you won't get involved in anything you can't handle."

"OK. Hey, let's hang out tomorrow. Just you and me."

He nodded on his way out the door.

After snagging some snacks from Mom's pantry and watering her houseplants, I folded the warm clothes straight from the dryer. Something clinked on the tile floor. It was the earring I'd stuffed in my pocket last night. I had forgotten all about it and studied the dangly silver earring. It looked expensive. I slipped it into my jeans pocket, vowing to put it somewhere safe when I got home.

Back at the shop, I secured the freshly washed earring in a snack baggie and lay it on my desk downstairs so I wouldn't forget to ask Marla about it.

I sat down to play solitaire on my phone and noticed a missed call. My phone was probably still on silent from the visit to the hospital. I listened to a voicemail from Fred Morris.

"Miss Nilsen, this is Detective Morris with Brookings Police Department." His introduction was comically formal for someone I'd known all my life. And besides, I'd recognize his whiny voice anywhere. He said, "I'm calling with updates concerning Ms. Pratt's autopsy. The preliminary results should be available on Monday. If you wish to hear the findings, simply contact my office…Goodbye."

There was one good thing about Morris; He would keep everyone involved in the case fully informed. But unfortunately, he would also attach himself to us like a leach. I'd be sick of him in days, but at least we might find out how Fiona died.

I wondered whether her funeral would be held in Brookings or Rapid City. I sure didn't want to call Fred back to ask. Besides, Peggy and Mike got the *Brookings Register* and would share that info once they knew anything.

On Sunday, I took Jon out for brunch before we packed up his stuff. I pointed to my dresser. "Can you believe I already took my winter stuff downstairs so Sarah can have an empty drawer?"

He joked, "I see how you are. You'll move your crap for her but not for me?"

I smirked. "Well, now you'll have more room to look forward to when you return – at least until October when I need to move the sweaters upstairs again.

"No offense, but I don't plan to still be living with my sister next fall."

We carried a few loads to my car and drove to Doc's house. After carrying everything up the ancient narrow stairway, Jon chose a room with a window overlooking the park.

I stood at the window and said, "I'm jealous of all the space you'll have here. I mean the whole top floor is yours!"

He winked, "I know. I may never come back to your lumpy couch."

I knew he was kidding but what he said made me sad. I hugged him. "I hope you're not upset with me for ditching you. I really want you back as soon as Sarah leaves, OK?"

He grinned. "I know. But remember, soon I'll have enough cash to get my own place. For now, you need to hang out with Sarah. I can't remember the last time you did anything with girls your own age."

Glad to have his blessing, I reached up and kissed my only sibling on the cheek and said, "Don't be a stranger!"

I went downstairs, thanked Doc again and made my way home to a silent apartment. Better enjoy it now, because once my wild friend moved in, it would be anything but quiet.

That evening, I was so excited about Sarah's arrival that I flitted around the room making the apartment look presentable. Her folks were picking her up at the Sioux Falls airport and would bring her here any minute. The Andersons live out on a farm 20 miles from Brookings. Since Sarah sold her car before she left for Africa, staying at my place made sense. Of course, we had a year's worth of catching up to do anyway so she might as well stay with me.

Not an hour had gone by when a buzz sounded. I raced down the stairs to meet my friend, but she wasn't there. As a matter of fact, nobody was at the door. I stepped out onto the sidewalk and looked to the right. A couple walked into Doc's hardware store. To the left, a group of kids came out of Prince's Pizza, but there was nobody around who could have buzzed my door.

Whatever. I was too excited to go back upstairs, so I turned to my bird. "Flash your cage is so dirty. Let's give you fresh paper." I picked up the soiled top layer of newspaper on his cage floor. Just as I balled it up to throw it away, a photo on the next clean layer caught my eye. It had been taken on Main Street when the construction project began. The ceremonial photo showed Fiona standing next to Carter Fox with the other City Council members on both sides inaugurating the beginning of the project. Carter was holding up a shovel ala Thor. Seeing him act silly, made me smile now that I had experienced his charismatic personality.

On the contrary, seeing Fiona's picture made me sick to my stomach. I studied the image. Her smile was open and wide, making her appear more friendly than I had seen in person. The date on the paper was a month ago. What had happened in that time to change her friendly face to the sour one we'd seen of late? Even with the grainy, pixilated photo, it was clear enough to see she wore a dangly earring. "Flash. Does this match?" I held up the baggie to Flash, but he ignored it. When I turned around to put the earring back, the obnoxious buzz sounded again. This time, I realized the noise had come straight from the bird's mouth.

"Seriously?" Although I was impressed with the accuracy of his imitation if Flash kept that up how would I ever know if the buzz was the real door or just the bird? I'd be running down the stairs all the time. "You are going to drive me crazy, mister."

Happy with my attention, Flash went through his whole repertoire of electronic sounds; the microwave ding, my phone's ring tone, a jackhammer, and the new horrible buzzer. I shook my head. Can you unteach a parrot a sound? I quickly googled that question on my phone, but the question that came up was, "Can a parrot unlearn bad words?" Bad words? Jeez, at least Flash didn't cuss. I retyped, "Can a parrot unlearn a sound?"

The article read, "Parrots can't unlearn any more than we can, but if they find something better, they may switch to a new sound that's more interesting."

I turned to Flash. "Well, let's just hope you find something better than the jackhammer and buzzer soon."

When there was a tap, tap, tap on the window. Sarah! I hardly recognized her. She had a tan and her hair was longer, but that contagious, gaping smile was undeniable. I leapt to the door.

We squealed and jumped up and down like crazies. "Come in out of the cold, girl!"

Once inside my studio, I got a good look at Sarah. Besides her new hairstyle, she had lost a little weight and was fit. I said, "You look amazing! Oh! I have so much to ask you and tell you. I don't know where to start."

In the excitement, Flash decided to show off with his horrid jackhammer sound. Sarah squinted and walked to his cage and stared at my green parrot. "OK Ande, but first things first. Is this Flash?"

I'd forgotten she had never met him, so I made the appropriate introductions; "Flash, meet Sarah, my best friend in the whole world. Sarah, meet Flash, my number one employee."

She cocked her head, causing her blonde hair to reach her chin. When she left in May, she shaved her head in solidarity with the starving Africans in a remote part of Ghana where she was heading. I couldn't believe she had discarded her long hair at the time. But then again, who else would finish medical school and volunteer to work in a third-world country her first year out?

She said, "Employee?"

I nodded. "And he works for peanuts – literally." She listened as I explained his job.

She raised her eyebrow and pursed her lips. "Prove it."

I took a confident breath, put Flash on my shoulder, and flipped on my main and fill lights. I pointed to the Blue Spruce and said, "Now Sarah, stand right there. Flash, ready?"

He squawked, "Say Cheese!"

She laughed with her eyes closed, but I snapped the shutter anyway.

Then I said, "Flash, I need your help."

"Pretty girl."

She made a flirty grin at him and that was it - the award winner. Sarah used to wear heavy make-up, blue hair, and a lip ring, but now her natural freckled beauty shone through.

We hauled her stuff upstairs and relaxed with wine, cheese, and crackers. "Thanks for letting me stay here. I will spend plenty of time with Mom and Dad, but I want to be nearer the action."

"Of course. So what's your plan?"

She sighed. "I don't really have one yet. I need to look for a job soon, but honestly, I want some time off before starting."

"Well, finding a position should be easy with your experience. Are you thinking of working at Brookings Medical Center? I mean, you'd better find a job close by." I gave her the evil eye.

"Oh, I'd love to be a general practitioner at the clinic if they are hiring."

Even though Sarah is two years older than me, we've been best friends forever. We were inseparable playmates in grade school, had countless sleepovers in middle and high school and were roomies at South Dakota State. I worried when she moved to The Cities for med school, but with Minneapolis only four hours away we managed to see each other often on weekends. This past year was our only significant time apart.

She pointed to the window. "So, what's going on out there? I nearly tripped over a pile of bricks. Are they re-doing Main Street?"

I nodded and told her the whole story of the mess, about the rude guys at the bar, Doc's car damage, and ended with the death of Fiona.

Sarah's face dropped. "You don't think it was murder, do you?"

"Murder?" I gave a nervous laugh, still thinking that was ridiculous. "There were no signs of a struggle. She must have had some health problem we didn't know about. At any rate, the autopsy report should reveal what happened. I didn't mention Carter's suggestion that it could have been suicide. "It's just so sad. And seeing her dead was awful."

Sarah put her arm over my shoulder and said, "Drink another glass of wine – that might help." She changed the subject to brighten the mood, "So….are you dating anyone?"

I rolled my eyes. "You sound like Mom. You know I broke up with Tony last fall?"

She nodded. "I can't blame you. He spent more time working on his motorcycle than he spent with you." She poured us each another glass.

"Since then, I've been so involved with my studio and the Mainstreet Merchants Association I haven't even considered dating." I suddenly remembered handsome James from the kids' party, but no use stirring that pot with Sarah. She'd go crazy.

Her hands went to her hips. "You're kidding, Ande. These are your prime dating years! You should be out mingling instead of hanging out with all those old shop owners. You're only 28! And what's up with the ponytail? You look sixteen."

My hand touched my hair and I shrugged. Before I could defend my lifestyle or ask her how I could look older, she continued berating me. "Speaking of old guys, tell me you're not still hanging out with Doc?"

I squared my shoulders. "All the time."

She scrunched her nose, "Any sparks?"

"Sarah! We're talking about Doc, right?" My nose wrinkled. "Half the time we're like oil and water." I sighed. "He's been a super friend and I needed someone when you ditched me."

She acquiesced with a nod. "So, how's his temper?"

We both had seen Doc blow up before, but I bristled a little at the question. She never understood my buddy. "He's fine. Even after his car was damaged, he was very calm."

She raised an eyebrow. "Kind of a coincidence that Fiona died the same day, don't you think?"

Irritated, I shook my head defensively and spoke in a screechy voice, "Doc had nothing to do with her death. I'm positive." I sure hoped that was true.

This time I changed the subject. "So, how about *your* love life? Did you meet a hot doctor while in Africa? Or maybe a cool Ghanaian you wanted to bring home with you?"

"Ha! I was too tired to even think about romance." She bit her lip and said, "But, there was this one night…"

We spent the rest of the evening giggling, telling stories, and getting reacquainted. She told me of some amazing adventures in Africa and promised more when she wasn't so tired.

I gave her a spare key to my apartment. "Make yourself at home, girl." I knew Sarah would have no problem doing that.

Monday morning, I smiled to see my friend snuggled safely on my couch. After a year of worrying about her living across the globe, it was a relief to have her back safely.

While she slept, I brewed a pot of coffee and took a cup downstairs to get set up for my first photo shoot. As I stood near the window, a woman walked by and waved at me. I didn't know her but smiled. How embarrassing. I was still wearing my Yoda onesie pajamas! With my huge windows, I was on full display in my second living room. Perhaps it was time to invest in window shades.

I moved to greet my bird. "Good morning, Flash!"

Flash didn't answer but rushed to the front of the cage and climbed onto the door. When I pulled the wire cage door down, he ducked his head and came down with it. I guess he thinks it's his own amusement park ride since he "rides" the door every morning. Flash climbed onto my hand and made his way up my arm, grabbing my sleeve with his beak to assist him while he ascended. Good thing I wore the thick fuzzy pj's. Yesterday, he inadvertently poked holes in my new white blouse.

Once Flash was in place on my shoulder, he nibbled at my hair, a favorite pastime when I have my hair down. I had just settled into my bright red upholstered armchair when the darned bird let out his horrible jackhammering noise.

"Flash! No!" I rubbed my ear. At least it wasn't the same ear Leo yelled into a few nights ago. I tried to focus on the bird's face which was difficult since it was one inch from mine. Despite the proximity, Flash looked awfully proud of his new imitation. "That is a terrible sound."

There was a knock at my door. I motioned for Doc to come in. He unlocked the door, walked in, and sat across from me. "Have you heard anything else about Fiona?"

I shrugged. "Only that they did an autopsy. Should hear something today."

He took off his hat and scratched his head. "So, did the world traveler arrive?"

I smiled. "Yes. It's so great to have her back. She's still sleeping."

A voice from behind startled me. "Not anymore. Not with all that pounding." I turned as Sarah entered the room with her hands wrapped around a coffee mug. She wore a long t-shirt and her hair stood straight up.

I smiled at my sleepy friend. "I should have warned you to wear earplugs starting at 7 a.m. And that noise..." I pointed outside, "could be worse since one of the jackhammers is out of service."

She shook her head, then blinked. In a groggy voice she said, "Hey Doc. Long time no see."

He gave a sup nod. "Sarah? So is the couch better than sleeping in a tukul?"

She gave an approving smile. "You know what a tukul is?"

Of course, he did. Doc knew everything, but I sure didn't know what it was and shrugged.

Thankfully, Doc wasn't the type to mansplain. He simply answered my shrug, "It's a traditional African mud hut with a thatched roof. Pretty primitive?" He directed the question to Sarah.

"Oh yeah. Ande's couch was like sleeping on a giant marshmallow compared to a mat on the hard dirt floor. And not having to heat my own water to make instant coffee…that was a real treat." She took a sip and smiled.

I was relieved about her sleeping conditions but cringed when a couple walked by and waved. I said, "Argh. I've got to get something to cover my windows. Lately, I've been on display like a zoo animal with the detour by my shop. Doc, do you have any window shades in stock?"

He pointed at my Yoda suit and said, "Well, you can't blame them. You look like a furry animal today. Got a tape measure?"

I found one and he measured the windows and door then said, "Drop by and pick out the kind you want, and I'll install them. I've gotta go open my shop now. Stay out of trouble today if possible." He walked over to Flash's cage and said, "Help! I've been turned into a parrot."

Flash paid no attention to him. After Doc left, Sarah took his spot, curling her legs underneath her on the small couch. "So, how's Jon?"

I smiled. "He's doing great. He loves school."

"He's such a sweet kid – and so hot too." She winked at me, knowing I hated it when she said that. I'll admit my brother is handsome, but it's creepy to hear friends say it like that.

Another person with a Viking Coffee cup walked by and I wondered how Marla was handling business with the crime tape in her shop. I went to the window. A few people stood outside her door.

I jumped when Sarah's hot breath tickled my neck. She said, "What's up?"

"Oh, just wondering what's going on at Viking Coffee. I think I'll put on clothes and check it out." I had an hour before my first appointment.

"Okay. I'll take a shower. Mom and Dad are taking me car shopping!"

"Fun! I hope you find a good one." I ran upstairs and traded my Yoda suit for jeans and a sweater.

Out on the street, the men were back at work as if nothing had happened to their 'boss lady.'

When I approached Marla's shop, I read the sign on the door. 'Viking Coffee is open. To-go orders only. Please knock for service.'

The solution worked and maybe business had even picked up. I scooted past the five people in line and said, "Excuse me, official business," then knocked on the door.

When the door opened, Marla held out two cups. Her eyes brightened and she motioned me in. As I entered I said, "Too bad you don't have a window to take…"

My sentence was cut short when I spotted the handsome man behind her counter. I sputtered, "James?" What was the nice guy from the birthday party doing in Marla's shop?

He gave me a smile. "Hey there. How did you rate getting past the door Nazi?"

I stammered. "Uhhh. Why are you here? Shouldn't you be teaching?"

Marla rushed over to him. "Save your chitchat for later. I need a tall Caramel Macchiato and a Grande Flat White, extra hot." She opened the cash register, grabbed change, and ran to the door.

I moved out of their way, avoiding the forbidden booth, and sat at a table. James ran the espresso machine like a natural barista. Was there anything he couldn't do?

Finally, the line dissipated and Marla sat down with a thump on her stool. "So, how do you two know each other?"

I said, "Um…we met Friday at Seth's 8th birthday party."

Marla gave a confused, "OK?"

James looked at me and answered my earlier question. "Marla's my aunt."

My eyes shot open. He was the nephew that moved to town. It all made sense. As I regarded them, I could see they had the same nose. "Oh!"

Marla said, "It was a zoo here over the weekend and Jamie's class is testing today. He found another proctor so he could help me out." She gave his arm a sweet hug.

I nodded. "Well of course he came to save the day. He's getting pretty good at that." I winked. "Marla, I'm glad you found a solution to your problem. I just stopped by to make sure you are okay." I stood to go. "Did Morris call you they are doing an autopsy?"

Her shoulders slumped as she nodded. "Yes. He's very thorough."

"That's one word for Fred. Well, guess I'd better get ready for my first clients, that is if they don't cancel." I turned to James. "After this, are you gonna rescue a girl tied to a train track?"

"I'm always on the lookout for damsels in distress." He winked at me nearly causing me to trip over my own feet.

While waiting for my client, I sat down and pondered my interesting new male friend while mindlessly fingering the baggie holding the earring.

My phone rang, startling me so much that I dropped the earring on the floor. I fumbled to answer the phone. "Hello?"

I recognized Morris's stiff voice immediately.

"Ms. Nilsen, can you come down to the police station?"

"Um. Sure. I have some time tomorrow."

He answered curtly, "No. I'm afraid I need to speak with you today."

Woah. "I can come over right after my next session." I looked at my watch. "It will be about an hour."

"You can't cancel it?"

"No, I can't Fred. Why the rush?"

"It's Detective Morris." He sighed. "Come As soon as possible and I'd suggest you bring a lawyer."

"Are you kidding?"

He said, "Have you ever known me to jest?"

Come to think of it, I had never known Fred Morris to show any sense of humor. "Right. Okay, I'll see you in a bit."

I called Mike and explained Morris's dramatic call. "I don't know what it's about, but is there any way you can meet me at the police station in an hour?"

Mike chuckled and said, "Well, you know Fred. He thinks everything is of major importance. But, sure. I'll take my lunch and eat it at the station."

Relieved that Mike wasn't too concerned, I scurried around finding props for photographing dogs.

My next client was Madison, the sorority girl who wanted me to photograph Pom Pom. I realized I hadn't asked its breed. I pictured a Pomeranian, but what if he/she was a big dog? Whatever breed, I would be ready and got my squeakers out.

A few minutes later the bouncy girl entered with no dog in tow. I said, "Hi Madison, where's Pom Pom?"

She laughed and opened her coat to reveal a tiny furry puppy. "Right here."

I moved closer and upon further inspection said in surprise, "Pom Pom is a guinea pig?"

CHAPTER 7

I stared at the tri-colored fluffball and said in astonishment, "I thought for sure Pom Pom was a dog."

She tilted her bouncy curls and squeaked, "Oh, didn't I tell you?"

"No." This was just plain weird, me taking photos of a guinea pig. I sighed and said, "Madison, I hate to tell you, but my sitting fees are the same, whether it's a child, a big animal, or a..." I tried to think of a nice word for the varmint and said, "little guy."

She said, "That's fine," with a shrug and a perky smile. "But, Pom Pom isn't a guy. She's a girl."

Ok then. Apparently, some people have more disposable money than others. "Well, she sure is a cutie. Let's get started!"

I set up the tall table so I wouldn't have to crouch down on the floor to take pictures. Starting with a white backdrop, I laid some white fuzzy fabric on the table. "We'll start with a more formal setting." I giggled at the idea of a formal photo of a rodent.

"Stand here, so you can catch Pom Pom if she gets too close to the edge." Madison stood just to the side and I set my camera to take the macro photos. I made sure the pet's eyes were clear before taking a shot. The mini pig was funny and actually kind of cute, rooting around making grunting sounds, and emitting high-pitched squeaks.

Upon hearing the little animal's sounds, Flash started beeping. That, along with my squeaky toy to get Pom Pom's attention, made it seem like we were in the middle of an electronics shop.

For the next setting, Madison pulled out a tiny hat from her bag. Then she dressed Pom Pom in a tiara, followed by a tutu. My eyes widened with each elaborate costume she put her in. I took photos of each outfit. For the grand finale, she dressed the poor, patient Pom Pom as a unicorn.

When I showed her the images, Madison squealed as loud as the pig. "I definitely want that one. And that! Oh, how cute!"

In the day and age of quality cell phone photos, why didn't she just take pictures herself rather than spend a fortune at my place? But who was I to turn away a paying client?

Finally, the odd duo left. I put on my heavy coat since the forecast was for a drastic drop in temps, and left to meet Fred Morris. The station was only a few blocks away, but I opted to drive. It was comforting to know I could escape the police station faster in a car than on foot. I chuckled at the notion.

When I arrived at the small precinct, I entered the lobby which was decorated with a spring theme. It was definitely the handiwork of my friend, Laura, who works in the billing department. I'd been here many times to pick her up for lunch and wondered if I had time to say hi. I started to peek in, but was stopped by a familiar hoarse voice that sounded like Roz from *Monsters, Inc.*

"Is that little Miss Nilsen?"

It was our ancient dispatcher, Ada. I turned around to see the woman in her mid-80s all decked out in a full police uniform and hunched over holding a cane. Her question wasn't rhetorical. She squinted and wobbled toward me to get a better look.

I spoke up so she could hear me. "Yes. It's me, Ada. Good to see you! I heard you got a stairlift installed at your house."

She nodded. "I did and I love it. You should see me zoom up and down those stairs."

I pictured her slow gradual ascent in the mechanical chair and suppressed a giggle. Ada had worked for Brookings Police since the stone age and had no plans to retire. A few years ago, a petition circulated to have her removed because of all her mistakes, but nobody in the department had the heart to force her out. As a compromise, the city required another dispatcher to be on duty whenever Ada worked.

Ada asked, "Are you here to talk to Freddie about that woman who was killed? Tsk tsk."

I frowned. "I know. It's awful. Yes. I'm here to see Officer Morris."

"Well, I'd better hurry back to my desk. Someone might call with an emergency."

I watched my spunky old friend inch down the hall until Morris' nasal voice said, "Ms. Nilsen? Please walk this way."

I so wanted to copy his walk, remembering all the times Sarah and I had done just that when anyone uttered those words. And his would be a good one to imitate since Fred was always in stealth mode - examining everything in his path. But alas, I walked normally and followed him to a small interrogation room. It was kind of cool to be questioned at a police station, even if it was by Fred Morris.

Mike was already sitting at the table eating a meatloaf sandwich. I nodded to him, grabbed a few of his potato chips, and crunched as I sat beside him.

Fred peered at me above his folded hands. "We got the autopsy report. It's not good."

Well, duh. Fiona died. But of course, I didn't say that aloud.

He went on, "Ethylene Glycol and a heavy dose of sleeping pills were in her system."

I stopped chewing the chips, horrified to think Carter Fox was right about Marla dying by suicide. "Oh no. So, you think Marla ended her own life?"

He cocked his head. "No. I think someone else did."

My eyes widened. "What? Murder?"

He closed his eyes as if I was stupid. "Nobody would kill themselves with antifreeze."

I said, "Antifreeze?" what did that have to do with anything? Maybe Morris was losing it, but Mike put his sandwich down and sat up straight.

Morris continued with what sounded like information memorized from recent online research. "Ethylene Glycol is the compound in antifreeze. It can be used as a poison because of its sweet taste. Consuming just three ounces is lethal to a person of up to 140 lbs. And ingesting it is very painful."

I couldn't believe it and said, "But who would want to hurt Fiona?" As soon as I said that, several names popped into my head: Mustache Man, Doc, Marla, and even me. Who knew how many others?

Fred said, "Andrea, I need to know everything about your relationship with Ms. Pratt."

I was still reeling from the news about the antifreeze. "But I already told you all that I know."

He put a 1990's cassette tape recorder on the table and pushed the record button. "Start from the beginning."

I told the story again, hoping I wasn't wavering on the details.

"And where did you go after you left Ms. White's shop Friday morning?"

"Back to my apartment, then to a kid's birthday party." I added, "Oh. Did I tell you I saw Fiona argue with a workman? I don't know his name, but he's tall and has a mustache."

Morris jotted the information down and said, "What exactly did they say?"

I stammered, "Uh. I can't say for sure, but he said something like 'that's what you get for playing with fire.'"

Fred leaned forward. "Exactly what time was that?"

When I shrugged Mike said, "Fred, Ande has told you all she knows. We need to get back to work unless there is anything else."

"There is something else…" Morris cleared his throat and his face paled; neither reaction was normal for the overly confident man. He took a breath and looked me square in the eyes. "Your DNA was found on her mug."

I shrugged. "What mug?"

He cleared his throat. "The one with the poisoned drink...that killed Ms. Pratt."

My breath caught and I tried to swallow the dread caught in my throat. That was impossible. Wasn't it? I frantically tried to recall my actions leading up to the discovery of Fiona's body. I said with certainty, "But, I never touched any other cup that day except my own."

Morris lifted an eyebrow, "But didn't you say you made lemonade for Miss White?"

Oh yeah. Flustered, I admitted, "Oh yes. Of course, I guess I touched hers too."

That omission probably made me look like I was trying to hide something.

Before I could ask if I was a suspect, Morris stood up and said, "Ms. Nilsen, you can go for now. But, don't leave town. I will definitely need to ask more questions. And don't talk to anyone about this except your lawyer. The cause of death hasn't been released yet."

In the lobby, I sat on a bench by Mike and explained to him in detail exactly what I had done all day Friday. Mike put his hand on my shoulder and said, "Don't get too worked up. There must be a good explanation."

I thanked him and said with a quivering voice, "I need to get to the bottom of this."

He eyed me suspiciously. "Ande, if Fiona was really murdered, you should be careful poking around."

I gave him a hug as we parted ways. Not only was I shaken from the thought of murder, but I shivered uncontrollably outside in the cold air. The Sioux Falls weatherman was right for a change. Within seconds of leaving the station, my black coat turned white. As I drove, giant wet snowflakes landed silently on my windshield. I was struck by the beauty of the intricate patterns of the flakes. I hated to destroy the scene by turning on my wipers and even welcomed the lovely distraction. I pulled over to the side of Main Street to study the designs and clear my racing mind. Despite being one o'clock in the afternoon, it was so dark outside some neon lights gave off a red hue to the complex designs. Unfortunately, the blood-red glow only made me think of murder, which snapped me back to my titanic problem.

I focused beyond the flakes to the neon sign in a shop window, surprised to read the words, Doc's Hardware. I had inadvertently parked in front of his store. I turned off my car and ran up to the door, shaking the snow from my hair as I entered.

Doc looked up from his cash register. "What are you doing out in this weather?"

I put on a bright face and said, "Not much. I Just stopped by to pick out my blinds and tell you I'm a suspect in Fiona's murder!"

I knew I wasn't supposed to tell anyone, but I had to confide in Doc.

"What?" His eyes widened and for once he was baffled. He put down the stack of bills and contorted his face. "So it was murder? Why are you a suspect?"

Still in disbelief, I rubbed my eyes. "I just left the police station. Fiona's autopsy showed high doses of sleeping pills and antifreeze...and apparently, my DNA was found on the cup or mug Fiona drank from."

He sat on his stool. "Wow. How did that happen?"

I leaned against a barrel of work gloves and threw my head back in frustration. "I have no idea. I mean, I was there that day and drank from a mug. I also made a cup of lemonade for Marla, but I sure didn't put anything in it." My mind went back to that day. "Surely Marla would have washed the cups. What do I do?"

Doc nodded. "Well, there's nothing that can be done about it right now. So...wanna look at the shades?"

I appreciated the distraction. "Sure." I looked through the choices and found some affordable blinds that would do the job. I got my credit card out to pay him.

He held up his hand. "Just wait until after we're finished."

"Well, please keep track." I said, "Hey, Doc, can I buy you lunch to help pay you back for the installation fee? I'm starving and don't have another session until three."

"Sure, let me lock up. How about Mick's?"

That was a silly question. I always wanted to go to Mick's. The tiny hamburger joint with tiny hamburgers had been a staple in Brookings for 70 years. With only 12 stools in the whole place, it was hard to get a seat, so I usually got take-out, but today I wanted to eat there. "Let's do it."

As we walked the block to Mick's, snow built up on my eyelashes and I could barely see so I pulled my hood around my face.

We got seats right away, probably because of the weather. The best thing about eating at Mick's is that all the seats face the grill. It's mesmerizing to watch Mick flip the little burgers. Today wasn't the day to worry about what I ate, and I devoured three small hamburgers. I deserved each bite and the chocolate malt too.

I wiped my mouth with a napkin and swiveled my stool to Doc. "Who in the world has access to antifreeze?"

With a mouthful of fries, he mumbled, "Everyone." He swallowed and sadi, "You can buy it anywhere, including my store. I keep in my basement toilet so it doesn't freeze in winter - hence the word anti-freeze."

My forehead puckered. "Hm. I thought it was just for cars. What does it look like?"

"It's usually blue or pink and comes in gallon jugs. The taste is sweet so it's a perfect poison if you want to off somcone." He slurped his shake."

The man was a master at making odd statements sound routine. I cocked my head, "You sure know a lot about murder by antifreeze. Should I be worried?"

He shrugged a shoulder, "I read a lot and watch detective shows, but it's pretty much common knowledge."

"Not to me. So, let's get this straight. If someone poisoned Fiona after I left but way before bedtime, why were sleeping pills in her system too?"

Doc blinked, took another fry, and said matter-of-factly, "Maybe whoever gave her the poison knew it would take several hours to kill her and didn't want her to call for help or be in too much pain so they added sleeping pills to knock her out while it kicked in?"

The notion made me cringe. "So, Fiona was probably still alive while I was across the street editing birthday party photos?" I felt sick to my stomach and the chocolate malt didn't help.

"Ande, don't blame yourself. A better question is; who did it?"

At that moment, I vowed to get to the bottom of this and get myself off the suspect list at the same time.

When we left Mick's, the snow had stopped, but I kept my hood up to cover my ears from the frigid wind. I had to turn my whole body to say goodbye to Doc before crossing the street to my place.

Before my next clients arrived, I sat at my desk and made a list on my phone of suspects and their possible motives. Mustache Man was an obvious choice. He seemed guilty at every level. I hated to add sweet Davis to my list, but he did say he would do anything to prove his love for Marla. Then there was Marla herself. She wanted desperately to get Fiona out of her shop. However, she was extremely upset when she found Fiona dead.

Last on my list was Doc. I only added him because Sarah reminded me he wanted to avenge his car. This was the worst list of suspects ever. I didn't want to blame one of my friends just to take the suspicion from me. If nothing else, I'd like to make sure they were in the clear.

Of course, there was always the possibility the killer was someone I didn't know. Fiona probably had no shortage of enemies.

Despite the snow, the family of five arrived on time for their photo session. They were bundled up and took a while to fix their hair and prepare themselves. I put my problems aside and concentrated on the job. In the middle of a particularly fun pose with the kids holding Easter baskets, Sarah burst into the room from my stairway, startling us all.

She squealed, "Dad helped me get a used Honda Civic! It's great! Gonna shop with Mom now." She rushed by and I worried the family would think the intrusion was unprofessional. But, Sarah has such a dazzling personality; how could anyone complain? And she was really cute in her new blue top.

Wait! Was that my shirt? I was about to question her but she announced to the children, "Smile for the birdie!" With a flourish, she put on her coat and disappeared through the front door. I may have to hire my whirlwind of a friend because the family beamed more for her than they had for Flash. They even held their smiles as they turned to me and I got the perfect shot of the whole family.

Later, after editing photos, I felt increasingly lonely and agitated. I called my brother and told yet another person about my situation.

He was dumbfounded. "You? How could Fred think you were smart enough to come up with that concoction to give the lady?"

"Wait a minute, mister. You're supposed to be on my side."

"I am, but do you even know what anti-freeze is?"

"Of course! It's a pink or blue liquid that comes in a gallon jug and it's used to keep things from freezing. It can be used as a poison because of its sweet taste."

"Sounds to me like you just Googled that."

"Well, I didn't." That was true enough. "So, what do I do? How can I clear my name?"

Jon was silent for a while and said, "Well, you can start by investigating your suspects. Eliminate those who have a good alibi and hopefully you can narrow it down. I really am sorry you're going through this, Sis. Let me know if you need help."

"Thanks."

"Oh, tell Sarah hi for me."

"I will if she ever comes home."

After I ended the call, I was surprised to find it was already seven. I didn't want to bug Sarah by texting about dinner plans, so I ate a salad and streamed a few shows before heading to bed.

Just after I turned off the light, Sarah entered the apartment, giggling.

I hollered, "Sarah? Come here."

She opened my door and bounced off my door jamb, apparently under the influence of something.

She spoke slowly but with way too much inflection. "Hi, Ande!" Her silhouette appeared in the doorway and she squealed. "What are you doing in the dark?"

"I'm trying to sleep. Where in the world did your mom take you?"

"Haha. She left hours ago. But I met this guy at Rob's Corner Bar. His name is Gary. He's so cute and tall. He bought me drinks all night long."

I started to say, perhaps a few too many drinks, but instead asked, "Is he an SDSU student?"

"Nope. He's older, has a real job, and is so cool."

I watched her swerve a bit and said, "Sarah, I think you need to get some sleep."

"OK." She stumbled over to the other side of my bed and climbed in with me. She was asleep as soon as her head hit the pillow.

I said to no one, "That wasn't exactly what I meant."

I had set my alarm to go off at seven so I could get the backdrops ready for a grandma and three children of indeterminate ages who were expected at eight. Unfortunately, I had already been awakened by the deafening construction noise long before my alarm sounded.

Apparently, none of the racket was loud enough to wake the zombie lying next to me. I drug myself out of bed and chuckled at Sarah. She probably needed a night to let her hair down and just be a silly girl after having to be professional for a year.

When Flash saw me enter his fortress, he started his usual montage of sounds. I listened and smiled as he rode down his door and hopped on his perch.

I said, "Ready to work?" as I put grapes into his cup.

While I waited for the clients, I looked out to the street where three inches of new snow covered the ground like white glitter.

The grandma and kids, all preschoolers, arrived and just loved Flash. The oldest, maybe four, asked me, "Are you a pirate?"

I looked at the green parrot on my shoulder then shouted to the boy, "Aye, Aye, Matey. Now sit right back and show us yer smile or I'll have to make ye walk the plank."

The boy giggled and I got a really nice shot. I may have to get a pirate outfit and brush up on the lingo. It would be a great idea for Halloween and I've already got the coolest part of the costume.

When the group left, I went upstairs to shower. From the bathroom, I could hear Sarah snoring. When I came out, she was rubbing her eyes with her fists like a baby.

I smiled. "Sounds like you had quite an evening."

She croaked, "Yeah. When I got here, I was putting my key in your door but saw Steve and the gang going into Rob's. I went across the street to say hi. I was going to call you to join us but got distracted when Gary started buying me drinks." She made a blurry face and squinted at the bed, "Thanks for letting me sleep here."

I chuckled. "It's fine. I'm not sure you could have made it to the couch. Glad you had fun."

CHAPTER 8

My hair was still wet when the front door buzzed. I assumed it was Flash and ran downstairs, towel in hand, to reprimand him but there was really someone at the door. It was my first grade Sunday school teacher standing with another woman. Surprised, I opened the door with my towel in hand. "Well hello!"

Mrs. Gaddis made her entrance, full of life as ever. After stomping the snow from her boots, she swooped in as if she was on a great expedition. Her exuberant, friendly air always made me smile. The woman studied my place with wide gleaming eyes, then gave me a bear hug. "Andrea, I just love your place!"

Mrs. Gaddis had been friends with my mother for as long as I could remember, but in no way resembled a typical 55-year-old. Her dark hair was cut in a short shag and she wore a cute sparkly outfit that accentuated her body with more curves than I would ever have.

I pulled back from her tight hug. "Thanks!"

She turned to the other woman. "This is my friend, Carol Hammond."

I smiled at the prim woman with mousy gray hair and wondered if she was a Sunday School teacher too. She looked more like one than Mrs. Gaddis ever had. Carol gave me a shy wave.

I said, "So, how are you, Mrs. Gaddis?"

"First of all, please call me Joy. You're not in my Sunday school class anymore." The woman truly embodied her name.

"Please forgive my appearance, Joy." I motioned to my damp hair. "I just got out of the shower. What can I do for you ladies?"

Joy pursed her lips and said seriously, "Well, you know I lost Bob a few years back?"

I nodded but remembered it was more like fifteen or maybe even twenty years ago.

"Well, after that my friends and I started a little social club called the Brookings Knitting Club – Your mother comes sometimes."

I was well aware of the group. Mom told me enough stories to know they were a fun bunch. I nodded again.

"Well, we're all snowbirds like your parents…" She pointed her finger at me. "Speaking of which, are your parents ever coming back from Alabama?"

I loved how she interrupted herself. I said, "Hopefully in a few weeks, but they may not want to leave the coast. Jon and I spent Christmas with them, and I can see why. The beach is amazing."

"And now you understand why we leave for the winter." Her head tipped as if to punctuate the statement.

Carol silently nodded in agreement, then Joy got back on track. "Anyway…for years when we all got back to town, we would get together to knit, drink tea, and catch up. But, over the years we've evolved and started taking our knitting to the café and having lunch out. Then eventually we stopped knitting altogether and just met for cocktails." She gave a hoity-toity head waggle.

I nodded again politely, thinking my head was going to come off if we kept this up. Would I ever learn why they were here today? Be patient, Ande.

Carol chimed in with a sweet voice, "Since we're all retired, we each volunteer. Some read to school children, others cuddle babies at the hospital, and some deliver Meals on Wheels, but we wanted our club to do more than just gossip and drink too."

Joy continued, "We raise money for a different charity each year. Last year, we held a bunco game at the rec center with proceeds going to the Boys and Girls Club."

I said, "I remember that. How nice." I glanced at my wall clock wondering when they would get to the point. My hair was going to dry like this and look like a mess.

Mrs. Gaddis finally said, "And that brings us to why we are here today..."

I raised my eyebrows, anxious to end the suspense.

"Since you do pet photos, we wanted to have you take photos for a charity calendar that would benefit the rescue shelter!"

I nodded. "Oh. That's nice. I can probably arrange that."

"Yes, well, we want to have 12 dogs and 12 of our members to be in the photos."

"Wait. A dozen people and a dozen dogs?" I surveyed my small space thinking it would be a tight squeeze. The logistics of such a session whirred through my mind, but the ladies stared at me with such excited anticipation that I couldn't turn them down. "It may be tricky squeezing everyone in, but sure. When were you thinking of doing this?"

Joy said with a huge smile, "We hoped for some time this week."

My eyelids fluttered. "This week? Um. Let me check my calendar." I wanted to say that would be impossible, but really my schedule was pretty light due to construction cancellations. Might as well get this crazy session over with soon. I looked at my phone calendar. "Actually, Thursday morning is wide open."

Joy led the two-person dance team in a full-out but awkward hip-hop session. She sang, "That's the way uh-huh, uh-huh, I like it," as they danced. She stopped and said, "And don't worry, even though it's for a fundraiser you'll get paid your regular fee and we'll take care of designing and printing the calendars."

I was so relieved to hear they would put the calendars together I said, "No that's okay. I'll donate my time."

Carol reached out and took my hands in hers. "Bless you. Bless you. Bless you!"

Joy added, "Aren't you just a doll? Oh. One more thing. Do you think we could put some sheets up on the windows? Some of the ladies are nervous about being watched as they pose."

That was an odd request, but I had a remedy at the ready. "As a matter of fact, my friend Doc is coming today or tomorrow to put up shades, so that should be perfect."

Carol gave a big sigh. "How wonderful."

Joy, on the other hand, said, "Doc? Do you mean Dave Johnson?"

I didn't know anyone who called him Dave and was surprised she even knew him. I said, "Yep. That's the one."

Her face softened and she said, "How is Dave doing? I haven't talked to him for a long time. Is he still working in Sioux Falls?"

"Oh, he's fine, and no, he owns the hardware store across the street. He loves it." I was surprised she didn't know he was Doc of Doc's Hardware, but then again, she didn't seem like much of a handywoman.

As if to emphasize that, she put her manicured hand with long tiger-stripe gel nails on mine. "Would you tell Dave hello for me?"

"Sure." I studied her face. Did Mrs. Gaddis like Doc?

They left and danced down the street like crazies. Funny ladies.

When I went upstairs, Sarah was sitting on the couch holding an empty coffee cup. She was way more alive than when I'd left her and said, "What was all that commotion?"

I said, "Remember Mrs. Gaddis?"

Her eyes widened as she said, "Our Sunday School teacher?"

"She's bringing in a dozen dogs and a dozen ladies this Thursday for a charity photo calendar. I might need your help."

With her hand to her mouth in fake remorse, she said, "Oh gee. I think I have to wash my hair that day." She tipped her head to the side and examined me. "Speaking of which, your hair looks really cute."

I stared at my friend assuming she was still being sarcastic since I hadn't done anything to it since jumping out of the shower, but she nodded and said, "Makes you look older."

I flew into the bathroom to get a look. Oh, my goodness. My hair was completely dry and sat at my shoulders with enough body and wave to look like an actual hairstyle. Why had I been drying, pulling, straightening, and pony-tailing for so long?

I nodded and said aloud, "Thanks for the eternally long story, Mrs. Gaddis. You saved me an expensive trip to the salon."

From the other room, Sarah said, "Huh?"

I emerged and said, "Never mind. Wanna get lunch today? It's Taco Tuesday."

She moaned with a smile. "Mmmm. I have missed those Potato Oles. I should be ready to eat by noon."

"Great. I'll run a few errands and be back for you. And I want to see your car!"

I made my way out onto the street and headed for Davis' flower shop. I needed to either eliminate or confirm my meek, lovestruck friend as a suspect.

When I opened the door I was happy to see his normal color had returned since the last time I had seen him. He didn't look shaky at all. Whew. "So how are you today, my friend?"

Davis grinned. "I feel like a new man!" Then he twirled around as if he was in a musical. I half expected him to jump on the counter and belt out a show tune.

I was surprised by his complete turnaround. "Really? What happened?"

"Well, I can credit you, Ande. You taught me to stand up for myself and stop letting people push me around. I'm starting to take matters into my own hands and it's so empowering! And it's all because of you."

Wow. What an improvement. Maybe I had some sort of magical powers to heal the weak after all. "Well, good for you, Davis. I won't take the credit though. You had it in you all along."

A thought hit me. What if by taking matters into his own hands, he meant he had killed Fiona? There was a tightening in my stomach. I cleared my throat and asked in a near whisper, "What exactly did you do?"

Davis practically glowed. "Just after you left, I wrote a brilliant letter. Then I walked right out to one of those hardhat men and told him to take it to Fiona. The guy took my envelope, saluted me, and said, 'Yes Boss!' and walked off towards the coffee shop." He threw his shoulders back and stood tall.

I was relieved to think Davis had only written a letter, but cringed at his naivety. He didn't realize the worker was mocking him by saluting. And more than likely his brilliant letter had been tossed into the trash before ever getting to Fiona.

"Davis, you do know that Fiona died that same night, right?"

He frowned then squeaked, "Yes. You don't think my letter upset her so much that she had a heart attack, do you?"

I shook my head and said, "I don't think so."

I certainly couldn't imagine anything Davis could write would have that effect on anyone. For my own investigation, I asked, "So what did you do after that on Friday?"

Davis pulled up photos on his phone and showed me snapshots from a wedding he had worked. I took the phone from him to view pictures of his flowers. According to the day and time stamp on the images, he was in Sioux Falls all afternoon and evening. That was a pretty good alibi. Whew.

I patted his hand. "I'm glad you have found your voice."

"Ande, you found my voice."

I sighed as I left, relieved to know he was in the clear - that is until I noticed a jug of pink antifreeze beside his door.

I crossed the street and maneuvered around chunks of Peggy's sidewalk and made it inside her shop unscathed. I walked through the L-shaped store to find her. I picked up a blue vintage vase, thinking it would be gorgeous on my windowsill, but returned it carefully to the shelf when I read the price.

Peggy stood behind her counter near the other entrance pricing a box of jewelry someone had brought in to sell. She looked up. "Hey Ande, I heard Sarah's back."

"Yep and crazy as ever." I nodded at the door. "Bet you were glad to get that fixed."

She nodded, "Indeed."

When Memory heard my voice, she came out from behind a bookshelf and meowed. I picked her up. Peggy shook her head. "I swear that cat only likes you. She stays hidden all day until you come around. What are you, a cat whisperer?"

I whispered into the cat's ear attempting to be funny. Peggy set a necklace on the counter and we moved over to a velvet love seat where I told her about my meeting with Carter Fox on Saturday.

"He showed me the plans and I'm not kidding Fiona's drawings were impeccable. I can see why they chose her, but I still don't know why the crew. Mayor Fox seems to think those guys will be happy to follow the new rules."

She nodded to the door. "I'm not sure that guy with the mustache follows any rules."

"No joke." I opted not to tell her about my run-ins with him.

Peggy put her hand on my shoulder. "Ande, Mike couldn't tell me much, but he said Fred suspects you?" She scrunched her nose.

I closed my eyes. "You know I would never hurt anyone, right?"

"Of course not. But, who would?"

"That's the million-dollar question." We both sighed.

At noon, Sarah drove me to Taco John's in her new car. While we ate, I told her about meeting James. I didn't mention being a murder suspect, hoping I could forget it for a while.

She said, "You go, girl! He sounds perfect for you. I can't wait to meet him. Hey, speaking of boys, mind if I bring Gary back tonight to watch some TV?"

I popped a potato ole' in my mouth. "Gary?"

"Remember? The guy I met last night?"

I nodded. "Oh yeah." I wondered why she couldn't go to his place. Surely, the older guy with a real job had a TV and probably more room than my tiny place. But since I had told Sarah to treat the apartment as her own I said, "Why not?"

She perked up and licked her lips. "Wanna go to the dairy bar?" I was glad the reason for her smacking was ice cream instead of some guy named Gary.

I nodded. "Absolutely, but I need to get back by one thirty.

The snow had already melted from the sidewalks so it was an easy jaunt from Taco John to campus. We crossed the street just as the chimes from the Campanile began to ring. I love the tall tower that stood in its spot since 1929. When the chimes rang, I knew what time it is since it rings on the hour. It was one o'clock.

I squatted so I could frame the whole unique obelisk in picture I'm pretty sure I have taken hundreds of similar Campanile photos, but the fresh snow and bright sun today made the red bricks shine. Sarah photobombed one picture and we ended up taking selfies.

She said, "Wanna race to the top like old times?"

"I'm not in any shape to do all 180 steps, especially after tacos."

She nodded. "Yeah, me neither."

We got our ice cream cones and ate them on our way back to her car. We were so lucky that SDSU had its own Dairy and Food Science Department so we could enjoy fresh ice cream and cheese whenever we wanted. The cold cookies and cream took my mind off my troubles.

Back at the shop, I set up my tree backdrop for a two o'clock appointment to photograph an elderly couple celebrating their 60th wedding anniversary. I was glad I hadn't turned off my cell phone yet since the man called asking if I could help them navigate the street from a parking spot behind my studio. They couldn't park in the handicapped spot since it was demolished.

I ran around the building and offered my arm to the woman and we slowly made our way to the front, being careful not to step in any slick spots or holes.

The couple was adorable and told me stories as I snapped pictures. One image caught them looking at each other so lovingly that I teared up. Afterward, I walked them back to their oversized Oldsmobile and thanked them for their business.

Upon returning to my studio, I gulped to find James inside standing in front of my backdrop. Did my heart stop for a second? Maybe not, but it sure pounded more than usual.

I stammered, "Well, hello there."

He turned and said, "Hi."

I was so unprepared to see him I just said, "Can I help you?" sounding more like I was an employee at Burger King than a friend.

He gave a warm smile. "I just checked in on Aunt Marla and thought I'd try to catch you."

I wanted to say, 'catch away' but said, "Well, good timing. I just finished a photo shoot."

He smirked, "I know. I walked by once, but you were busy snapping pictures of a couple, so I went over to Rob's corner and kept an eye out until they left."

I was touched that this guy had made such an effort to see me. "Here. Have a seat." I ushered him to my seating corner, and he sat in my comfy wingback chair.

He said, "So, I need to know the story behind the spelling of your name."

I rolled my eyes. "To be honest, I may never know for sure. My name is actually Andrea, but my family and friends have always called me Ande. Mom spelled it with an e instead of a y when I started kindergarten, so that's just how I've always done it. Sometimes Mom says it's because she wants to remember her trip to Bolivia and the beautiful Andes Mountains. Other times she says it's because she likes the mints. So who knows?" I shrugged.

"Well, it's certainly different and kinda cute." He looked around the studio. "How long have you been interested in photography?"

"Ever since third grade when my parents gave me a point and shoot. But when I was in high school and my grandpa gave me his Pentax K1000, I became obsessed. Even when I don't have a camera, I take pics constantly with my phone."

I sat across from him and asked, "Have they removed the crime tape from the coffee shop?"

He shook his head. "Said it might be today."

"Poor Marla. What a mess. Is she alright?"

"Hard to tell with her. She's always been the best actress in the family." He laughed.

I scrunched my forehead, not getting the joke.

"Didn't you know Marla is an accomplished actor? When she lived in Omaha, she starred in numerous plays. Not big-time Broadway sorts, but still she's really good."

"I did not know that." As I pondered the information about one of my suspects, Flash ended the silence by saying, "Pretty girl." He often spoke out of context.

James turned to see the parrot who was standing out on his perch. "Well, who do we have here?"

"That's my sidekick, Flash. He helps me get the attention of unruly children – kind of like you do."

He laughed. "I like the way you taught him to call you pretty girl."

I held my palms up in protest. "I didn't teach him that. That's one of the many phrases he came equipped with when I got him a year ago."

James said, "Well, it certainly fits. You are very pretty. And I like your hair down."

My blush came on as fast as one of my mom's hot flashes. "Thanks." I wanted to return the compliment by saying something nice about him, but I held back – I needed to confirm he was single before flirting. I stood and walked to Flash. As I stroked his feathered head, I asked, "So, do you have any other family here?"

With a slight shake of the head, he said, "Nope. Just Marla."

I sat back down and just came out with it. "No wife or children?"

Leaning so far forward in his chair, I could smell his minty breath, he gave a crooked smile. "No. No wife. No children."

I nodded approvingly and said, "Me neither. Just a bird."

James said, "Well, I'm sure he's good company."

I laughed but all I could think was; "Had this man brushed his teeth just for me? Ahh."

He looked at his watch and got up from his chair. "I need to get back to school."

Just as I leaned forward to stand, he bent to the ground and we bumped heads. I said, "Ouch."

He pulled me in close and touched my forehead where I'd been hit. "I'm so sorry, Ande."

I gazed up into his blue eyes. "It's fine. Just startled me."

James cleared his throat and pulled back a little. "I was picking this up from the floor." He held out a small baggie to me. The one with the earring.

I took it, still a little flustered from our close encounter. "Thanks. It's just an earring I found last week. You've never seen your aunt wearing one like this have you?"

He shrugged. "I'm not good at noticing that kind of thing."

I found that interesting since he did notice my hair. Hmm. I said, "Thanks for stopping by, James."

He took one of my cards from my desk. "Would you like to do dinner sometime?"

I smiled. "I like dinner."

"Great. I'll call you soon. But if you ever need to reach me, here is my card." He pulled one from his pocket and handed it to me. I was surprised to know teachers carried cards. It read, "James White, Special Education Teacher Certified in Speech Pathology and American Sign Language." Then of course it included his contact information, including his cell phone number. Hmm, nice.

He said, "Talk soon," and left.

I leaned my head against the wall and closed my eyes. Wow. I liked this guy.

Alone again, I worked on editing photos from the last two sessions. After about an hour, the door creaked open and Fred Morris literally tiptoed into my studio. He crept around as if he was a cat burglar.

"Fred,? Are you trying to be sneaky? You know I can see you."

He stood erect and spoke through his nose., "I'm trying not to disturb anything."

"Well, I've had people in and out of here for days so the only thing getting disturbed is me. Why are you here?"

"I've come to inspect your place of business for further evidence in the murder of Fiona Pratt."

I let loose. "Do you honestly think I would hurt somebody?" I could speak more freely when a tape player wasn't recording me. But knowing Fred Morris might be recording me now.

"I'm sorry if you feel unjustly accused, but I am strictly going by the evidence. I have a search warrant if you would like to see it. Otherwise, I will look around to see if anything strikes me as odd."

I wanted to say, 'You strike me as odd,' but refrained. Weren't there other officers that could be assigned to this case instead of Fred?

Morris scoured my studio. I knew I didn't have sleeping pills, anti-freeze, or any weapons, but my nerves jangled anyway. The strange officer crouched, dusted, picked things up, and even put something tiny in a baggie as if he was Inspector Clouseau. I wondered if he could get any information from dog or guinea pig hair. As I watched the curious man with his magnifying glass and scotch tape, I held Flash and smoothed his ruffled feathers, just like he had done so many times for me.

When I noticed the earring laying on my desk, I stiffened. That could be considered evidence, especially if Fiona had been wearing the matching one at the time of her death. What should I do? He would surely notice if I snatched it up.

My breathing grew shallow as Fred finished the slow lap around my studio and approached the desk. He stopped and stared, causing my heart to skip. Instead of picking up the bag with the earring, he bent down and got a Viking Coffee cup from the trash and sealed it carefully in a bag. James must have carried it in with him. I prayed Fred wouldn't hear my heart pounding, but figured the obnoxious street noise should cover that up.

I attempted to distract him from seeing the earring. "Find anything to convict me yet, 'Detective' Morris?"

Upon hearing his preferred title, Fred stood a little taller and turned to me with a nod. "Nothing conclusive. But you never know what the lab will say. I will keep in touch." He moved away from the desk without seeing the earring and left.

Within five minutes, there was another knock. I turned the handle on the door before realizing it could be Sherlock coming back. The earring was still on the desk and I started to fret, but I relaxed when my new guest was just Doc. He stood outside holding an awkward bundle of window blind boxes. I grabbed what I could and helped him inside.

He huffed, "Is this a good time?"

"Oh, you betcha." I frowned. "Unfortunately, my schedule has been pretty light lately."

He nodded. "I get it. I drove to Sioux Falls this morning. Jack and Sydney said we only had two customers while I was gone."

When I pictured him driving, I thought of his convertible. "Doc, did you get your car fixed?"

"They're working on it."

I wasn't going to ask where he had gone Friday night, but couldn't hold my tongue completely. "Did you file a report and make an insurance claim?"

He turned to me with eyebrows raised. "Don't worry about it."

I watched him open the packages and I said, "Oh, guess what? I just had a visit from Inspector Gadget. He went over my studio with everything but a fine-toothed comb – and maybe even one of those when I wasn't looking."

"Did he find anything?"

"No. And I didn't expect him to. I don't have any anti-freeze or sleeping pills here."

Doc shrugged. "Probably looking for fingerprints, fiber, and hair samples to put you at the crime scene."

"Well of course I was at the crime scene! He saw me there."

"Hey. Don't get mad at me. I'm just suggesting what he may have been doing."

Frustrated, I needed to get away to think. I said, "Want some iced tea?"

"Sure." He took the ladder and a set of brackets to a window.

As I climbed the steps, a million thoughts zoomed through my mind. So many people and pets have been in my studio lately. How could Fred even find my fingerprints and hair? And what about everyone who had been in the coffee shop?

I filled two glasses with tea and added a dose of powdered Stevia to mine. As I stirred in the sweetener, I pictured the murderer mixing crushed sleeping pills into Fiona's drink, and shuddered.

Back downstairs, I was surprised that one shade was already installed. I handed him the glass. "It looks perfect. You're a fast worker."

"Did you think I would just pretend to put them up?"

I rolled my eyes, but the word pretend reminded me of James' comment about Marla's acting. "Hey Doc, were you aware that Marla is an actress? My new friend, James happens to be her nephew. He said she is quite good."

"No. I hadn't heard that. So?" He took a drink.

I sat in my chair with my tea. "Well, I was just thinking…" I tucked my legs underneath me. "What if Marla was so upset about Fiona taking over her shop that she found a way to get her "out" and then she just acted distraught to cover it up?"

He arched an eyebrow. "Now, do you really think that?"

I took a deep breath and said, "No, but I want to find the killer, so all kinds of scenarios keep bouncing around in my brain."

"Now let's get back to your new friend. You like him?" He winked at me.

My face grew hot and I shrugged. "Maybe?"

He picked up his drill. "It's about time someone made you blush."

This comment prompted me to say, "Well, speaking of which...a group of ladies is coming in Thursday for a calendar shoot. And I believe you know their leader, Joy Gaddis?"

He froze at the mention of her name. "Joy?"

Aha. He did know her. "She asked me to tell you hi."

He gave a smile. "Yeah. We used to date a long time ago. A few years after Bob died."

How had I not known that? Of course, I was probably in middle school, so even thinking of adults dating would have been gross to me at the time. "Well, she's still a wild and crazy lady."

"That's good to know. Tell her hello for me." The pleasant grin remained on his face as he worked.

By the time the windows had been sufficiently covered, it was six o'clock. I said, "Can I take you to O'Hare's for dinner?"

"Sure, but you're not going to owe me anything if you keep buying my meals."

"No way. I haven't even begun to pay for those blinds. I'm just paying off your labor right now."

As I put on my coat, Doc repeated his phrase, "Help! I've been turned into a parrot," to Flash. We crossed the street and went downstairs to the pub underneath Rob's Corner, stopping to talk to a friend as we entered. My favorite booth in the corner was taken, so we sat at a high top in the center of the small space.

I ordered a salad and snagged some of Doc's enormous plate of nachos. I rolled my eyes. "Sarah invited a guy to come back and watch TV tonight. I don't want to intrude, so have another beer."

Doc brightened. "How about we see the new Vin Diesel film?"

I could think of a more appealing movie, but said, "Sure."

After we watched the extreme action movie, Doc dropped me off at home. I put Flash up for the night and said, "I love you," hoping the bird would echo it back.

He replied, "What's in your wallet?"

I chuckled but was glad he didn't have a TV downstairs to learn any more silly phrases. I climbed the stairs, hoping Sarah's friend was gone. The only light in my apartment emitted from the TV. I saw the outline of Sarah and a guy on the couch and walked past them to the kitchen for a drink. I'm always thirsty after popcorn.

Sarah chided, "Just ignore us, why don't you?"

I said, "I didn't want to interrupt your show."

She muted the sound. "It's lame anyway. Gary, this is Ande. Ande this is Gary."

I couldn't see the man, but said, "Hi Gary"

"Hello, Ande." The voice sounded familiar, but when Sarah turned on the lamp, I almost dropped my glass of water. It was Mustache Man! The jerk was on my couch! In my apartment.

CHAPTER 9

Gary, AKA, Mustache Man, smirked, then winked at me, obviously enjoying the irony of our meeting more than I did.

My first inclination was to scream, 'take your hands off my friend' or 'get out of my house,' but Sarah would think I was nuts. I'd have to endure this and explain it all to her later. When she turned her head, I gave the jerk a hostile glare.

I couldn't stay in the same room with this man any longer. "I'm going to my room to work on some stuff. Sarah, I'll need you to help me early in the morning." That was my sneaky way of encouraging her to cut the evening short. I hated to think of her getting very involved with this guy.

She wrinkled her nose at me. "Okay? Wake me when you need me." She turned back to the despicable Mustache Man who might just be a murderer. Just as I turned toward my room, she brushed her hand along his cheek. Gross!

I tried to calm down enough to read a book, but that wasn't possible with 'you know who' in the next room. So, I got my phone and scrutinized my list of possible suspects and motives again. I still couldn't believe I was using the term – murder. My brain hurt trying to conjure up motives so instead, I watched some old episodes of Bob's Burgers to get my mind off the whole thing.

An hour later, I went to the bathroom to brush my teeth. When I came out, Gary stood blocking my doorway.

I took a step back and said, "What do you want?"

"I want you to keep your trap shut. If you say anything about me, you'll regret it."

"That's twice you've threatened me." I wanted to call Sarah over and tried to look around his big body for my friend, but she wasn't in the apartment.

He sniffed. "Don't worry about Sarah, little bee, she went down to answer the door. It's just you and me here…"

My cheeks heated as I considered what to do. This guy was threatening me and now I had even more reason to tell Sarah all I knew about him.

When Sarah appeared in the doorway from the stairs out of breath, Gary moved away nonchalantly. She didn't seem to notice the close proximity of the creepy guy and her best friend. She said, "Ande, your bird is crazy. His buzz was so realistic I thought someone was at the door."

I cleared my throat and said with a wobbly voice, "Yeah. It's his newest annoying habit. He'll talk all night if I leave the lights on." My anxiety was real.

Sarah said in a playful voice, "Well, I turned them off. You're welcome."

Gary lifted his eyebrow to me as a warning sign. I returned to my room and locked the door behind me, crossing my fingers that the two of us would be safe with a madman in the apartment.

When morning came, I found Sarah all alone snoozing on the couch. An empty bag of chips and a few beer bottles littered the coffee table. I made coffee and headed down the stairs, my mind consumed with the events of last night. I refused to be bullied by that Gary guy with the creepy mustache. I should have stood up to him and alerted Sarah. He could really be dangerous. I mean, he threatened me! Telling Sarah about him was a no-brainer. I just had to figure out how.

After putting Flash on his morning perch, I lifted my new shade and stared out the window at the progress, or lack thereof, on the street. The sun shone, making the remaining snow patches sparkle. I contemplated how to tell Sarah about her awful date when I noticed an orange safety cone leaning against my door.

I stepped outside to move it and found Mother Nature had tricked me with her gorgeous sunshine. Instead of the warmth I expected, the temperature couldn't have been more than ten degrees. I tossed the cone further away and jumped back inside.

I picked up my feathery buddy and took a sip of lukewarm coffee. Without warning, Flash made his loud jackhammer sound right in my ear, causing me to spill my coffee down my front. Yet again, I was glad I was wearing an old shirt.

"You are so annoying." I put him back on his tall stand perch and wasn't that gentle about it. I said sternly, "I was trying to be nice and spend quality time with you, and that's the thanks I get?"

He made his new equally annoying buzz and said, "Pretty girl".

"Don't you even <u>try</u> to butter me up." I shook my head and climbed the stairs, wiping my wet shirt with a napkin as I went.

When I opened the door, Sarah rubbed her eyes and blinked a few times. She said groggily, "So, what do you need me for today?"

I stared at her, confused, then realized she spoke of my feeble attempt to have her send Mustache Man home early last night. "Oh, never mind...but I do need to talk to you about something."

In the kitchen, I wiped down my shirt and got two cups of black coffee. I handed one to Sarah and watched her drag herself up to a sitting position so she could drink.

"Nice coffee stain, klutz."

"Yeah. I'm blaming it on Flash this time."

She smiled. "Okay? So what do you need to talk to me about?"

I looked at my sleepy-eyed friend and started, "Remember how I told you about the worker guy at the bar harassing me and later, threatening me?"

She yawned and nodded.

"Well...that guy was Gary."

She snorted. "Right."

"Sarah, I'm not kidding. Of course, I didn't know his name then so I just called him Mustache Man, but it was definitely him."

She cocked her head at me as if I was crazy, but I continued even more animated, "Then, last night while you were downstairs, he told me not to tell you anything about him. But I don't care. You have to know that he's not who he appears to be. He's scary."

Her smile faded. "Gary did that last night?"

I nodded. "I'm really sorry. I know you like him, but I think he could be dangerous. You need to be careful around him."

She said, "You really think he would hurt you?"

"I don't know, but I don't think he was joking either time he threatened me."

When Sarah remained silent, I worried she might be mad at me. But then she said, "Well, it's not like he was Mr. Right. I was just enjoying some male attention." She smirked. "Ande, don't worry. I won't tell him you said anything. I'll just brush him off like I do when I get tired of any guy. It would have happened sooner or later. He just talks about himself anyway."

I bit my lip wondering if he would get angry with her.

She picked up on my worry and said, "Remember, I've been around the world and have seen things. I can handle myself."

My anxiety decreased with each of her words. I hugged her and said, "I'm glad you're not crushed."

She smiled and waved me off.

I said, "You know, I really could use your help today. I have to shoot the Brookings High track team at 3:30. Wanna come?"

"Do I get my own gun and will they actually be running, 'cause that would make it more challenging."

It took me a sec to catch her joke. "Very funny. Guess I should be careful in using the word shoot."

She said, "Sure, I'll go along. It'll be good to see our old stomping grounds again."

"Great. Be ready by three."

"Okay. Oh!" She beamed with excitement. "I found out yesterday that the Medical Center is expanding and needs general practitioners, my main interest. I have to update my resume' this morning. Then later I'll stop by and drop it off. I hope I get an interview."

"So quick? Sarah, that's great."

She shrugged. "We'll see. Cross your fingers!"

I wasn't surprised to hear they needed more doctors. This is the fastest-growing area in South Dakota. "I'll root for you. Are you sure you have time to help me today?"

"Yep. Besides, if I get an interview, you'll make it up to me by doing a mock interview."

"Deal! Now I'm going downstairs to set up for yet another Easter session."

After I'd gotten all the bunny-eared kids safely out the door, I started cleaning up the mess. When there was a knock at the door, I looked up to find Carter Fox standing outside. The tall, dark-haired man was unmistakable.

I walked casually to the door. "Hey, what brings you by?"

He entered and smirked. "Having a party?"

I brushed away the pastel Easter grass clinging to my hair and chuckled. "No. It's just that time of year."

He leaned against the door and crossed his arms in a confident manner. "I stopped by to see if we could schedule that big family photo shoot. Any chance you would be available this weekend?"

I tore my eyes away from him and grabbed my phone from the table. The calendar confirmed my weekend was indeed free. I said without looking at him, "I have Friday or Saturday available. Which would be best for you?"

"Saturday is the health fair. How about Friday, at say five o'clock? Could we meet at my house and take a few photos, then possibly go down to the lake for a few more?"

My eyes rounded with the excitement of seeing their house. He waited for an answer and I said without reservation, "Absolutely!"

Remembering to act less starstruck and more professional, I asked, "Do you have a terraced area, a deck, or a large stairway that could fit your whole family? Logistics, you know."

In a casual tone, he said, "We actually have all three. You're more than welcome to come early, say at 4 or 4:30? I'll make sure that Debra or the housekeeper lets you in to set up."

Ick. I didn't want to be anywhere near Debra until I had to, but I put on a nice smile anyway. "That will work. Oh, and is your house on the east or west side of Lake Campbell?"

"Our home is west of the lake."

I lit up. "Awesome! Then, the lighting should be great for afternoon photos." I used my hands to describe the scene. "The sun will illuminate the faces…and with the lake in the background…" I kissed my fingertips as if I was an Italian chef. "It will be perfection."

He grinned, looking amused. "We haven't discussed a fee."

I wasn't worried, since my prices were affordable. When I gave him a quote, he said, "You really should charge more than that, my girl." He jotted down his address and cell phone number on a piece of paper and handed it to me.

I started to thank him, but Flash interrupted me by whistling the Andy Griffith theme song my dad had taught him.

Carter stared at Flash with a curious look. He walked toward the birdcage and said, "What an interesting bird. So, he's pretty smart, huh?"

I laughed. "I'm not sure about that, but he does like to mimic what he hears."

He nodded. "Look, I need to catch lunch before going to my office. Can I bring you something?"

I stammered in surprise, "Uh. No. That's fine. I have food upstairs."

He looked behind me at the door leading to my stairway. With an eyebrow raised, he said, "So, you live up there?"

"Yes. I got a much better deal on my studio rental if I combined it with the upstairs apartment unit. It works out perfectly."

He nodded. "Did one of your clients lose an earring?" He cocked his head at the baggie on my desk.

I shrugged. "Maybe. I found it the other day on the sidewalk and I'm trying to find the owner. It's not yours, is it?"

He chuckled and said, "Not mine. Guess I'll see you at my place Friday afternoon."

I caught him before he reached the door. "Oh, Mr. Fox. How many people should I plan for in the photo?"

He calculated the numbers on his fingers and in his head. "I'd say about 25? And some are a handful."

I wondered if he meant his own kids and wife.

Before opening the door, he turned and pointed at me. "And Ande, please call me Carter."

After he left, I added the contact information for the most important man in Brookings into my phone. I added his family photoshoot to my calendar. Woohoo! I finally hit the big time.

I drove to the photo lab and picked up my latest prints. The huge canvas enlargement of little Emma and Snowball was spectacular, but it was so big it barely fit in my SUV.

After hauling all sizes of prints into my studio, I got ready for track team photo shoot. I collected my camera, tripod, lenses, and finally Sarah, who helped haul it to my car.

Sarah and I arrived at Brookings High and carried my gear to the stadium where years ago we spent many a Friday night watching football games.

Sarah pointed to the concession stand and said, "Ahh. Remember when I kissed Brian Jacobs over there? It was so romantic…until my parents walked by and caught us."

I laughed just as a tall man walked up to us. He wore a ball cap emblazoned with the school's bobcat logo. I said, "Coach Hanson?"

He nodded and we introduced ourselves. The coach led us to the stands and then asked, "Mind if we do both outdoor and indoor photos?" His face was hopeful.

I smiled. "Whatever you want. We're yours for an hour and a half."

I set up my tripod as the student-athletes meandered into the stadium wearing matching shorts and sleeveless jerseys.

Sarah nudged me and said, "Jeez, aren't they freezing?"

I wondered that myself as the sparsely dressed kids scuffed through the snow in their running shoes. I was plenty warm in my jacket, but even in a heavy parka, Sarah rubbed her arms to warm up. I'm guessing she didn't come across much cold weather in Africa and had lost some of her northern hardiness.

I took pictures of the 40-plus athletes in various groupings while my silly friend made faces at them. "What are you doing?"

"What? You don't have your bird to entertain them. Isn't that why you invited me?"

Half of the kids smiled at her while others rolled their eyes. Was this knucklehead really a doctor?

We moved into the gymnasium and took more photos of the team. When we finished and everything was loaded into the car, I said, "Want to run by HyVee? I'm out of coffee and TP."

She said, "Sure, but I'm buying. It's the least I can do to earn my keep."

We pushed a cart around the grocery store, picking up way more than planned. As we neared the bakery aisle, Sarah squealed, "Hey, let's make snickerdoodles!"

Oh my gosh, that sounded so good. "Yes! We'll need some eggs."

"I'm on it." She sprinted to the other side of the store to get a carton.

I had just picked up a bag of flour when Leo materialized out of the blue. He said, "What the heck, Ande? Channel 7 news just announced Fiona was murdered and…" He glanced around and said quietly, "…and you are the prime suspect."

As soon as I processed his words, the bag of flour slipped from my hands and exploded on the floor.

I slowly looked down at the huge pile of white powder covering our jeans and shoes. My tongue was completely dry as if the flour had burst in my mouth.

Leo closed his eyes and said, "Sorry to upset you. The anchor didn't actually use your name, but said a Brookings photographer is the number one suspect in the case."

Might as well have said my name since I'm the only professional photographer in town. Who had told the media? Fred? Only a few people knew my DNA had been found on the cup. I hadn't told anyone but Doc and Jon that it was a murder- not even Sarah.

I pulled myself together and moistened my mouth enough to speak. "Leo, you know I didn't do it right?"

He shook his head. "Of course you didn't! Nobody who knows you would believe you could do something like that."

I squeaked, "But others will. This is going to ruin my business and my reputation."

He put his hands on my shoulders. "We won't let that happen. We'll figure it out." He stared at the floor and said, "I'll go tell the manager about the mess."

As he walked away, I stood frozen in my pile of flour trying to comprehend the news.

"I leave you alone for a second and you cause an explosion?" When Sarah looked up from the mess to my furrowed brow, her tone changed. "What's wrong?"

By the time I finished telling her what Leo had said, a kid arrived with a broom and dustpan. Leo was right behind him and gave a nod. "Sarah?"

"Hey, Leo."

On a normal day Sarah and Leo would have a gabfest when seeing each other, but today they held back.

I came to my senses and moved aside shaking off my feet so the teen could clean up the mess.

Leo adjusted his ball cap and said, "Ande, don't worry, my brother will fix it."

We stood in uncomfortable silence as the kid swept. Leo changed the subject in an upbeat tone. "You two coming to Spinners tomorrow night?"

Sarah said, "Wouldn't miss it."

I nodded. "Thanks for telling me, Leo. I'm sorry I floured your shoes."

He shrugged. "It covers the dirt. I've been working on digging my pond. Later." He nodded and turned towards the beer locker.

We went ahead and bought our supplies, including a fresh bag of flour. We didn't say much until we got in the car. I started the ignition and turned to Sarah before backing out of the parking space, "I didn't do it, you know."

"Duh!" Sarah picked up her phone and dialed a number. Her voice was loud and slow as she spoke. "I need to speak to Officer Morris...No. It's not an emergency...Sarah Anderson. S.a.r..."
She blew out a puff of air in frustration. "Come on, Ada. You've known me all my life. My uncle is married to your daughter. You even helped deliver me. Can I please speak to Fred?"

I tried to keep my eyes on the road, but couldn't keep from staring at Sarah. What was she doing?

Finally she barked, "Fred Morris, how could let them announce on TV that a Brookings photographer is your main suspect in Fiona's death? Now the world thinks Ande is a murderer!" She paused then said, "Channel 7."

Sarah was silent for a while then hung up and turned to me. "He hasn't talked to any reporters and is pretty angry that the cause of death was announced. He said the only people who knew your DNA was found on her cup were you, Mike, and Marla. And the lab in Pierre only had a numbered specimen."

"Then, how did the station find out? I know Mike told Peggy and I told Jon and Doc but..." When I saw Sarah's face, I expected her to have a 'Doc may be guilty' look, but instead, she pouted.

She said in a choked voice, "You told Doc and Jon, but you didn't tell me about this? When did you find out?"

I pulled int a convenience store lot next to a six-foot pile of snow and turned to Sarah. "I'm sorry. I stopped by Doc's on my way home from the Police station on Monday because I was upset. You were still out, and later you were so excited about applying for a job. Then the whole Gary thing came up."

"You've known since Monday?"

"Yes, but we haven't had that much time together. I'm sorry. I promise you'll be the first to know every update from now on."

She softened. "You must have been very upset. I feel bad I wasn't there for you."

"Well, you would have been if I had told you. Besides, just having you around kept my mind off of it and that's what I really needed."

She twisted her mouth and said, "Okay. Just remember, we're in this together from now on."

"Okay. Deal." I shook her hand and motioned to go in the store. We got slushies and drove home.

As we approached my door I was shocked to find it ajar. I looked at Sarah and pushed the door open with my foot, ready to throw my icy drink at a perpetrator. But there, sitting on my couch was Jon playing with Flash.

He did a double-take when he saw me and said, "Woah, Flash, who's that girl with her hair down?"

"Oh. You scared me!"

"Why? You gave me a key. Am I not supposed to use it now that you have a new roommate?"

When Sarah finally peeked her head inside, Jon stood. "Hi, Sarah! Come on in. I won't bite."

She blew out a sigh as she came through the door. "Hi, Jonjon." She had called him that ever since he was a baby. I smiled when they embraced. She looked up at him, "You must have grown another five inches this year."

He chuckled and said, "Are you glad to be home?"

"Yeah, but it's a little nerve-wracking to leap feet-first into a detective drama."

He said, "How's all that going? You both are so skittish."

I said, "Well, it could be better. Did you hear I'm now a suspect?"

"I told you not to get involved." He shook his head at Flash. "She never listens to me." Then turned back to me. "Ok, spill it."

I explained most everything, then threatened him with his life to keep his mouth shut about it on campus or I'd never get to do another Greek photo shoot.

"Have you told Mom or Dad yet?"

I swung my head back and forth dramatically. "No way I'm getting them involved."

"OK, but Mom will be furious if she finds out on her own. And if you're in prison when she gets back, heads will roll."

"Good. They deserve a dose of Mom if I'm put in prison. So, did you just come by just to scare me, pet Flash or are you hungry?" My little brother was always begging for a home-cooked meal.

"I wondered if you still have those leftover powder packets from the color run you photographed last fall. I'd like to use some for an art project for my mixed media class."

I put my camera down. "I do. I've never found a use for them. I'll go get them. You can have them all if you'll help Sarah bring in the groceries."

As I left the room Sarah said, "Did you know Ande's got a boyfriend?"

I rolled my eyes then ran upstairs and made a beeline for the closet. I dug around until I found the box and checked inside to make sure the packets were still there. I was surprised I'd collected so many unbroken bags of the powder.

While Sarah put the food away, I handed the box to Jon. He said, "Wow. I don't need that many. I just want one of each color." He grabbed an empty plastic bag from Sarah and put one each of the pink, green, blue, purple, yellow, and orange powder packets inside. I said, "If you need white, I've got flour." I showed Jon my shoe that had the white powder in every crevice.

Sarah laughed as she joined us. She picked up a blue bag and squeezed it. "What's it made of?"

Jon sat down and answered, "I think it's just cornstarch and dye. It has to be food-safe since they throw it at people in the race and it can get in their eyes and mouth."

She shrugged, not quite getting the concept of throwing powder at runners.

Standing by Jon, I ruffled his long hair. "Looks like I should donate my ponytail holders to you since I'm not wearing them as much anymore."

"Yeah, yeah. Hey, when are they starting the real excavating of your street so they can pour the new concrete? It all looks so haphazard."

I rolled my eyes. "Hazard is the key part of that word. It's like they just throw a dart and that's the place they tear up for the day. Then they leave it a mess and throw another dart the next day and start somewhere else."

He shook his head. "My boss wouldn't put up with that. Well, I've gotta go. I'm meeting a buddy at Viking Coffee."

"Let me know if you find something that vindicates me."

He saluted and walked to the door. "Be careful, or I'm telling Mom."

We said in unison, "We will."

CHAPTER 10

Sarah waved as Jon left. "He is so darned cute! That hair! I'm surprised some girl hasn't snatched him up yet."

"From what I understand, they've tried. I guess he's just too focused on school and his job now to get involved in a relationship. And that's a good thing."

Sarah nodded and went upstairs to prepare for her possible future interview. While packaging the new prints in my new 'Picture This on Main' envelopes, I tried to process the fact that my picture may soon be hanging on the post office wall.

All the photos of little Emma in her lace dress were darling just as I had expected. I called Anna to say the prints were ready. She was thrilled to talk to me and anxious to pick up the photos. She told long stories of what little Emma did today and then she asked if Jon would be at my studio when she dropped by. Wow. Being a stay-at-home mom must be terribly lonely.

I inspected the images of the Fox family and the quality was good. Most pictures had both kids smiling and even captured the threads of silver running through Carter's thick black hair. I studied his chiseled face, so full of warmth. On the contrary, his wife, even with an open smile, had that look of superiority that put me on edge.

I called the number on their order form and Carter's liquid-sounding voice came over the recording with a welcome message. At the beep I said, "Mr. and Mrs. Fox, this is Ande from 'Picture This on Main'. I just wanted to tell you that your photos are ready to be picked up at your convenience."

I hung up just as Sarah appeared at the bottom of the stairs. "Gary texted and asked if I wanted to go out tonight. I just wrote back. 'Thanks, but got plans with my BFF.'"

"Whew! I'm glad you still want me as your BFF." I winked. "How did he take it?"

She shrugged. "I don't really care. So, how about we go out and get dinner. Then we can come back and make snickerdoodles?"

"Sounds perfect. Let me call Mike first. I've been putting it off."

Sarah nodded and went back upstairs as I called my friendly lawyer. I sure hoped he would still want to represent me. "Hi Mike, have you seen the news?"

"No, I just got off work. Heading home now." I could hear him huffing and figured he was walking to his house from his office. "Should I?"

"Probably." I told him what his brother had told me. "I'm furious. Isn't this defamation of character? I mean I haven't been arrested. And Fred said he didn't know anything about the broadcast. I swear the only people I told were Jon and Doc and they are the last people to inform a TV station of anything – you know how Doc hates the media."

"I'll call the studio and ask where they got their information and get back to you. Don't worry."

"I'm afraid I can't stop worrying, but thank you, Mike."

When we hung up I yelled up the stairwell. "Ready to go?"

Instantly, Sarah came down the stairs in a one-person stampede. The girl must be hungry. "How about O'Hare's?"

"Perfect." I didn't mind going there two nights in a row.

We made our way down the narrow stairs of the pub. The little place was crowded, but this time we got to sit in my favorite booth, hidden in the corner opposite the popcorn machine. I ordered a French Dip sandwich and a Coke. As much as I wanted to drown my sorrow with something stronger, I needed to keep my head on straight. She ordered two orders of chislic and a margarita.

"Chislic?" I was surprised she was only ordering an appetizer.

"I've been craving it for months. They sure didn't have deep-fried cubes of garlicky meat on toothpicks in Africa." She stared at an empty space on the wall, thinking. "As a matter of fact, I never saw a toothpick the whole time I was there. Although I did see a man yank a piece of wood from a tree and pick his teeth."

I was thinking about the rich buttery meat when a couple from my church came in. I watched as the woman recognized me and pulled her husband right back up the stairs.

"Did you see that? They acted like I'm a leper!" My eyes filled with tears.

"Stop it. We're going to get to the bottom of this," Sarah said forcefully. "But first, I want to hear everything you learned during that interview with Barney Fife."

After the server brought our drinks, Sarah licked the salt from the rim of her glass and took a sip. I took a long drink of Coke and a deep breath before starting. "Well I don't know how it happened, but my DNA was on the cup. I don't know how it got there."

"Tell me again what happened that morning."

I described exactly how it had gone down in Viking Coffee with my Matcha tea and making the drink for Marla. "I never touched another cup!"

Our food arrived and we put our conversation on hold while we ate. Sarah gave me a bite of the chislic and I nearly melted with the burst of flavor. I should order it more often.

"Well, it sounds like we need to find the real killer." She whispered, "Have you given any more thought to Doc?"

Oh boy. Why did she have to bring that up? My stomach sank. Doc couldn't do something like that, could he? Without answering, I lay my arms on the sticky table and put my head on them, wishing I was home, sleeping it all off.

Sarah backpaddled and said, "You're probably right. Of course he didn't do it. Just thinking of all possibilities. Sorry."

With my mouth buried in my arms, my voice came out muffled, "It's OK. I get it. I'll show you my suspects list tomorrow." When I raised my head I was greeted with even worse news. That stupid Gary/Mustache Man came through the door with his gang of unsavory work buddies.

Sarah raised her hand to wave him over, but I grabbed it and pulled it down. "What are you doing? We don't want him to see us."

I scooted to the corner of the booth, pulling Sarah with me. We were pretty well hidden, but still had a clear shot of the guys. Luckily, the place had thinned out so they didn't have to scour the room for seats and consequently missed seeing us. I breathed a sigh of relief when they sat at a high-top table across the room.

The men were not wearing their orange vests but managed to stand out on their own with their crude behavior. When one guy yelled some profanity at another, Sarah's eyes widened.

I whispered, "Just you wait, girl, you may get to see them in their full glory."

Although we couldn't hear their conversation, we watched their body language. Were they celebrating something? I leaned in to Sarah. "It doesn't look like they are mourning the loss of their boss, does it?"

Before Sarah could fully shake her head, a cute young server walked to the men, her ponytail swinging. Gary put his arm around her waist and whispered something into her ear. The teen pulled away and practically ran back to the bar with a beet-red face, not realizing she had just entered a lion's den. When the lecher said something to his buddies, they laughed and one even gave him a high five.

I turned to Sarah in time to see her jaw drop. She said with a nod, "OK, so thank you for warning me about that creep."

The male bartender walked to their table. He said something and Gary shrugged, then the guy walked back to the bar.

The room seemed to shrink with those men in the joint. I whispered to Sarah, "I would totally ignore Gary except for the fact that he is one of my suspects."

She looked at me, "What do you think he would he gain from killing Fiona?"

I ventured, "Well, maybe he was mad at her for admonishing the crew and giving them new rules? The two of them were arguing the day she died, he had easy access to the coffee shop, and I know from experience he likes to threaten people."

Sarah laughed, "Every place I ever worked had rules. That's no reason to kill someone."

I had to agree it was a flimsy motive but said, "Well, I think we should investigate this Gary guy anyway."

"Definitely. Who else is on your list?"

"I know you don't know Marla well since she moved here just before you left. I think she's a nice lady, but..." I held up one finger. "I just found out she's an accomplished actor. She could have been putting on an act when she was so upset about Fiona's death." I held up a second finger. "She had access to my cup." With a third finger, I said, "And Marla was the last person to see Fiona alive." She could easily have framed me and she has more of a motive for killing Fiona than most. She hated her for taking over her shop."

"Woah. We definitely need to talk to her too." She leaned in closer. "Is anyone else on your list?"

"You know Davis?"

"The meek little flower dude with the round glasses?"

"Yep. He's got a huge crush on Marla and keeps asking her out. He sent her flowers on Friday and the note said, 'I would do anything for you.' Maybe he killed Fiona for making Marla so miserable, but I talked to him and he seems to have a good alibi."

Sarah said, "And then there's Doc with his damaged car."

Our heads were nearly touching as we whispered. I was getting ready to defend Doc again when a deep voice interrupted. "Are you two hiding?"

We slowly looked up to find Gary looming over us, with his gross mustache and a sly smirk on his face.

I glanced at Sarah, hoping she would follow my lead. We had to pretend I hadn't told her anything about him. Even though it nearly killed me to say it, I turned and spoke in a semi-pleasant voice. "Gary, is it? Nice to see you again."

Sarah added in a flirty tone. "Hey, mister. I saw you come in but didn't want to bother you and your buddies. Have a seat." She scooted over so he could climb in between us.

I cringed at the idea of the jerk sitting next to me, so I moved to the other side of the booth.

Sarah excelled at faking with our little ruse. When she snuggled up next to him and asked about his day, I had to fight to keep my sandwich down. She was so good I almost believed she liked the monster.

A cute male server came to our table and asked if we wanted to order more drinks. Gary said, "Set these girls up. It's on me."

Sarah ordered another margarita. As much as I wanted to get the heck away from this guy I said, "Can I have a Grainbelt Premium, please?"

Gary slung his arm over Sarah's shoulder as if he owned her and taunted me with a sharp stare. "So, what brings you two out tonight?"

Sarah said, "Oh, Ande and I both had a busy day and we didn't feel like cooking."

An uncomfortable silence filled the space as Foreigner played "You're as cold as ice" over the speakers. Ironically, the whole scene gave me chills.

When the drinks arrived, I sipped on my beer and nibbled on my cold fries, trying to focus on anything other than the lovebirds.

Finally, I couldn't stay quiet any longer and threw out the first hook and line. With an attempt at naivety, I said, "So, didn't you work for the woman who died last week? Fiona something?" I watched closely for his reaction.

Gary didn't flinch but rather, stared into my eyes so fiercely I had to look away. He said, "Yes. Such a shame. Must have had some heart problems."

When Sarah opened her mouth in protest, I was afraid she might tell him we knew her death was determined homicide, so I kicked her foot under the table.

"Ow!"

I was impressed when Sarah aptly qualified her outburst with, "It just makes my heart hurt to think of someone dying."

Both of their eyes were still fixed on me. Gary said, "I guess the stress of the project got to her. She had a lot of angry business owners to contend with too. That didn't help."

Well, that was clearly directed at me. He turned to Sarah and pushed a piece of hair behind her ear. He changed the subject and murmured, "How about we do dinner tomorrow night, Sarah?"

Ick. Did his porn stache just touch her cheek?

While his head was turned away, I mouthed the word, "Spinners'."

She gave a slight nod and cooed to him, "I'm busy tomorrow night, but how about Friday night?" She perked up and squealed, "Ooh. I know! We could have a double date? Ande, you could bring your new friend, James?"

Gary gave a slight eye roll, but mine was more extreme. Just the thought of spending an evening with him sickened me. At this point I didn't even care if Gary noticed my look of horror. But since I wanted to investigate him further and figured that must have been Sarah's plan, I said with as much cheer as I could muster, "Oh, yeah. Great idea. I'll ask him."

Gary gave me a smug glare and kissed Sarah's cheek which gave me the heebie-jeebies. Finally, he stood and said, "I'll text you about Friday." He left to join his friends, but not before giving me another warning stare.

I exhaled and asked Sarah, "How could you stand him being so close to you?"

"Well, I couldn't let on that I knew he was a jerk. It's called acting." She shrugged. "I just pretended he was Chris Hemsworth and it wasn't so hard."

"Chris Hemsworth? Girl, you have a phenomenal imagination."

I caught the eye of our server and he came over to check on us. I said, "We want to cash out.'

He motioned across the bar, "That guy took care of it."

Sarah said, "Who? Chris Hemsworth?"

I rolled my eyes at the confused server. "Never mind. And thank you."

He walked away, probably thinking we were nuts. We left a good tip and put on our coats before leaving the stale joint. I sensed Gary's stare as we climbed the steps to Main Street.

As we crossed the street, I said, "I about died when you suggested a double date. I'm not sure I can stand to watch him paw all over you again."

"Well, I wasn't about to go out with the creep alone. It will be the perfect time to investigate him with a plan. We weren't prepared tonight, but we did get free food and drinks, so that was good."

"I guess so if you want a possible killer footing your dinner bill. No more talk about murder tonight! Let's talk snickerdoodles."

While I got everything out to make the cookies, Sarah turned on the TV so we could watch *Bob's Burgers* as we baked. A special report came on and a picture of Fiona popped up. Sarah grabbed the remote to turn it off, but I said, "It's OK. Let's hear what they have to say."

My stomach sank in anticipation of the broadcast.

The anchor with false eyelashes and perfect hair said, "Friday evening, 48-year-old construction project manager, Fiona Pratt, was found unresponsive in a Brookings coffee shop. She was later pronounced dead at Brookings Regional Hospital. The cause of death has not been officially released."

The reporter went on to tell some personal information about Fiona, but by then, Sarah had turned down the volume. She said, "Hey, she didn't mention a photographer this time!"

I let out a slow stream of air. Maybe Fred Morris or Mike had contacted the station. Hopefully, only a small audience had watched the noon report. But I've lived in Brookings long enough to know that secrets don't stay secrets long in a small town. The news about me has probably been spread across the state by now.

We watched several episodes of *Bob's Burgers* and topped off the evening by eating way too many warm cookies.

Thursday morning, Sarah and I set up the studio in preparation for a whole gaggle of older ladies and rescue dogs. We followed Joy's specifications and started with a white backdrop. She also asked me to have a dressing room so the "girls" could change, so we cleared out both the storeroom and my downstairs bathroom, hoping that would suffice.

Sarah said, "You are awfully quiet this morning. Are you nervous about the big group of dames and dogs or …other things?"

I caught what she meant about other things and answered, "Both. This is my first session since the news broadcast. What if the ladies don't show?"

"If you build it, they will come!" she said dramatically. "Besides, wouldn't Joy have called to cancel? Hey, why are they making a calendar in March, anyway?"

Anticipating a rowdy group, I stabilized my tripod with the sandbags I use for outdoor windy days. "Oh, most of them are snowbirds and will head down south in the fall. They wanted to get it done before summer hits and they get busy golfing and gardening. Plus, this way they'll have plenty of time to sell the calendars before the new year."

Sarah's phone rang. Upon seeing the caller ID, she waggled her eyebrows at me and ran upstairs to take the call. Within minutes, she came running back downstairs yelling, "I got an interview! They want me to come in today at 4!"

"That's wonderful! You're gonna ace it. As soon as this session is over, we'll practice for your interview."

Promptly at eleven, an endless line of women ages 55-90 burst through the door full of energy. Well, burst may be an exaggeration since a few were slowed down with walkers and canes. Joy's friend, Carol, seemed to stand taller than before. She held the door for the crew and introduced me to each lady "This is the adorable, Andrea!"

The gals, each carrying a bag of props, stamped the snow from their shoes as they entered. I recognized at least half of them; one was my mom's hairdresser another was my old cafeteria lunch lady and some others were Mom's friends. One large woman with an equally large voice bellowed, "I nearly fell in a hole in the street!"

Could I be sued for the poor conditions outside my shop if someone got hurt? I chose not to worry about that now.

Joy made her appearance carrying a stack of colorful signs. She made several trips from her car carrying plastic step stools, folding chairs, and even a box of wine with clear plastic cups. She said with a wink, "For emergencies."

That seemed pretty weird, but I had a feeling I'd be needing the emergency elixir by the time I was done with this crew.

Joy sidled up to me and whispered, "I have to find a substitute for November because after the news report yesterday, her husband wouldn't let November come."

She must have seen my face drop for she said, "Don't worry, Darlin', nobody else believes you could hurt anyone. You are just the sweetest thing around."

I felt a bit better after hearing that but was sorry to cause a hiccup in their big plans. I watched Joy and Carol conspire over their problem and make phone calls.

I was distracted when a woman backed into my tripod. Despite my precautions and no camera attached yet, I instinctively bounded over and grabbed the stand.

Sarah chuckled. "Gee. I didn't know you could move that fast, Ande!"

"Yeah, well I don't want anyone to get clobbered by falling apparatus." With my shop so full of bodies and gear, it was a possibility. What would it be like when twelve dogs arrived? I whistled to get the ladies' attention and pointed out the two "dressing rooms."

One lady spoke up. "Where are the puppies?"

Joy announced, "Not to worry. They'll be here. Let's get ready for the cover photo. Black robes please." She marched to the back and started leading the women like she was the Pied Piper.

Carol stayed behind, glancing at the uncovered windows. "Can we shut your shades? Some of the women are a little bit shy."

I nodded. "Of course. We'll do that now."

Sarah and I pulled down my new blinds, making the room much darker than I expected. With the shades drawn, I couldn't depend on natural light so I plugged in all the other light sources which took up even more of the limited space. "Hey Sarah, pick some music on my phone so we can liven the mood."

She found some tunes and before long Alicia Keys' "Girl on Fire" was blasting through my Bluetooth speakers. I hoped it would get the gals in the party mood.

In a cacophonous entrance of giggles, Joy led the women from the storeroom. They were all dressed in matching black robes and carried signs brandishing their month. Some ladies strutted to the music. The one with the best rhythm was steadied by her walker.

Standing behind four stools, Joy announced, "I'll stand here. February here, March..." She directed the first four months to stand in a row. "May through August, you are on the stools in front of us." I noticed this group needed a little help getting in their places.

"September through December, please sit on the chairs in front." Joy took her place and stared at the empty spot. "I haven't found anyone for November yet." She faced Sarah and clasped her hands in prayer. "Do you want to be Miss November?"

Sarah's mouth was as round as her eyes as she said, "Um. No thank you."

Joy's pout was pitiful. "Please? We don't have anyone else."

Sarah's shoulders slumped and she closed her eyes. Just as she was about to succumb to the pressure, somebody tapped at the door.

A silver-haired woman entered and everyone cheered "Rachel!" Joy ran over and hugged her.

The lady said, "I couldn't let you down. As soon as George left, I changed clothes and drove over here."

The person most relieved was Sarah who gushed, "Thank you, Rachel!"

The door buzzed and I peeked through the shades to find three girls, each with four leashes attached to four dogs. I opened the door and said, "I guess you brought the pups?"

The first girl was out of breath as she tried to control her pack. She said, "Yes. And we're supposed to stay with them until they are finished."

"Come on in!"

The girls, probably university students, stumbled inside almost tripping over the leashes and all the extra feet below them. The dogs were of all breeds, sizes, and activity levels. Upon their arrival, the room felt even smaller. Why had I pictured quiet little puppies when I agreed to this? This was anything but quiet and one dog had to be 150 pounds or more. Still, I wished I had time to pet every one of the precious critters.

A few pups cowered in the new surroundings and some pulled at their leashes. One medium-sized dog spotted Flash and took a flying leap toward the cage, only to be stopped by the tether around his neck. Flash was on high alert and retreated inside his cage.

I laughed when a Border Collie immediately went for a tennis ball on one woman's walker and had to be pulled back.

A stocky dog, maybe a terrier, lifted its leg on Emma's enormous canvas and I shouted, "No!" The girl yanked him back just in time to save the print. I ran over and lifted the canvas up onto a table, out of aim for a dog. That was the last thing I needed to do; pay for an extra expensive print out-of-pocket.

The women couldn't get enough of the dogs and squealed in delight. Sarah leaned in to me and shouted, "It sure is loud with all this whining and yapping."

"Yeah, and the dogs are noisy too - ba-dum-bum."

We laughed and I turned off the music which helped lower the noise level a bit.

Joy clapped her hands. "OK gals, this is what we're going to do…" Everyone, except the dogs, looked her way. "For this shot, the largest dogs will be on the floor in front of those on chairs. Medium and small dogs should be held by the ladies in the other two rows."

A lady with silver hair in long braids held up a July sign. "How can I hold this sign and a dog at the same time?"

Joy bit her lip, trying to solve the logistical nightmare. I piped up with my own suggestion. "I know you spent a lot of time and effort making the signs, but if it would make things easier, I can super-impose similar-looking month names while editing."

There was a collective smile. When Joy nodded, the signs were tossed to the side. The young girls handed over dogs and leashes as the women cooed.

I shut Flash's cage, turned on the bright lights, and attached my camera to the tripod. As the ladies got to know their assigned dogs I took some candid shots of the big group just for the heck of it. Tails wagged, tongues flew, ladies giggled and kissed the dogs back. All the while I snapped the shutter. Nobody was posing for the camera but I could tell the pictures were going to be fun with the unbridled happiness.

I cleared my throat to get ready for the posed photos. "Let's get started, shall we?" The ladies stared at me as if they had forgotten completely where they were, and why.

I started to take a picture when Joy yelled, "Showtime, ladies!"

In a bizarre move, all twelve women untied their robes and let them drop to the ground.

My jaw dropped as 24 bare breasts suddenly loomed in front of me. What in the world?

CHAPTER 11

Shocked at the sight of twelve naked women, I turned to Sarah, whose mouth was also agape. The poor girls from the shelter were traumatized.

Joy gave an innocent pout and said, "I didn't know if you would be willing to photograph us in the buff, so we kept it a surprise. But don't worry. We promise to cover our parts for the photos – like in the movie, *Calendar Girls.*"

She acted like that explained everything, but I didn't know what she was talking about and shrugged.

Sarah surprised me by nodding and smiling. "Oh, that's cool."

I turned to her with a blank face. "What?"

She leaned into me and explained, "You haven't seen it? It's a cute British movie about these older women who make a calendar by posing in the nude. It's really funny. The ladies cover themselves by holding a cake or a vase of flowers or something like that."

I had not seen the movie and the scene in front of me was starting to overwhelm me. My reputation was already at stake with all the murder talk. Would this hurt or help my business? On one hand, it was for charity, on the other....jeez.

I finally gave a big sigh and said gave in. "Well, let's get this ball rolling?"

The gals who had been watching me nervously cheered and I used Flash's signature line and yelled, "Say Cheese!"

The nervous women made forced smiles, which was not a good look. They also tried to cover themselves up with their furry friends, a feat more difficult with the wiggly animals.

Dogs faced every which way and nothing about the scene seemed natural or joyful. I tried a few more shots and called Joy over to me. Without a shy bone in her body, the naked woman strutted over to me carrying what had to be the oldest, ugliest dog I'd ever seen.

I whispered, "Joy, I just don't think this is going to work. The women look like scared rabbits. It's going to be nearly impossible to get all dogs and ladies to face the camera at the same time."

I showed her the last photo I'd taken and said, "See?"

She scrunched her face in horror at the images.

I said, "But...I do have an idea. How about we use one of these candid shots I took before they disrobed, and use it for the cover?" I showed her the first picture. "Just look at those faces! It's precious. We can't possibly recreate that moment."

Her face melted. "Oh, that is absolutely adorable! But..."

I interrupted, "I know they still have their robes on. But wouldn't it be better to have the surprise inside the cover?"

Her mouth twisted. I could tell that wasn't her plan, but she nodded. "Well, Sally, Mrs. October, didn't think children should see the cover on the counter for sale at Mac's diner or the Quickie Mart anyway. You're right. And we're too classy for a brown paper cover. This will be perfect."

Joy faced the group in all her glory. "It's time for individual pictures. Since I'm January, I'll be first." She turned to the young girls and said, "The handlers can watch your dog while you get your props..." She held her hand to her mouth and added, "or wine. Andrea, can I have the gold backdrop?"

I tried to avoid her full-frontal nudity as I walked up and said, "Coming up!"

Joy swaggered off to the dressing room as the women quickly put their robes on. She turned around and hollered, "Monica and Sally, can you move the stools and chairs to the side? Just leave one stool, please."

The frazzled dog wranglers retrieved their retrievers and other breeds from the scene and gathered in the corner to commiserate with their peers. I overheard one of the college students say to another one, "Now we know why she only wanted female dog handlers."

While Sarah and I put up the backdrop of shiny gold strips, most of the calendar women lined up for wine. I turned to my friend and said, "Now I understand why they would want to drink in the morning."

She nodded. "I may want to get drunk just to forget what I'm seeing."

Our attention was hijacked again by Joy, who strutted out carrying a black cane and wearing a top hat with nothing else. She gracefully bent to pick up her dog and walked to the backdrop. I had to admit she looked amazing for someone in her 50s.

The heavy-set lady I remembered as being July yelled, "I'd like to see you try to cover everything with that little dog, Joy."

Everyone laughed, but I wondered the same thing. I said, "Don't worry, we'll try our best to make sure you are covered, but if any questionable body parts show, I will edit them out."

I made my way to the camera as Joy positioned herself on a chair. One manicured hand held the dog across her chest while the other lay across the cane in her lap.

Sarah ran forward to tip Joy's hat down a little and reposition the dog and cane so all was rated PG. Now I had to get the dog's attention, so I picked up a squeaky pig I'd gotten at the rummage sale. When I squeezed it, all the dogs in the room looked right at me. I laughed and snapped the photo. Perfect.

I announced. "One down, eleven to go. February, it's your turn."

Once the requested red backdrop was up, Ms. February, a woman with beautiful white hair, held a huge sparkly pink heart. She wrangled a brown Pit Bull in front of her.

When they were in position, the dog looked up as the toy squeaked, but sadly the woman was looking away. I realized I'd need to rectify this. "Ladies - just a reminder; once you are in place, hold your smile and never let your eyes leave the camera. Getting the attention of the dog is my priority and I need you to be ready the moment the dog looks up."

We tried it again, but the Pittie wasn't falling for the squeaker again. He pulled at his leash to go to the door. I was frustrated when I realized this may happen with all of the dogs. They couldn't be tricked by my squeak to look up again.

Thankfully, one of the animal rescue workers handed me a bag of treats and said, "Crinkle this."

I did. Ms. February and the dog posed perfectly. Each of them got a treat - one being a cup of wine.

We went on to March who held a purple kite and a tiny Chihuahua with enormous ears. Right in the middle of a shot, the door opened and Mrs. Fox walked in carrying a Viking Coffee cup and wearing a fur coat that resembled the black chow at the end of Ms. November's leash.

Oh great. This would be interesting. Debra Fox took off her sunglasses casually and instantly frowned when she saw all of the dogs. But her face was aghast when she took in the naked woman holding the kite. She scowled. "What is going on here?"

I hurried over to her. "I'm sorry, Mrs. Fox. We're in the middle of a calendar photo shoot for a fundraiser. It's not as weird as it looks."

Everyone could tell she was repelled by the whole scene. Ms. August, a woman in her 80s sure didn't care what the mayor's wife thought. She uncovered a shoulder, gave a silly shimmy, and said, "What's wrong? Don't I look like a perfect pin-up girl?" The other ladies chuckled softly.

I scurried to the desk and handed the Fox Family photo packet to her. "Is this why you stopped by?"

She grabbed it out of my hand, her face full of disdain, then sneered loud enough for all to hear, "I almost didn't come, you being wanted for murder and all, but Carter wanted the photos." She huffed, "You might as well kiss your business goodbye once people learn everything about you."

Debra Fox gave disapproving glare and stomped out the door.

Sarah spoke to the closed door, "Oh yeah? Well, you can kiss…" She stopped in the middle of her too-late rant and came to me. "Don't listen to her. She's just a bully."

The other ladies joined in and commiserated by nodding in solidarity. I figured I'd better keep going with the session or we wouldn't finish December until December.

After I finished photographing April, one of the college girls gathered up the first four pups to take back to the shelter. Before she left, Ms. February begged her to put a hold on "Bubba." She had gotten so attached to the Pit Bull, that she promised she'd be over later to start adoption proceedings.

A few of the ladies, anxious for their turn, had drunk several cups of wine, poured by Sarah of course. It made the day more fun to see the older women relax and get silly. After spending time with the pups and clever, sweet ladies, I had forgotten about their wrinkled nakedness. The happiness they exuded crossed over into the finished images. It almost made up for Debra's rudeness.

At one point, when I was shooting June, Flash came out of his cage and announced, "Help, I've been turned into a parrot!"

Everyone laughed and my mouth dropped open. I couldn't believe what he just said. I explained to the group, "My friend, Doc, has been trying to teach Flash to say that phrase for a month. He'll be thrilled."

Joy, now wearing street clothes, perked up and said, "Doc?"

I'd forgotten she knew him. "Yes. As a matter of fact, he said to tell you hi." I watched as an eyebrow lifted and a smile crept on her face. "He did? So do you see him often?"

"Almost every day – we go rummaging together."

She nodded. "Still looking for tools?"

Wow. She did know him. I nodded then brightened. "And every Thursday, our group meets at Spinners Pub for beer and Prince's Pizza. You should come tonight and catch up."

She acted shy for the first time. "Oh, I don't know."

Sarah joined in and said, "We'll both be there. Come anytime between 7 and 9."

"I'll think about it." She nodded.

I continued with my monthly task, marveling at how well-behaved the dogs were, that is until a speckled hound dog peed on the leg of my desk. Poor guys had been inside a long time. When I kneeled to mop up the mess, the fluffy black Chow licked my face with its black tongue. I couldn't help but giggle at the gesture. Being around all the doggies just made me want one even more.

The 12 months seemed like they took a year to shoot, but long before Ms. December hid behind a stack of Christmas presents, I was convinced the calendar would be a big hit. It was clever and funny. Everyone was bound to love the dogs and maybe even the women.

After the boisterous crew left, we poured cups of wine from the box Joy left for us. I lay back on the couch in exhaustion and rolled my head to face Sarah. "Thanks so much for your help. Who knew I'd need wranglers for the dogs and another for the women?"

"It was really fun. Those gals have spunk. I sure hope we're fun like that when we get old."

I checked the time on my phone. One o'clock already? "We'd better start your mock interview!"

After a quick ham sandwich, Sarah and I sat at my studio seating area and prepared for the interview. I said, "Do you have a list of questions for me to ask?"

"Nope. You're a smart cookie. Come up with some things they might ask, and I'll answer."

I know very little about the medical field, but shrugged and used the most professional voice I could muster, "Ms. Anderson, why are you interested in working at this clinic?"

She sat up straight. "First of all, Brookings Medical Center is a first rate clinic with superior physicians. I would be proud to be part of the team. On a personal note, Brookings is my home. I would like to give back to my community by contributing skills that I gained while here and while practicing medicine in Africa."

With a serious face, I asked, "Have you ever been part of a nude photo shoot?"

She snorted. "Just think, if that Rachel hadn't shown up, I would have been in my birthday suit as Ms. November holding a plastic roast turkey!"

I found it hard to stop giggling at the thought but managed to continue with the fake interview for another half hour. I had to google appropriate questions to ask a prospective physician. Sarah gave thoughtful responses with a professional demeanor.

When finished I said, "Thank you for coming in, Ms. Anderson. You're hired."

She laughed. "I wish it was that easy. Too bad the interviewers won't have birds on their shoulders. Flash distracted me from being nervous."

"Well, you know how they say if you're nervous, picture the audience with no clothes on? Well, we've had enough of that for one day, so if you get nervous, picture Flash biting their hair."

As if on cue, Flash made a microwave beep then stood on one foot and scratched his head with the other. I covered my ear in case he beeped again.

Sarah stood. "Thanks so much, Ande. I feel much more confident now. Hey, did you ask James about tomorrow night?"

I took in a sharp breath. "I totally forgot about our spy date, but I'll call him. Oh, can you tell Mustache Man it has to be after seven? I have an afternoon photo shoot tomorrow."

She frowned. "Ick. I almost forgot who my date is."

I cocked my head. "Hey. Want to go with me tomorrow at four? It's a big family photo shoot at Carter Fox's house on Lake Campbell. I sure could use the help. And unlike today, I could pay you for that one."

"Who, me? Go see a beautiful mansion on the lake, owned by the hunky rich guy who donated money for the new Fox Residence Hall on campus? And get paid? Uh…heck yeah."

"Well, don't forget, we have Mrs. Fox to deal with."

She made a face and said, "Well, then I'll be there to back you up if she's rude."

"Not if, but when. I just hope she hasn't poisoned the whole family against me or the session will be torture."

Sarah gave a sympathetic sigh. She walked to the window and opened the blinds, blinding me. "Ande, you should take a nice relaxing walk to clear your mind. It's gorgeous outside. The snow is almost gone."

"I think I will."

She smiled. "Meanwhile, I'm heading upstairs to gather my thoughts and get beautified."

"Sarah, you could walk in just like you are and kill it."

She chuckled. "Oh right. Everyone wants to hire a doctor covered in dog hair."

I smiled and put on my jacket as Sarah climbed the stairs. She was right, a nice walk could be relaxing. Before shutting the door, I turned the hands on my door-clock to, 'Be back at 3:30.'

You couldn't ask for a prettier day. The sun was sure doing its job. As soon as I hit the sidewalk, it warmed me all the way down to my bones.

I took a different route from last week as worries about my possible arrest crept back into my mind. I had just turned a corner and was looking down to avoid stepping in snow when a thunderous roar made me jump. My right foot took an icy bath in a slushy puddle as the horrific noise continued above me. I feared an airplane or asteroid was about to crash into me. I held my hands above my head to shield myself from whatever was there and peeked between my fingers.

It was neither an airplane nor an asteroid. There, looming directly above me, stood a huge Tyrannosaurus Rex with its mouth open baring sharp, foot-long teeth! Its giant head and short arms moved eerily along with its incredible roar.

As soon as my brain registered the scene, I relaxed. I had inadvertently wandered by the Children's Museum where lifelike dinosaurs stood in the courtyard year-round. According to the museum, the mama and baby T-Rex are the only full-size, permanent animatronic T-Rex dinosaurs in the U.S.

Once my heart rate slowed, I scolded myself for not paying attention to where I was going. I shook the cold water from my shoe, then since I had my camera with me I snapped some photos of the two giant creatures. I waved to my big noisy friends and continued onward staying more observant.

I brightened when I spotted my first Pasque Flower of the season. I squatted down and took a photo of the dainty purple state flower, which is always spring's first bloom.

Mabel's house was up ahead, so I decided to stop by. After I knocked, it took a while for her to get to the door but she smiled when she saw me.

"Hi Mabel. I was passing by and have my camera with me. Is now a good time to photograph Bubbles?"

She took my hand and pulled me inside. "Oh my. That would be wonderful."

I took several shots of Bubbles from various angles. There isn't much diversity in photographing a fish, but I caught Bubbles with her mouth open, mouth closed, and fins in different positions. I even got one shot where Bubbles magnified eyes looked head-on into the camera. The rest of my magic had to depend on lighting and perspective changes. A stack of multi-colored blankets caught my eye and I asked Mabel if I could hang some behind the aquarium for different colored backdrops.

After capturing all the views of Bubbles possible, I asked, "Do you want to choose the photos now?"

She scrunched up her nose. "How can we do that? You haven't developed them yet."

We sat on her loveseat, having hot tea and cookies as I explained the new-fangled world of digital photography to the octogenarian. She giggled and beamed at the sight of each image.

It was funny. After all that work, Mabel made the smallest order in 'Picture This on Main' history - one 4x6 print. She said she didn't want to bother me by ordering more. Instead of trying to explain it wouldn't be more work, I just planned to order a print of all the best photos and give them to her gratis and maybe even deliver them in a little photo album.

The glorious walk and impromptu session with Mabel and Bubbles had done the trick. My shoulders, jaw, and forehead were finally relaxed.

With my focus on sidestepping pavement cracks, I was halfway across the street before noticing two men standing at my door. I froze. One of the men was obviously Fred Morris standing erect in his police uniform. I didn't recognize the other man who wore a sleek black suit. Could I turn back and hide in the flower shop? When the two men looked at their watches, I realized I was later than my door clock indicated. I sighed. I had better face whatever music they had to play for me. Please let them have good news.

The tension crept back into my shoulders as I approached the men. "Hello, Officer Morris, I mean, Detective Morris. I'm sorry I'm late. I took a little walk. How can I help you?"

Instead of his overly professional manner, Fred's head hung low as if he'd been reprimanded. The other man stood tall. He had a clean-cut face with a square jaw but I couldn't see his eyes because he wore dark sunglasses. He shook my hand with a strong grip.

"Ms. Nilsen, I'm Detective Jones from the South Dakota State Police in Pierre. I've been assigned to oversee the Pratt investigation."

My eyes darted between the two men. They called in the state police? Why? Was his presence good or bad for me? If this new guy thought I was guilty, I could be arrested today. But, if I was deemed innocent, I might be exonerated. I must convince the new officer I'm not a murderer.

Attempting confidence, I said with a bright voice, "Welcome to Brookings, Detective Jones," but then I had trouble unlocking the door with my shaking hand.

Once inside I ushered the men to the couch. "Can I get you something to drink?"

It was eerie how both of them shook their heads no in unison without smiling. It was like I was in the company of two robots. Jones, still wearing his shades, motioned for me to sit and I took the chair across from them.

The silence was killing me. I turned to Fred and blurted, "Did you find out who contacted the TV station? More importantly, have you found Fiona's killer?"

Fred cleared his throat and sounded defeated as he spoke. "Um…I'm not at liberty to discuss the investigation." He looked at Jones as if waiting for permission to continue. After a nod from the new lead detective Morris said, "But, I can share that your attorney was in touch with me. I, in turn, contacted channel seven. The station manager agreed not to make any more announcements until they get confirmation from us."

I let out an audible sigh. That must be why they changed last night's report. I said, "Speaking of Mike, is there any reason I should have him here with me today?"

The real detective said, "Your attorney? It's up to you."

Mike would still be at work and I hated to call him away again, so I said, "So…why did you come to see me?"

Jones said, "Ms. Nilsen, we're here in response to an anonymous call we received from someone who heard you say in public that you vowed 'to straighten Fiona out or die trying.'"

What? Did I say that? I sputtered, "I may have said something, but I just meant I was going to talk to Ms. Pratt and the mayor about the mess on Main Street. Who called you?"

In a belittling tone, Jones repeated the word emphasizing each syllable. "A-non-y-mous."

Fred piped up and added, "For now, it's your word against h…" He caught himself before giving away a hint, "the person who called."

I could sense Jones rolling his eyes behind his dark glasses at Fred. He said, "Ms. Nilsen. I'm sure you would like to clear your name, but in all honesty, it doesn't look good for you. Your DNA was found on the murder weapon and now we have a witness that said you made a threatening comment."

I gulped in disbelief as the detective continued. "Unfortunately, you are still our main suspect in her murder."

My voice elevated even more than my heart rate and it sounded like a screech. "I would never hurt Fiona or anybody. You've got to believe me."

He lifted a shoulder. "Well, DNA doesn't lie."

My throat thickened but before I started to cry, I pleaded, "I think I was framed."

He may have looked at me with sympathy or disgust, but I would never know which. He picked up a notebook and flipped it open. "I've studied Officer Morris's notes, but I have questions myself." He said flatly, "I'll need you to retrace the events of the day leading up to finding the body."

Again? I took a deep unsteady breath and wondered if I had it in me to repeat the whole story. But I managed to go through the whole day starting with Matcha Tea. I told about Mustache Man arguing with Fiona and said, "I found out his name is Gary. I don't know his last name." He jotted that down as I continued reciting the timeline through the birthday party, Doc's car being vandalized, finding Fiona slumped over the table, and ending with the arrival of Fred Morris and the EMTs. When I finished, I rolled my head around my shoulders trying to loosen the knots which were re-forming.

Jones flipped back a page in his notebook. "I'd like to go to a comment you just made. Tell me more about the doctor."

I shrugged. "Well, I didn't know either of the EMTs. I didn't even talk to them."

He said, "No. The doctor whose car was vandalized."

That question was comic relief. "Doc? He's not a doctor."

Jones nodded. "So, he's a professor at the university?"

The idea of Doc being a professor was so ludicrous I almost laughed. Although plenty capable, Doc would never want to deal with the paperwork required to be a professor. I expected Fred to snicker along with me, but he kept his typical stoic face. With unbelievable control, I said, "No. Doc is not a professor either - although he's one of the smartest people I know."

Jones sat back and put his hands on his hips. "Then, why is he called Doc?"

I explained, "He used to work for the Department of Corrections in Sioux Falls. You know, where the incarcerated wear D.O.C. on the back of their orange jumpsuits? He's had the nickname for at least 10 years."

The inspector didn't react to the clever nickname. "And what is this Doc's real name?"

Fred answered this time. "His name is Dave Johnson. He owns Doc's Hardware store across the street."

The man nodded as he wrote the name down. "And did he file a police report?"

Fred said, "Not with me. This is the first I've heard about the vandalism."

They waited for me to answer. "I think he did. When I left him, he said he was going to take care of it."

Morris told Jones, "I'll check on that."

Jones asked, "Did this Doc person have any idea who might have damaged his car?"

The two watched me intently, but I wasn't about to incriminate Doc and said casually, "You'll have to ask him that." After giving him Doc's phone number, Joe Cool stood and said, "That will be all for now. We will be in touch. Don't leave town."

The more they told me not to leave town, the more I wanted to hop on a plane and fly far, far away.

I watched the officers cross the street, Jones leading the way and Fred following like a sad puppy. I think his ego had been squashed when the big dog from Pierre took over. As much as Fred Morris annoyed me, he was very thorough, kept me in the loop and he was familiar and harmless. I had known the odd duck all my life and I felt bad for him.

On the other hand, maybe this haughty detective had big-city skills and could find the actual killer. I could only hope.

CHAPTER 12

After the officers left, a woman and a little girl walked past my studio holding hands. The scene evoked a wistful feeling in me. I could sure use my mother today. Not only because I miss her and could use a little coddling, but because she would probably have the murder solved by now. Elaine Nilsen had a way of asking just the right questions to get a confession. Jon and I sure never got away with anything as kids. We have told her repeatedly she should be a detective.

I took down the cardboard clock on my door, hoping nobody else had come looking for me when I was 30 minutes late. From now on I would just hang the closed sign up when leaving. An appointment-based business is great but I need to be here when promised.

I plopped down on the couch and called Mike to fill him in on the visit from the Blues Brothers.

"Are you OK?"

"Well, I'm not going to jail. Not today anyway." I described the pompous new detective and poor Fred's apparent demotion. "I told them I'm convinced someone is trying to frame me. Otherwise, why would anyone incriminate me by calling the TV station and the police department?"

Mike sighed. "You may be on to something. I should have been there for the interrogation. Next time, call me no matter the time. And Ande, just remember you didn't do anything wrong."

When I hung up, I frowned at my messy studio. How embarrassing that cops visited with dog hair and slobber covering the place. Wait. I don't care what they think. But I didn't like the mess and started sweeping. I stopped when Anna's huge canvas caught my eye. Why hadn't she come to get it yet? I picked up the phone and called her again.

"Anna? Hi. It's Ande. Did you stop by today? I was out for a walk and got back late. I hope I didn't miss you."

There was silence after my ramble and I wondered if I had reached a recording. Finally, Anna's voice came on, but it was strained. "Um…Ande? My husband and I discussed it and we have to cancel my order. We just can't have anything to do with you now that you've been named as a murder suspect. I'm afraid every time I looked at the pictures, I would think of that poor woman." Her voice warbled a little then got really quiet. "We'll need a full refund."

Her last words though hushed were loud enough to echo around my head. I almost choked. "But, Anna. I didn't do it. I had nothing to do with her death. I promise. You know me!"

She said, "I'm sorry Ande. We have to protect Emma." Click. She was gone.

Well, my world was now upside down. I was losing business and losing big. There was no way I could return the outrageously large photo order. I would have to eat the printing cost, and of course, my profit was gone too. So much for a beautiful day.

I took out my frustration by vacuuming dog hair and spraying pee spots. Flash tried to cheer me up with his version of the Jeopardy theme song, but all that did was make me nervous.

When I finished cleaning the studio, I climbed the stairs as if ascending Mt. Fuji rather than just one flight. At the summit, I debated whether to take a nap or make cookies. I opted for the more productive choice and washed my hands. I started on a quick batch of chocolate chip cookies since we already devoured the snickerdoodles. Cookies always help my mood and Sarah would appreciate a treat to celebrate a good interview or console her if it went bad. We could take the rest to Spinners tonight.

While the cookies baked, the words, 'find the murderer' kept going through my head. I should definitely start with Mustache

Man. I got James's card and called to ask him about the double date. As the phone rang, there was a pounding in my chest. It wasn't the same feeling as my impending-doom thump, but different in a good way.

After four rings I almost hung up. Then I heard a low, "Hello?"

I cleared my throat. "Hi James? It's Ande, from Picture This on Main?"

In a playful voice, he said, "I'm having trouble remembering. Tell me more."

I smiled. "Well, I'm very short, have blond hair which is often in a ponytail. I can usually be seen with a camera or parrot."

He chuckled and said, "Now I remember. What are you up to Ande?"

"Um James...I have a proposition for you."

I could hear his smile through the phone. "Oh Yeah? I'll probably accept."

"OK. Well, this is going to sound really weird, but I need you to go on a double date with my roommate and me so we can get information on a guy we think may have been involved in Fiona's murder."

"Let me get this straight. You want to go on a double date to investigate a possible murderer?"

I said weakly, "Sort of. It's not official or formal or anything - we just want information about someone I suspect."

He spoke in a serious tone, "So, who is this guy and why do you think he could be involved?"

"His name is Gary. He's one of the construction workers. My roommate, Sarah, went out with him a few times, but he's not a nice person. He's been very rude to me on several occasions and..." I started to say he threatened me but chose not to mention that. "I just want to check him off my list of suspects."

"You have a list of suspects?"

Oh brother. This wasn't going nearly as smoothly as I had hoped. I just came out with it. "Well, yes. Since the police consider me as their prime suspect, I'm determined to discover who may have actually killed Fiona."

I closed my eyes, wishing I had never called him for this. Why am I trying to get this innocent guy involved? The oven timer went off and the annoying beeps continued as I waited for his reply.

He said, "Sorry. Had to go turn down my TV. I wasn't sure I heard you right. Did you say you are suspected of killing someone? I find that very hard to believe."

"Good. Please don't believe it, because it's not true."

"Ande, I'll be glad to be a part of your private investigation evening, but I want to know more about this man before walking blindly into something like this."

I was relieved he was open to going on the weird date, but could hardly think with all the beeping. "Great! We're going to meet tomorrow night at a restaurant to be determined later at seven. So…about Gary… Wait. Can you hold on a second? I have cookies in the oven and the timer is relentless."

"Of course."

I managed to pull the tray out before the cookies burned and put it on the stovetop.

Back on the phone, I said, "OK. I guess I should give you some background on Mustache Man." I went ahead with the reasons I suspected the jerk. I even told him about his advances and how he threatened me.

At that point, he said, "Oh. I'm not sure I'll be able to control myself around this guy."

I smiled at his chivalry. "Well, you'll have to for at least one evening."

I explained how Sarah had been taken in by his charm, and despite Gary's threats, I had told her the truth about him.

I couldn't resist and took a bite of a hot cookie. I mumbled, "Now that Sarah knows the truth, she wants her own sort of revenge. Gary's probably not thrilled that I'm going to dinner with them since he despises me, but at least he thinks I kept my mouth shut and didn't tell Sarah anything."

"He sounds like a real winner."

I said, "Oh he is. Not. I'll text you the place when we decide."

"OK. I will await further instructions."

I could envision him saluting the phone and clicking his heels, so I added, "That will be all. At ease."

Before hanging up, he said, "Save a cookie for me."

"Oh, I can arrange that."

I was glad James was willing to go along with our plan. It was smart to have him on board anyway. As a bonus, I'd get to spend time with him.

Feeling much better, I baked the rest of the cookies and put a few in a baggie to give to James tomorrow night. I opened my purse to put them inside and found a wadded-up piece of paper. Assuming it was a receipt, I opened it, but it was a typed message. *Stop snooping around, or I'll find a permanent way to stop you. I will know if you take this note to the police. PS I have a gun.*

I gulped. Who wrote it? And when? I started to panic. Anyone could have slipped it inside my purse over the past week. Could I trust anyone enough to show them this note?

I quickly locked my door and sat frozen on my couch for a good long while, then poured a glass of wine in hopes it would make me relax. I turned on the TV but a rerun of Criminal Minds played. That wouldn't help at all, so I blindly changed channels as my mind whirred. Someone was indeed framing me and he or she knew I was asking around. The killer was on the loose and could come after me! Who do I know that has a gun? That was a silly question. Everyone does. This is South Dakota for heaven's sake. It's full of hunters.

Just as I closed my eyes, there was a loud bang. Something warm spread across my chest. There was no immediate pain, but I understood your body could numb you briefly in a severe injury. I leaned back, realizing I was going to die from a gunshot wound.

Just as I was about to faint away, Sarah yelled, "I got the job!"

From my prone position, I focused my eyes on Sarah and said weakly, "Was I shot?"

She took one look at me and threw her hand to her mouth. "Oh My Gosh!"

I sat up and touched my wet chest then looked down to see the huge red blotch growing on my white shirt. It was weird that I still had no pain. Then I noticed my empty wine glass laying on my lap. I shook my head, unsure if I was more relieved or embarrassed that my "gunshot injury" was just spilled Cab Sav.

I sat up and wiped the stain with a napkin. "Sarah, you scared the life out of me."

She ran to tend to my wound and upon closer evaluation, rolled her eyes. "It's just wine? I thought you were stabbed and I would have to perform my first emergency medical procedure as a Brookings doctor - on your couch!"

I gave a meek, relieved chuckle. "Well, I thought I was shot."

Her hand was still at her throat when she said, "Ande, don't scare me like that!"

"Me scare you?" I let loose, "Why did you slam the door so hard? In my head, you were coming to murder me!"

Her face scrunched up in confusion. "What? Why?"

I regained my composure; happy I hadn't been shot and relieved to have company. I said, "It's OK. I'll explain in a minute. But first...Yay on the job, Dr. Anderson! Tell me more."

Sarah's demeanor changed as if she had switched the channel from a horror to a comedy. She grabbed the wine bottle and filled two glasses, then started in with excited babble. "They asked questions similar to yours, but without a bird. Anyway, I guess I did OK. It turned out they need both an internist and a general practitioner. They said I could choose!"

Listening to my excited friend was just the distraction I needed as I sat in my cold wet shirt. I said, "Someday, you'll have to explain the difference between an internist and a general practitioner to me. Wow, you sure work fast! When do you start?" I stood and locked the door before going to the kitchen for more paper towels.

"In May! So I have a little time to just chill." When she collapsed on my couch, I put a warm cookie in her hand.

"Ahhhh. That's the best prize. You made these?" She took a bite and acted like she would melt as she chewed. With her mouth full, she mumbled, "Who knew a dead girl could make such yummy, gooey cookies?"

I felt a pang in my chest at the thought and said weakly, "Save room for pizza and beer, for tonight we celebrate! Tell me about the job!" I sat next to her and dabbed my shirt while she talked.

"It's a great way to start out since I'll be salaried and working for the health system. They'll provide equipment and staff. Then, someday when I want to start my own practice, I can. And since I don't start for a while, I can help you out until then."

I smiled. "That would be great!"

She narrowed her eyes and touched my belly, where the shirt was beginning to dry. "So, tell me why you thought I came to shoot you?"

"Oh." I rolled my head around my shoulders. "Well, first of all, it wasn't you I thought would kill me."

I thought about how much to tell Sarah and decided even though I promised to tell her everything, I would sit on the threatening note info. for a bit so I didn't ruin her excitement.

I went on, "First of all, I had a visit from Barney Fife and a state detective who said they got an anonymous call saying that I may be the guilty party. I think I'm being framed! So, that had me spooked."

Sarah shook her head as she munched a cookie.

"And I was also depressed because Anna Tripp canceled her order. Apparently, she can't do business with an accused murderer. I paid a lot for her order and now she wants a full refund. I've never had to issue a refund. Everyone loves their portraits."

"What? You'd go broke if you didn't get paid for that order. The life-sized picture of her kid must have cost a fortune. And nobody else would want it."

"I know. What am I supposed to do?"

Sarah bit her thumbnail and then got indignant. "I can see giving her a refund on the session or your upcharge, but heck no. She ordered the prints and can pay for the printing fee at the very least."

"You think so?" I started thinking about it. That was right.

She said, "Now that I work for you, want me to call her back and be your bulldog?"

Normally, I'd handle it, but today I was tired of defending myself so I said, "Would you?" I gave her the number and she placed the call.

In a friendly voice, Sarah said, "Anna. Hi! It's Sarah Anderson. How in the world are you?"

She held the phone away from her ear while Anna did her usual thing and jabbered non-stop. Finally, Sarah got a word in. "Listen, I understand you are uncomfortable working with Ande's Picture this on Main, but I assure you Ande is not guilty of anything except being a good friend and community member. These are false accusations, but you can choose to believe whatever you want..."

She took a breath and added, "But as Ande's temporary employee, you are responsible for the cost of the prints themselves, whether you take the photos or not." Sarah read the amount she owed from a paper I handed her. "If you aren't happy with the quality of the photography, we can arrange to return the session fee to you, but not the cost of printing."

There was no sound for a moment, then Anna's voice came through the phone like a little mouse. "So, I can't get a full refund?"

Sarah nodded into the phone. "Right. But you will need to view the prints to see if you are satisfied. We will keep them here for one week so you can view the absolutely adorable portraits of..."

I whispered, "Emma."

"...Emma. But if you don't stop by, you'll still be charged and the prints will be destroyed. It's just standard procedure."

After a few more minutes of listening, Sarah hung up and smiled. "Well, she's changed her mind and wants to see the photos before making a decision."

I took a deep breath of relief. "Is there anything you can't do? Thank you so much!"

"You would have handled it if you weren't in such a funk."

Indeed I would have.

I changed out of my "bloody" clothes and put the remaining cookies in a tin. As we walked to Spinners, I couldn't help but look around for someone lurking in the shadows. Maybe I should have told Sarah since the fear of being shot was too much for me to handle alone.

When we entered Spinners, we were surprised to be the first at our table. We waited a while until the server came over and said with a wink, "Your gang's out back."

A crease appeared between Sarah's eyebrows.

I stood and explained to her, "Believe it or not, Spinners has a new beer garden. I didn't know it was open yet for spring!"

On our way through the crowded bar, I scanned the people, looking for anyone suspicious. My nose wrinkled as I passed the table where the workmen had sat last week. As soon as we walked through the back door, Leo's voice boomed across the outdoor patio, "Ande! Sarah!" We smiled at the warm, albeit loud welcome.

Sarah took in the new outdoor space with globe lights glowing across pergolas. Ten sturdy wrought iron tables and chairs dotted the area. Her eyes lit up to see patio heaters standing near each table. She said, "I can't believe Spinners is so cool. I want to sit by the heater." She ran over to the two seats Doc was saving for us near the warm flames. I glanced at our group and prayed that none of them had written the note.

The sight of Doc reminded me of my conversation with the police concerning him. When he smiled at me, I assumed they hadn't contacted him yet. I'd better tell him before the odd couple made a surprise visit.

Just as I pulled out my chair to sit and talk to him, a slurred male voice behind me said, "There she is. How'd you do it, hit her with your camera?"

My stomach dropped. I turned around and recognized the workman with the green feed store hat. He was sitting with a few of the other guys, all of whom stared at me. When his buddies snorted with laughter at his remark I wanted to run back to my studio to hide.

In an instant, Doc was by my side, his face red with rage and eyes fixed in an unblinking glare. He growled, "What did you say?"

Now, at the hardware store or just hanging out with me, Doc was never intimidating, but the face he showed these guys was rough enough for them to retreat and stare silently into their beer mugs. I wouldn't want to endure his menacing glare either. Once the guys had sufficiently backed down from their taunts, Doc gently helped me from my frozen stance to my seat.

Sarah shook her head in disgust and put her hand on my shoulder. My other cronies gave me looks of sympathy, or maybe pity.

Peggy said, "Don't listen to them. They are a bunch of jerks who don't even know you."

Davis changed the subject. "Sarah, your hair grew fast in Africa. You look great!"

Marla cocked her head at me. "And Ande, you did something different to your hair. It's really cute. You could actually pass for 20 now."

I smiled at the compliment. Even though my nerves were still in a bundle, I said as casually as I could, "I just let it dry on its own. Who knew I had waves?"

Once everyone had a beer in hand, Mike lifted his mug. "May the Road Rise Up to Meet You!" We toasted his abbreviated blessing and took a drink, then he and Leo called in the pizza order.

Peggy said, "Well, would you look at that?"

Marla and Davis stared behind us and clapped. I turned, surprised to see Stan hobbling through the door on crutches. Mike jumped up and scooted a chair out for him. Leo started a round of applause for the professor. Once Stan was seated, we raised a beer to toast him.

I asked, "How did you get here?"

Leo said, "I'm pretty sure he didn't ride his bike."

Stan waved to the server, then answered, "I took a taxi."

Sarah turned to him. "Lookin' good, Dr. Landry – except the leg, of course. Sorry about the accident."

He nodded. "Good to see you again, Sarah. And call me Stan - You're not in my class anymore."

Mike leaned forward and said, "Are you going to sue the construction company?"

Stan opened his mouth to answer, but the server arrived with his Dr. Pepper. He mouthed, "Thank you," then took off his hat and rubbed his balding head. "I just don't feel right suing now that that woman died. I hope she didn't feel so bad about my accident that it contributed to her death."

He obviously didn't know she had been killed by someone else.

Leo said, "Stan, believe me, it wasn't your fault..." Stan cocked his head in interest and then Leo shared the gruesome news, "Fiona was murdered."

Instead of focusing on Stan's reaction of surprise, I watched the person who was still on my suspect list - Marla. She didn't look up from her beer but shook her head slowly. Davis, who sat very close to Marla, was visibly shocked.

Stan's eyes were big. "How was she killed?"

At this, Marla's expression was hard to read. Her face was passive. I wondered how much she knew?

Mike responded, "Um. It's not been announced publicly yet, so those of us who know aren't at liberty to say."

Leo twisted his mouth and speculated, "I know you can't tell me, but I'm betting on poison. Otherwise, there would have been outward signs when you found her, right Marla?"

Marla shrugged, not giving anything away. As a matter of fact, nobody agreed or disagreed with his guess, and we sat numbly drinking our beer. Looking at this group, I found it hard to imagine any of these friends capable of poisoning Fiona, framing me, or most recently, threatening to kill me. At least I hoped not.

"Hey Doc, isn't that Joy Gaddis?" Leo's loud stage whisper shook us from our contemplative state.

When everyone turned again, I watched Doc's expression. His eyebrows went up about two inches. She stood by the door dressed in a turquoise quilted jacket and a black beret.

Since I had been the one to invite her, I jumped up and ran to welcome her. "Hey, Joy. I'm so glad you came. Some members of our group are silly, but they're all sweethearts."

She scanned the crew and said, "Don't worry about me. I can handle myself. Besides, I know most of them, Leo included."

Sarah pulled up an extra chair by Doc and we scooted ours over to give her room.

Doc's eyes sparkled as he said, "Been a while, Joy."

Joy smiled. "Hey, Dave. She looked around the table and greeted each person without an ounce of insecurity. She knew them all. "Ande urged me to come tonight. She did a photo shoot this morning for me and my friends."

Doc said, "Oh, yeah. She mentioned that. How did it go?"

My eyes darted from Joy to Sarah, wondering which one would spill the beans about the bizarre session. The rest of the group was focused on the confirmed bachelor and his old flame.

Joy spoke in her usual loud, animated way, "Oh, you might as well know. The Brookings Knitting Club is doing a fundraiser and Ande took photos of us with rescue dogs for a calendar."

Everyone nodded approvingly until she winked, "But we were all in the nude."

All eyes brightened except for Davis whose face turned pink as bubblegum.

Leo erupted, "Sign me up for one of those calendars!" Then he turned to me. "Now Ande, why didn't you call me to help with that photo session? The only time you need my assistance is with my grandson's little league team pictures."

I reached across and punched his arm playfully. "You were the last person we needed. And I hate to break it to you, but the ladies will be semi-covered in the calendar."

He snapped his fingers as if to say, 'Oh darn.'

Peggy put her beer mug down. "Like in *Calendar Girls*?"

Again with the reference to the movie. I must watch it.

When Joy nodded, Mike said, "I imagine they will sell quickly – out of curiosity if nothing else." Then he looked at his watch, stood, and said, "Oh! Pizza's ready."

Completely out of character, Doc spoke up and offered to go get them. "Joy, wanna come along?" He turned to her with a smile.

She stood. Maybe they wanted some alone time. Mike handed over the wad of money to Doc and we watched the couple exit through the gate to the alley.

As soon as they disappeared, the table was abuzz with the possibility of a rekindled romance. Davis said, "You know back when those two dated, I thought it was a strange match, but they always looked happy."

It surprised me that everyone knew all about Doc and Joy. But then again, I was probably 13, and wouldn't have been interested in anything adults did.

Sarah leaned over and asked the million-dollar question. "Why did they break up?"

Blank faces stared at her. Peggy said, "Doc wouldn't talk about it, so no one knew. But I'm glad you invited her tonight. It's nice to see him with that look in his eyes again."

A strange feeling came over me. I was thrilled for my buddy but sad that he might not spend as much time with me if they got together. Stop being selfish, Ande.

Stan spoke up. "Hey Leo, when is your mail-order bride arriving? I sure hope you got the insurance plan, cause when she sees you, she's bound to high tail it back to the Philippines or wherever you ordered her from."

Leo boomed back, "I've already got my harem. You're the one who needs a mail-order bride."

We all laughed at the two single guys who frequently made jokes about it.

Doc and Joy returned with the pizza. I held up my tin and said, "Save room for cookies! We have reason to celebrate tonight." I pointed ala Vanna White, to Sarah.

All eyes shifted to my giddy friend who did a little dance in her seat and sang, "I'm the new general practitioner at Brookings Regional Medical Center!"

After several congratulatory remarks. Leo extended his hand and said, "Dr. Anderson, I presume?" I snapped a photo as they shook hands.

Doc topped off Sarah's beer and we toasted her. Once conversations ping-ponged in different directions, our new resident doctor sat by Stan and discussed his treatments. I only heard snippets of their conversation, but Sarah sounded very knowledgeable about his injury. What an impressive girl.

Mike said, "Are we ready to place bets on when the biggest pile of snow will melt?"

Davis said, "The big one by the elementary school, right?"

Mike nodded and said, "A dollar per bet. Peggy, can you keep track?"

She opened a note on her phone and said, "Ready."

Leo barked his bet, "May 20. I'll be there with a camera to prove it." He threw a dollar across the table.

Stan said, "You'll be there with a blow torch to make it happen."

I laughed. "I'm betting on June 15th." Some eyebrows raised, so I qualified my choice, "Last year, all the snow wasn't gone until June first. And this year, we've had two more feet of snow, so I'm sticking with June 15."

The other bets ranged from May 1st all the way to June 10th. Peggy, our official bet keeper, typed the dates into her phone and collected the dollar bills.

Sarah asked, "What does the winner get?"

Leo said, "Duh? A 12-pack of Grainbelt."

I leaned in and said, "Beer is always the prize with this gang."

She shook her head as if it was the dumbest thing she'd ever heard of. "Well, we had a bet in Africa to see who would get the first mosquito bite of the rainy season this year."

Mike said, "Who won? Or should I say lost?"

With a grimace, she held out her arm, showing a small red bump in the crook of her elbow. "I was the lucky one."

Leo bellowed, "What did you win? Malaria?"

Everyone laughed at that and Sarah said, "Thankfully, no. I took the pills regularly so I was good. My prize was this:" She pulled a small gadget from her purse.

Doc inspected the tool. "Nice. A screwdriver, knife, and flashlight all in one."

"I've already used it several times, but TSA in Amsterdam almost took it away."

Doc passed it to Leo who inspected it. "That's a pretty good tool, so I say." I always grinned when the guy finished a sentence that way.

CHAPTER 13

When our Spinners group dispersed, Sarah and I walked down the dark street toward my apartment. Shoot. I forgot to tell Doc what I told the police. I would have to call him tomorrow. As I carried the empty cookie container, I asked Sarah, "Don't you think Doc and Joy got cozier as the evening went on? I still wonder why they broke up?"

"Maybe she couldn't put up with him killing people."

I stopped just short of my door and said, "Sarah! Doc didn't kill anyone. Why are you so determined to accuse him?"

"I don't know. He's just got quirks I don't understand."

"You've got quirks I don't understand."

A loud 'hoot' stopped our squabbling. We tried to find the source of the sound. I pointed and whispered, "Look! On the street lamp!"

There standing on the lamppost was a beautiful owl. I carefully took my phone from my pocket and snapped a photo of the majestic bird.

Sarah whispered, "It's so beautiful!"

I nodded. "And it's asking the same question we are, "Who?""

She nodded; eyes affixed to the creature.

The owl made another 'hoot' and took off flapping its enormous wings as it flew down Main Street. We stood awestruck.

Sarah said, "It's a sign. We have to be wise to find the murderer."

"Speaking of which, when we get inside I have news."

I unlocked the door. Once we were inside, I locked it and pulled Sarah over to my downstairs couch. "Check out what I found in my purse today."

Sarah took the wrinkled paper from me and read it. "No. That's not real."

"Well, what is it then?"

She studied it again. "Hmm. Who wrote it?"

I cocked my head. "I only wish I knew. That's the main reason I thought someone shot me today."

She nodded and said, "Now I understand why you were so skittish as we walked to Spinners today. Why didn't you tell me about this?"

"I didn't want to ruin your happy moment."

"Okay, but I wouldn't worry a whole lot about it. I could be a prank."

I bellowed, "A prank? I don't know anybody who would use a threatening note as a prank."

"Okay. Well, let's just be very careful and wary. I'll stick to you like glue for the next few days until we figure out this whole thing."

"Thanks. Let's start with tomorrow's man."

Sarah closed her eyes and said in a dreamy voice, "Yes. Carter Fox."

I sighed, "No. The double date with Mustache Man."

With a sour expression, she said, "Oh yeah, him. Did you ever invite James?"

I walked to Flash and put a small piece of pizza crust in his bowl. "Yes. James is in. Here's your pizza. Now hop in, buddy. It's bedtime." The bird rushed through the door to get his treat and I shut it behind him.

"Good. I can't wait to meet your hunka, hunka, burnin' love."

I turned off the lights and grinned as I followed her up the stairs. The girl sure loved to exaggerate.

"Sarah, we need to have a plan so I can fill James in before we go. Do you think I should tell him about the note?"

"Probably. But, let's discuss it tomorrow. Tonight, I just want to revel in the fact that I'll be making real money soon. And please don't bring up my student loans."

I locked the apartment door and grinned at her. She was as excited as a child on Christmas and deserved to celebrate. "Of course! What do you want to do?"

"Sit on the couch, watch reality tv and eat cookies."

"I can do that except we'll have to settle for popcorn since the cookies are gone."

She held up a finger. "But I saw a baggie with some in your purse."

"Sorry. I'm saving those for James."

"Ooooh. Must be love."

I waggled my eyebrows, then we spent a good two hours trying to figure out which guy would get the rose from *The Bachelorette*. At least for a while, my mind was wiped clean of murder.

I awoke to another bright sunny day with afternoon temps forecast for the 50s. Perfect for the afternoon photo shoot.

I spent an hour in bed with my laptop open, trying to ignore the noise outside. Once I placed the small order for Bubbles' photos, I tackled the calendar pics, which were especially fun to edit. Most of the images were adorable. Of course, one photo showed a little too much skin despite our obsessive checking and rechecking. It was an easy fix. I just duplicated the flowers Ms. May held to cover the objectional body part.

Sarah tapped on my door. "Who wants coffee?"

"I do!"

She walked in with two mugs in hand and gave me one. She sat on the end of my bed and looked at her phone. "I'm working on tonight's agenda. We should, "1: Mention Fiona's murder. 2: Ask him if he liked her. 3: Ask who will replace Fiona. 4: Ask when the project will be completed. And 5: See if he's packing a gun."

Her suggestions were good, but I winced at number five. I sure hoped he wouldn't shoot me at dinner! "Hopefully, Gary will reveal a strong motive so I can tell Fred and Detective Joe Cool."

"Why do you think the state police got involved?"

"I guess the biggies in Pierre don't think a small-town cop can handle a murder investigation. You should have seen the new guy. He was so smug he never took his sunglasses off, like a Men-In-Black wannabe. I can't believe I'm saying this, but I'd rather have good old Fred Morris in charge."

"Well, that is saying something. What did they want?"

I sighed. "Mr. Big Shot made me relive the whole day again. I didn't have anything new to report, but they did. Apparently, somebody called in anonymously and said I had announced publicly that I would take care of Fiona, or something like that."

She leaned forward. "Did you?"

"You know me…last Thursday at Spinners, after Fiona came in and bullied us, I stood right up to our group and said something about getting to the bottom of it, but it certainly wasn't a threat."

"Who heard you say it?"

I listed the people who were there that night. "The usual crew; Doc, Mike, Peggy, Davis, Marla, Stan, Leo, and one of his new lady friends from Mitchell. Nobody who would want to frame me." At least I hoped not.

"Did someone at another table hear you? A server? Or Gary?"

I tried to recall how crowded it was that night. "Maybe? I don't remember who was around. I do know Gary hadn't arrived yet, so he didn't hear me."

She cocked her head, "Are you still considering Marla or Davis as suspects?"

"Not Davis. He just doesn't have it in him and has a good alibi. I haven't checked out Marla enough to cross her from my list."

Sarah jumped up so fast my computer fell over. Her eyes gleamed. "Let's go to Viking Coffee!"

"Really? Now?" I laughed at Sarah's spontaneity and was touched to know she was determined to help me. "Let's do it! I'll get dressed."

Before we put our coats on, I ran to my desk, picked up the earring, and held the baggie out to Sarah. "Look at this!"

"Hmmm. It's an earring. Nice." She gave me wide eyes like I had lost my mind.

I said, "But wait! There's more," as if to prove myself even nuttier. I whispered, "I haven't told anyone about this, not even the police. I found the earring outside Viking Coffee after Fiona was taken away on a gurney." I shuddered at the memory. "It could belong to Fiona or maybe the murderer? I don't think Fiona was found with only one earring or Morris would have noticed the baggie on my desk when he searched."

I could see her wheels turning as she stared at the piece of jewelry. "Have you asked Marla if she lost an earring?"

"No, but I plan to now."

Wearing only a light jacket I stepped off the curb with a pep in my step. Spring was here!

Down the street, I was surprised to see Carter Fox in an animated discussion with Gary. I nudged Sarah and she looked up. "Is that the mayor?"

I nodded. "I wish we could hear what they're saying."

"He doesn't look too happy – look at his hands."

He was making wild motions with his arms. My attention was hijacked by a voice calling from the other direction. "Hey girls!"

We looked to the right where Davis stood in front of his flower shop, hands on hips and face to the sun.

I shouted, "Hi, Davis. Soaking up some Vitamin D?"

"That's right. What a glorious day."

Sarah shouted, "I haven't even been here four days and was about to go back to Africa, so I'm really happy it's warming up."

When the two men noticed us, Gary gave a sly wave to Sarah and Carter nodded at me with a smile.

Before reaching the coffee shop door, I stopped and pulled Sarah back into the defunct bookstore alcove so we wouldn't be seen. "Wait. What else are we going to ask Marla? We already know she left her shop last Friday afternoon and didn't return until she found the body. What else is there?"

"Does she know Fiona was poisoned?"

I said, "I'm sure she does. Morris is pretty good about updating interested parties and she is certainly an interested party. No point in searching her shop for anti-freeze or sleeping pills. What kind of killer would leave the murder weapons out in plain sight?"

She twitched her mouth and said, "Well, let's just go in and see what happens."

I took a deep breath. The door jingled and Marla stood, broom in hand smiling. "Hi girls, what can I do for you?"

Sarah held her arms out like a zombie. "Cooofffffeeeee." She dropped her hands and said, "Can I get a venti half-caramel, half-vanilla latte, double espresso heated only to 100 degrees with caramel drizzle on top."

I stared at her. Didn't the girl just return from a third-world country where she had to heat water over an open fire just to have instant coffee? How in the world did she get so picky? I said, "You've got to be kidding. How did you survive in Africa?"

"Well, I didn't have a choice there and was happy with whatever I could get. Here, I can order anything I want. Right, Marla?"

Marla chuckled. "That's right." She stood the broom in the corner and began making Sarah's drink as if it was a normal order. She asked, "What do you want, Ande?"

"Um…I'll have a tall caramel macchiato?" I added sheepishly, "Extra hot?"

Sarah patted me on the back. "Atta girl."

I leaned against the counter. "So, Marla, did you get to meet Detective Jones from Pierre?" We watched her reaction.

She nodded. "They stopped by yesterday to check out the scene. That guy was something else. He really likes to do interviews and wouldn't let poor Fred say a word."

I agreed, "Right? At first, I thought he was kind of cool with the sunglasses but when he didn't take them off inside and started talking, I quickly realized he was a jerk."

She said, "Me too. I actually felt sorry for Fred." She handed Sarah's complicated order to her and started on mine.

The door opened and a young couple walked up. The two of us moved aside so they could order. Sarah held up her paper cup to cover her mouth and whispered to me, "So which is *the* booth?"

I pointed to the spot where Fiona's body had been found. Without any crime tape, it was back to its normal state - a clean and inviting place to enjoy a cup of joe for someone who didn't know at least. I, however, doubted I would ever sit there again.

As if I'd pointed the booth out to the girl, she sat right where Fiona's body had been slumped. I cringed. The girl took her phone from her pocket and scrolled while the guy paid and waited for their drinks.

Marla called my name and I accepted my cup and watched her make the other order. Once the man had their drinks and was seated, I spoke quietly between creamy sips, "Marla, did Morris tell you how Fiona was killed?"

She rinsed a rag and cleaned the area, nodding. "When I showed him the sassafras tea she normally drank, he took the pitcher as evidence. He later called me to say it was laced with poison!" She stopped wiping and said, "I don't know how the killer knew she drank that."

I remembered Marla telling our group about the special tea Fiona required, but didn't want to remind her and somehow incriminate myself further. I said, "How could someone get into the fridge without you noticing?"

She scoffed, "Fiona sent me away so many times to have her little meetings, anyone could have been behind the counter without me knowing it. And half the time she left the door unlocked when she was gone. That's exactly what I told Morris."

I cleared my throat and said, "So did Fred tell you they found my DNA on the cup that held the poison?"

She stopped wiping the counter and her eyes grew huge. "No. How did that happen?"

"Believe me. There is no way I would hurt Fiona or anyone." I bit my lip and asked, "Do you remember what you did with my matcha tea mug when I left."

She shrugged. "I was pretty upset that day, but I probably either washed it or put it in the sink." Her face changed from surprised to defensive and she barked, "Wait. I would never serve a drink in a dirty cup if that's what you're implying?" She put her arms out straight against the counter.

I glanced at the couple in the booth, glad that they were engaged in their own conversation and not paying attention to us. I motioned for my friends to follow me to the hallway. I whispered, "Of course not, Marla. I'm just grasping at straws trying to figure out how it could have happened. All I know for sure is that I left and didn't come back until you called me that night."

"Well, I was gone all day too!" Marla's face was now red and she breathed hard through her nose dramatically.

I remembered the 'accomplished actor' statement James had made. It would have been easy for Marla to poison Fiona, frame me, and even drop the note in my purse, but I couldn't believe it.

Sarah squinted. "If Ande left the rinsed cup on the counter, could Fiona have poured her own drink into it thinking it was clean?"

Marla seemed to calm a bit when this sunk in. "Well…maybe. Fiona did get tired of waiting for me to serve her and sometimes got the pitcher herself."

I nodded, picturing the scenario. I said, "That's as good a theory as any."

Sarah said, "But how did someone know it was your cup to frame you, Ande?"

I said, "They probably didn't have any idea until my DNA was found on the mug." I lit up. "Marla, I'm sure the police already asked this, but do you have an interior security camera?" I walked back into the front room, and spotted a small black camera hanging in the corner. I brightened.

Marla nodded. "Oh yes. They checked. It must have been shut off because there is no recording for that day."

I released the big breath I'd been holding. "Of course it was. Why in the world did you turn it off?"

She folded her arms and said with an edge in her voice, "I didn't."

Sarah asked, "Well then who did?"

"The only other person who knew how to work it was Fiona." After a beat, Marla answered our unspoken question. "She told me her clients may not want to be seen on camera. I thought that was odd, but I showed her the controls in the storeroom." Her frustration was mounting. "I told you she ran my life."

Sensing her tension, I diverted the conversation. "Marla, did you lose an earring recently?" I hoped she wouldn't be upset with this question too.

Her brow creased at the change of topic. "I don't think so."

I pulled the baggie from my pocket and said, "I found this outside your door that night. Is it yours?"

She took the baggie from my hand and examined the earring. "It's definitely not mine. I'm allergic to silver."

"Could it have belonged to Fiona?"

"I don't know. I tried not to look at her any more than I had to. Did you show it to Fred?"

I shook my head, no. "I'm just trying to get to the bottom of it myself."

"Oh. He's not going to like that."

The young couple left their booth and walked to the door. Marla said, "Thanks for coming in!"

They waved as they took their coffee out with them. I really hoped they hadn't heard us.

Marla led us to a different booth where we were free to talk as loud as we wanted. I handed her a $20 and said, "We haven't paid yet. Keep the change. I know I upset you."

She pushed it back across the table and grabbed my hands. "No. That's OK, Ande. You must be going through a lot right now." She took her hands away and said, "Besides, business is picking up. I can handle comping a drink or two."

That was nice of her. With Marla's warm, kind touch, I was finally convinced of her innocence. In retrospect, I probably would have reacted the same way she had in every situation. Time to focus on someone else.

Sarah read a text on her phone. "Ande, I'm running to Mom's to get more clothes. Besides, she made lemon bars!" She beamed. "Don't worry. I'll be back in plenty of time for our trip to the lake." She bounded out, car keys in hand and ready for a mom fix.

I shook my head. "Hard to believe that girl will soon be giving advice on healthy diets." I gave Marla a hug and said, "If you think of anything that may answer questions, please let me know."

She replied, "I will, but be careful. A murderer is out there."

I nodded and left. I planned to go fess up to Doc but headed home first to grab my phone I had left upstairs.

Back on my sidewalk, I threw my head back in aggravation to see my door ajar yet again. I pushed the door open and yelled, "Jon, what the heck? Twice in one week? Please keep the door shut."

As soon as I stepped inside my coffee cup slipped from my hand and the extra-hot caramel macchiato splashed on my running shoes, electrifying me with the burn. But that wasn't my biggest shock. My entire studio had been ransacked.

CHAPTER 14

What in the world? Should go in or flee? What if the trespasser was still inside? I focused on Flash's cage and gasped to see it tipped over on the floor. My heart pumped with adrenaline as I ran to check on him. I reached the cage to find my sweet parrot climbing up the wire bars to greet me. Thank God he was fine.

I took him out hoping to comfort him by cuddling and petting his head. I put him on my shoulder to lift the cage up so it stood the full 5-foot height. I said, "Flash. Who did this?" I looked around and whispered, "Are they still here?"

He didn't answer, but I decided to get out. Without my phone, I couldn't call the police. Instead, I ran like a maniac across the street to Doc's store, holding Flash tightly in both hands.

I pushed the door open with my foot, not wanting to lose control of my bird who might panic and fly away. Sydney came to the door with hands up. "You okay?"

"Is Doc here?"

"Yes. He's with the police in the storeroom."

"Please get them now. It's an emergency."

He let me in and turned to hurry past the row snow shovels and the wall of garden tools to the back room. I cooed to Flash. "Everything is just fine, buddy."

Within seconds, Doc rushed toward me. "What's wrong?"

"Someone broke into my studio! I was only gone 20 minutes!" My voice sounded weak and babyish.

Doc charged across the street with two officers and me close behind. I could tell Flash was anxious. He wiggled and I expected him to bite me any minute, but I held him so firmly he couldn't.

Once we entered the studio, I put Flash back in his cage. The silly bird calmly walked to a sunflower seed on his cage floor and ate as though nothing had happened. I was glad he wasn't upset.

I stood by the birdcage next to Fred who already had his notebook flipped open and pen poised to write. "Ms. Nilsen, where did you go, and was your door locked when you left?"

I opened my mouth to answer but was interrupted by the real detective who said, "Morris, I'll handle the interview. Check the back door to see if it is locked."

In his robotic tone, Fred replied, "There is no back door to her studio."

With a sigh, Jones ordered, "Then, check the front door to see how they broke in!"

Apparently, Fred didn't mind changing jobs. Inspecting the door was more up his alley. He rushed over with all his tools and the poor door never knew what hit it as Fred measured, took photos, and dusted for fingerprints. Doc stood over his shoulder and the two discussed the mechanics of the break-in.

Jones repeated the same questions Fred had asked plus many, many more. Still shaking from fright, I answered them all.

"Do you have a cash register?"

"No. All my transactions are done through an app on my phone. I get an occasional check, but nobody pays me with cash." Except for Mabel who counted out five dollars in change into my hand, but I didn't mention that. I was frustrated to be stuck answering the blowhard's relentless questions when I just wanted to take stock of my photography equipment. At least, from my vantage point, I could see that my expensive camera was safe on my desk – that was lucky its tripod lay tipped over on the floor.

As if he read my mind, Doc blurted out, "Ande, you should look around to see if anything is missing."

I watched Jones for permission like a child wanting to be released from time-out. He said in a snippy voice, "Not until I'm finished with the questions."

I turned to Doc and scowled. "I guess I'm not excused yet." A horrible thought struck me and I begged him, "Doc, can you check and see if the intruder got into my apartment?"

He shook his head, disgusted with the man in black, then ran up the steps taking several at a time, from the sound of it.

"Any idea who would want to break in?" Jones asked.

"Probably whoever has been trying to frame me." I was getting more irritated by the minute. Why wouldn't he let me look around my own place?

Doc came back downstairs and gave me the A-OK sign which was quite a relief. Finally, Jones said, "I need you to look around your studio and tell me if anything is missing."

The detective, who did way less detecting than officer Morris ever did, sat on the couch reviewing his notes.

I felt sick as I looked around my place, but at least I had Doc to accompany me. What were they looking for? The top layer of backdrops had been pulled down and hung at an angle.

Doc noticed my angst and said, "I can fix that."

A table was overturned and Emma's photos were strewn across the floor. I bent down to pick them up, but Fred said, "Don't touch those yet. I need to dust for fingerprints."

"Please don't get dust on the front of the photos or they'll be ruined."

He nodded. "Duly noted."

I was happy to see the huge Emma canvas standing unharmed against the wall. Even if Anna never came to get it, I would hate to have the amazing photo ruined. I stood and carefully stepped around other items. Back at my desk, the drawer had been emptied onto the floor. I panicked. Where was the earring? I scanned the floor for the tiny baggie then stopped short remembering it was still in my pocket from my visit to Marla's.

It was hard to recall what should be in the drawer. I said to Morris and Doc, "This is difficult. How am I supposed to notice if something missing?" I took a cleansing breath. "All my camera equipment seems to be here. As far as I can tell, things are just out of place. Flash is fine and no real harm has been done. Of course, I may miss something tomorrow."

Fred said, "Good. You may go if you want. I'll call when we're completed."

When Jones stood up it startled me. I'd forgotten the detective was even there. But to assert his authority and to contradict Fred's suggestion, he said in a deep voice, "No. You'll need to stay and confirm that we don't take anything."

Doc said, "Seriously? Hasn't she gone through enough?"

I really wanted to leave and said, "I trust you." I really did trust Morris. He was as by the book as you could get. I turned to Doc. "I'm going to run upstairs and get my phone." I did that and came back then took Doc's arm. "Fred, call me when you leave – we'll just be down the street."

Jones sputtered, "That is not advised."

Doc added, "Too bad. We're going for coffee."

Out in the fresh air and away from my invaded space, I took a deep cleansing breath. It was creepy to think someone went through my private belongings. My stomach churned and even though most of my drink was on my shoes, I could tell I didn't need any more coffee. I said, "Can we go to Mac's Diner for food? I've had enough coffee today."

We found seats at the crowded greasy spoon and the waitress, Sally, whom I've known all my life, came to us wearing a checked apron and a giant smile. "What will you kids have today?"

I returned the smile and wondered as I always did, why she dyed her hair cherry red. It was a completely unnatural look, especially on a woman of eighty. I said, "Sally, today I need some comfort food. How about French toast and ice water?"

She nodded and said, "How about you, Doc? Gonna have Mac's special?"

He nodded, "Yep. Heart attack on a plate and coffee, please."

She said, "Coming up!" and walked off with the limp she's had as long as I've known her.

While we waited for food, Doc said, "I'll install a new doorknob and deadbolt this afternoon."

"Oh thank you. I don't understand who did this, why, and how they got in and out in such a short time."

He shrugged. "Did anyone see you leave your studio?"

I recalled the walk to Viking Coffee with Sarah. "Well, Davis said hello, and we saw the mayor talking to Mustache Man down the street." My lips tightened, just thinking about Mustache Man. I said, "I'll find a way to ask him about it tonight."

"Tonight?"

"Yes. Sarah wants to help investigate him. We're going on a double date with him and my new friend, James."

He lifted an eyebrow and said, "Let me know how that goes. So, what about the other two? Davis or Fox? Would they have reason to trash your studio?"

I considered his question. "Well, Davis was a suspect for about a minute, but I'm not sure he has it in him."

Doc nodded in agreement.

"And Carter Fox? Can't imagine why he would need anything from my studio. His wife had already picked up their photos. I guess anyone could have seen us leave, but we were just across the street. How could someone risk being caught? Man, I should get a security camera!"

"You really should."

Sally brought our food. I said, "That was quick. Mac is sure speedy today."

"He wants to go golfing today since it's so nice out. He's working double-time hoping we can close early."

After she left, I took a bite of the buttery, syrupy bread, and nearly melted. I watched Doc dig into his eggs, toast, bacon, cheesy hash browns, biscuits, and sausage. I snagged a piece of his bacon, saying "You really don't need all that, right?"

He sure didn't seem mad at me for the bacon or me telling the police about his car. "Hey, Doc, I need to tell you something."

He swallowed. "Okay?"

With trepidation, I confessed. "I meant to tell you last night, but that lovely state officer, Jones, interrogated me yesterday. When I went through Friday's events again, I ended up telling him about your car being vandalized. It just slipped out."

He chuckled as he dipped his bacon in my syrup. "I know. They asked me about it."

My mouth dropped open. "I was afraid you'd be angry."

He waved a bacon slice at me. "Nah. You just told the truth, right? Never be ashamed of telling the truth."

What a refreshing way to look at the whole thing. I'll just keep telling the truth and it shall set me free. I blew out a big breath and said, "Thanks, Doc."

After a few minutes of eating and pondering the break-in, I wondered if I should tell Doc about the note in my purse. He would know whether I should tell the police or not.

Before I could tell him, my phone rang. A picture of Barney Fife appeared on the screen. I know it was juvenile of me, but I had added the photo to Fred's contact years ago and couldn't bear to change it to his actual face. "Hello?"

"Ms. Nilsen?"

"Yes, Fred?"

"We have completed the examination of your studio. You are free to return."

"Thanks. We'll be right back." I hung up and flagged Sally over to get the check.

"Time to get back to the Keystone Cops?" Doc asked, pulling his wallet from his pocket.

"Whoa, buddy, I'm still paying for the work you did for me last week. We've got a long way to go."

After I paid, we walked down the street, surprised to see workmen hard at work. Maybe the complete turnaround had something to do with Mayor Fox's visit earlier.

Morris was alone in the studio. Joe Cool probably left him to do the dirty work, but the scene surprised me. "Fred! You put my studio back together!" Everything was in its proper place. The photos lay in a perfect stack on my desk. The fallen backdrop was neatly folded, and the tripods and light stands were upright. Honestly, the place was tidier than before the break-in. I wondered if Fred would be interested in being my regular cleaning man.

The strange officer didn't look me in the eye, but said stiffly, "Since I didn't have to protect the area with crime tape, I just straightened up a bit." For once I was glad the guy was OCD. He saved me a whole day's work.

Doc looked at the door and said, "Did you find evidence as to who broke in?"

"Nothing conclusive as of now, but I'll..." He corrected himself, "...we'll keep in touch. Make sure to replace that lock right away."

I nodded and led him to the door. "Thank you again." I touched him on the arm. "Fred, are you okay?"

He flinched at my touch and said flatly, "I'm doing well, Andrea. I've been learning a lot working with the state police."

When the door shut, I told Doc, "Poor guy is not acting normal, I mean not normal for him. He's such a rule follower he wouldn't dare say anything derogatory about another officer."

Doc huffed. "I, on the other hand, don't have anything good to say about that state jerk."

As Doc ran to his store to get locks and tools, I took a closer look at my belongings and the tidy space didn't feel so creepy anymore. I pulled the earring from my pocket and set it back on the desk and played with Flash until Doc returned.

"I'm going upstairs to shower unless you need help."

"Nope."

The shower was just what I needed. I felt refreshed and ready to tackle the rest of a busy day. Since my weather app predicted wind, I put my hair in its signature ponytail so it wouldn't blow in my eyes while working. I dressed in my uniform of jeans and a white long-sleeved 'Picture This on Main' shirt. A few months back, I traded a cat photo session with a girl from the neighboring town of Oldham to embroider several shirts, which was a good deal. I should barter more often.

I lay a clean blue company shirt on the couch for Sarah to wear to the Fox session. It's nice that we are the same size.

Downstairs, I was happy to see Doc had just finished fixing the door. He said, "You are safe now – assuming you keep it locked." He winked and handed me a key. "I'll make copies for Sarah and Jon. Still want me to keep a set?"

"Yes, please. Thank you so much."

When he opened the door, two men stood there. Why? Why? Why couldn't they leave me alone?

Jones spoke to me in a clipped tone, "We never finished our interview with Mr. Johnson and have more questions for you."

Doc started to leave and Jones said, "Let's do it here so we have a place to sit."

I rolled my eyes as the men barged past us. Jones walked around inspecting the area. When he stuck his finger through the bars of the birdcage, I started to warn him, but it was too late. There was a flash of green as Flash rushed over and bit him!

He yelled, "What the blazes?" The detective held his forefinger up and for the first time, took his sunglasses off to get a better look. Even from a distance, I could see blood on his finger. Flash hadn't bitten anyone in ages, but better him than little Emma. Seriously, what adult sticks his fingers in the cage of an animal he doesn't know?

Jones mumbled something. The only words I picked up were: "Stupid bird." "Disease." The worst was "Sue."

I was flustered and ran to the bathroom, grabbed a Band-Aid, and gave it to him. "I'm so sorry. I would have warned you but I didn't dream you would poke your finger in his cage."

His steely blue eyes flared as he said, "You should post a warning sign."

Maybe I had sounded kind of snarky earlier, so I nodded. "OK. I'll do that, but he has never attacked anyone before. He must have been startled."

Was it bad that I wanted to go console my frightened bird rather than this jerk of a detective?

Once we were settled in the seating area, Jones put his dark glasses back on and composed himself. I noticed him staring at his finger as if he was trying to see through the bandage.

He growled, "I did some checking on your story, Mr. Johnson. Your friend corroborated your visit to his auto repair shop, but I find it hard to believe you chose not to contact the authorities about the damage."

Doc shrugged. "I'm not surprised you don't believe me. I haven't had faith in law enforcement ever since I worked at a federal prison."

Fred hesitated, then said, "Mr. Johnson, you said you thought Ms. Pratt did the damage. Didn't you want to ask her if she had anything to do with it?"

"I planned to confront her the next morning, but by then as you know, it was too late."

I listened to the discussion carefully. Doc sounded like Doc – honest, blunt, and calm. I believed him and hoped they did.

Jones, turned to me with a smug look that sent my composure out the window. He said, "I assume you haven't come up with a viable reason your prints were found on Fiona's cup? No proof to exonerate you?"

I was tired and aggravated enough to snap. "No. I have no proof I didn't kill Fiona. I may only be 5' 2" and look 18, but I'm not stupid. Any murderer would cover his or her tracks unless wanting to get caught. The only explanation is that someone is framing me. Think about it; two anonymous calls were made where I was the subject. And how stupid would I have to be to use my own cup to poison Fiona?"

I paused to take a breath and then with even more force said, "Your job is to find out who is framing me." My face was red and I breathed hard. I was happy to be back to my old self and speak my mind without cowering to this jerk, but I doubted anything would come of it. In fact, it was possible my request would backfire and they would lock me up. I studied their faces. Jones's frown wasn't a positive sign. Fred gave a slight nod that made me feel a smidge better. Neither of them had a rebuttal and they soon left, after again reminding us both not to leave town.

Doc stayed a few minutes more and said, "Too bad we can't be cellmates if Starsky and Hutch decide we're guilty."

I wanted to laugh, but with the stress of the situation, tears formed in my eyes. Doc surrounded me in a warm hug - something I needed more than I realized. His flannel shirt was soft and smelled of a mixture of laundry detergent, grease, and beer. After a few seconds, I pulled away and said, "Thank you. I really appreciate everything you do for me."

After Doc left, I had time to work on my recent orders. A light tap on the window interrupted my concentration. It was Anna standing outside without Emma. With a huge sigh, I let her in. "Hey. girl. Did you come by to see the photos?"

She wrung her hands and glanced around as if she walked into a haunted house. "Yes. My husband wouldn't let me bring Emma along."

"Anna, believe me. I would never hurt anyone, much less a child." I could feel tears welling up again and I blinked my eyes before handing the packet to her. "I hope you like the prints. I think they came out perfect."

She took the envelope and stepped back a bit as if I was a snake. I've heard people say they felt like a pariah but couldn't empathize until now. I bit my lip as she carefully opened it.

Her eyes lit up when she viewed the very first sheet and within seconds, the old Anna was back. "Oh, Ande, these are just adorable." She flipped through the portraits, oohing and aahing in her squeaky baby voice.

My breathing became smoother and I stepped around my desk to retrieve the giant canvas. When she looked up, her mouth and eyes got so wide, that I thought she would scream. And she did, but with delight.

"Oh my God! It's perfect. I don't care what my husband says. I'm taking them all home and that one is going over our mantle."

"So, you are happy with them? If not, I can refund part of…"

She interrupted me and said, "Oh forget about it. Anyone who can capture my baby so beautifully couldn't hurt anyone." She touched my hand. "I'm sorry if I hurt your feelings. It's just that the newsman said…well, you know."

I nodded. "I know. I'm trying to find the actual killer so I can clear my name."

She said, "Well, please be careful." She bundled up all the photos and practically skipped to the door.

I said, "Can I help you?"

"No. I've got it."

Whew. I dodged a bullet there and could pay my rent after all. And better yet, I changed one person's mind about me being a killer.

CHAPTER 15

A few hours later, when Sarah came home I hugged her.

"Wow. I've only been gone a few hours and you missed me that much?"

"You saved my business, girl. Anna came by and she loved Emma's portraits. Thank you! But you have to hear about my crazy morning before she came to collect the photos."

Once I had filled her in on the break-in, I relaxed.

She shook her head. "Your life has sure gotten exciting."

We collected my gear for the Fox family session and by 3:30 the two of us were decked out in Picture This on Main uniforms and driving to Lake Campbell.

As I drove the seven miles southwest of Brookings to the Fox home, Sarah asked, "Do you really think they live in a mansion?"

I shrugged. "I've never seen it, but it wouldn't surprise me if it's a doozy. Some of the newer builds on the lake are pretty fancy."

I pulled over to the side of the road and put the gearshift in park.

She stared at me. "What are you doing?"

"Roll down your window!" I grabbed my camera from the back seat and zoomed in past Sarah's face to two pheasants standing on a hay bale. The sun lit their multi-colored feathers perfectly and I snapped several photos. "That is why I love South Dakota."

"The birds?"

"Yes! I love the pheasants, the snow geese, and cormorants, And the jackrabbits, the prairies, the sundogs, everything! It's just so beautiful."

Sarah sighed. "Yeah. I missed it a lot while gone."

I started my car back up and followed our GPS down Sunrise Drive along the shoreline. The view of the lake between the large houses was amazing. I said, "Ahh to be wealthy and live here."

We turned onto a circular brick driveway the length of a football field which was lined with alternating White Pines and Blue Spruce, two of my favorite trees. Sure enough, a mansion loomed in front of us.

Sarah said, "Holy Guacamole!"

As much as I agreed, I snickered at her response. "You aren't going to say that when a patient comes to you with a broken knee or disgusting rash, are you?"

"I'll try to keep my surprise in check when it comes to my patients. But, honestly, why does someone around here need a place this big? How many kids do they have?"

"Just the twins as far as I know."

I parked in a rectangular bricked area at the end of the driveway, perfect for about eight cars. Seriously, who has their own parking lot? When we got out of my vehicle, I looked at the size of the place. Although not a castle, my mind went to Downton Abbey because of the majestic feel of the place.

Sarah gaped. "Look at that porch!"

A stairway made of rounded rock led up to the covered entryway that had to be 20 feet high. "I doubt it's called a porch. They probably say 'portico or use some other fancy word." The door alone was probably ten feet tall, with a huge chandelier overhead.

We each gathered an armload of gear and made our way up to the grand entry. Climbing the wide steps, I said, "I'm pretty sure Cinderella lost her slipper here."

"Yep. And I can't wait to meet Prince Charming."

I smirked in agreement. "Carter Fox is definitely charming."

The doorbell played a fifteen-second song. Maybe it took that long for the sound to reach the opposite end of the house. But someone must have been nearby because the tall door began to open. I prayed the person behind door number one wouldn't be Mrs. Fox. My prayer was answered when a dowdy-looking lady in her early sixties answered with a smile. "You must be our photographers?"

"Yes, Ma'am. I'm Ande and this is Sarah."

"Well, come on in, dears. I'm Karen. I've been given the honor of showing you around today. This is the foy-yay." She waved her hand across the area in a flourish. She continued talking as we followed her inside. "I used to say entryway, but Mrs. Fox instructed me to say foy-yay. Or if I prefer, I can call it a vestibule, but honestly, that's even worse, don't you think?"

I was surprised by the woman's straightforwardness. She was a hoot – not at all the stoic maid I expected, but more like a heavier version of Alice from *The Brady Bunch*. I answered, "I probably would say entryway myself, but this place is amazing."

The large "foyer" was just as grand as the exterior. Two enormous curved staircases led to a loft. Directly above our heads hung a beautiful chandelier of multi-colored glass. This would be a perfect place for photos if I used a wide-angle lens.

We laid the gear in the corner, all but my camera, and followed Karen on a tour.

Sarah scanned the space and said with wide eyes, "Karen do you have to clean this place? I mean this is really big."

"Well, I'm more of a Karen-of-all-trades. I get the kids ready for school, make their lunches, and oversee the other staff; the gardeners, cleaners, and the pool boys – which I'm telling you now, are not boys. One is older than me. But, to answer your question...my only cleaning duty is dusting. Mrs. Fox doesn't trust anyone else to dust her fine artwork."

We nodded. I wondered if she had to dust that chandelier but wasn't going to take the time for another long answer.

She led us into the living room. The moment I spied the plush white carpet, I wondered why. Why in the world did they have any carpet much less white carpet with young twins?

We took off our shoes and placed them by the staircase before stepping into the deep luxurious carpeted area. The walls were decorated with large modern paintings, all probable originals, and two red and orange lighted glass sconces. "Are those by Chihuly?"

Karen turned and nodded, "Oh yes. Signed and dated. The Foxes are proud of them. I have to be very careful when dusting."

I shook my head in awe. "I wouldn't want that job."

She ducked her head and looked around to make sure nobody was listening, then whispered, "One time, I knocked one off the wall, but I actually caught it before it hit the ground."

I shuddered just to think of dropping a piece that would cost upwards of $30,000.

As we walked past the white furniture, it was the view that blew me away. Beyond a series of eight tall, crystal-clear windows was a large cedar deck overlooking the expanse of Lake Campbell.

I sighed. "I'll bet sunrises are amazing here."

"Oh yes. And in the evenings, we get the reflection of the sunsets on the water." Karen put her hand over her mouth. "Almost makes it worth working here." She straightened and took a more serious tone. "Mr. Fox said you might find a good spot for photos out here."

She led up out onto the vast wooden deck that could easily hold a party of fifty. Built-in cedar benches surrounded the perimeter. Patio heaters stood by each of the wooden tables, extending the outdoor living season by a few months. Poor old Spinners didn't hold a candle to this professionally designed outdoor space. A massive, cedar stairway led down to a covered dock with a speed boat and a large pontoon ready to hit the water. A manicured lawn cascaded down to the water's edge with a large in-ground swimming pool nestled in a sunny spot of grass.

A park-grade wooden playset stood on the other side of the stairs.

Sarah shook her head in wonder at the place. "Those lucky, lucky kids."

I stared at the engaging play area. "Seriously. Remember our plastic kiddy pool and the rickety swing set? I think Dad found it on the side of the road when he was curb shopping."

Sarah nodded, reminiscing, "I do remember. I remember it was so rusty, my finger ripped open on the chain and I had to get a tetanus shot."

Standing next to us, Karen joined in shaking her head, "I know…" as if she was reminiscing about my swing set too. "And to think these two kids barely appreciate it."

I snapped out of my awe and tried to focus on my job. I was supposed to be looking at locations for the photos. I said, "Sarah, stand there."

She leaned against the sturdy wooden rail, smiling provocatively, and through my lens I could see the lake beautifully behind her with no playset or swimming pool in the shot. OK. That would be one perfect spot. "May I go down the stairs for a sec?" I asked.

Karen nodded. "Of course."

Karen jabbered to Sarah as I ran down about ten steps, still wearing only my socks. Looking back up at the house, I snapped a picture of the two of them on the deck. The speckled shadows from the tall pines weren't helpful at this time, but in an hour or so, it may be perfect.

As we made our way back inside, I counted the locations for photos. The front steps, the indoor staircase, the deck with the lake in the background, and another with the house in the background. All four would be great settings. Heck, I'd like to bring all my clients here.

"Thank you, Karen. I think we've got it. I'll start with the front steps since the sun isn't so low yet as to blind people."

"Well, don't forget the garden."

"A garden? Okay, well, let's check it out." I wasn't expecting much since it's barely spring, so nothing should be leafing out or blooming yet. We walked downstairs and through a playroom stocked with a pool table, and foosball table. It even had a row of real pinball machines and arcade games. Another door led to a media room that was the size of a real movie theater.

Sarah whispered, "Where did these people get their money?"

I shrugged thinking mayors didn't make that much. Karen led us to a side door, and we walked outside to what I could only describe as a professional botanic garden. Rows of various species of full-sized trees surrounded a lovely gazebo. As we walked, I noticed that each plant, tree, and shrub was labeled with its name.

I shook my head. "This place is beautiful and another great location for photos." That was an understatement. I could take all of the pictures in this lavish garden. The evergreens would be so nice for a background. "How long has the Fox family lived here?"

She twisted her mouth, thinking, then said, "We moved to Brookings about three years ago when Carter decided he wanted to raise the children in a smaller town. Anyway, they started designing the house right away. It took a good year and a half to build. I was never happier than when the yard and garden were completed. You wouldn't believe all the mud that got tracked in during that time."

I was surprised at this. "So, you've worked for them a long time?"

"Oh, yes. I moved with Carter and Debra from Minneapolis. I used to work for Debra's parents."

I said, "Wow. How long have you known her?"

"I practically raised all three girls. Their mom was the most amazing woman, a pure jewel. You would never know she was so wealthy. But she was sick for a long time and died of cancer five years ago. She made provisions in her will that I would always have employment with the family, which is a blessing and a curse." She laughed a little then said, "I opted to move here because Mr. Fox was the nicest of the three husbands."

Sarah said with an impish look, "So, you can do or say anything you want and can never be fired?"

Karen said, "Pretty much. I do get in trouble for my big mouth sometimes, but otherwise, I do what they pay me for and more. I hate to brag, but I'm the one who keeps the household afloat."

I said, "Karen, you are amazing." I turned my attention to Sarah. "Let's get everything set up on the front steps first."

We took the tripod through the front door and set it at the bottom of the steps just as a few cars arrived. A silver Mercedes pulled in next to my car and a black Lexus SUV zipped up to the four-car garage. Once the door lifted, the vehicle disappeared inside.

A striking woman with red hair and a well-dressed man carrying a toddler exited the Mercedes and walked up the steps past us. I smiled and said, "Hi."

The couple walked by, noses in the air, without comment but the baby gave a pudgy wave.

They entered the house without ringing the doorbell. I leaned to Sarah. "Friendly, huh?"

She grimaced. "I hope they aren't all like that."

"She must be related to Mrs. Fox, but Debra's even worse."

"Well, I did get to see her in action this week. Can't wait for more."

Out of nowhere, Carter Fox bounded over to us with a huge smile on his face. He must have been the one in the SUV.

"Hello, m' ladies! I'm so excited you're here. Did someone show you around?"

I said, "Yes. Karen took us on a tour of your amazing home."

He nodded. "She's a peach, isn't she? And you found some good spots for photos?" Before I could answer, he held out his hand to Sarah. "I don't believe we've met."

She took his hand. "No sir. I'm Sarah Anderson."

He shook his head at the two of us. "They sure do grow 'em pretty here in Brookings." I couldn't help but stare at Carter's thick black hair. In the direct sunlight, the strands of silver shimmered throughout. With his charismatic personality, he could easily be a celebrity of some sort. By the look on Sarah's face, she was helplessly enamored.

I cleared my throat, "Sarah and I have been friends since childhood. She's starting a job as a physician at Brookings Medical Center starting in June."

His eyes twinkled as he said, "Well if I ever feel ill, I'll call on Dr. Anderson."

Sarah turned to mush. She probably shouldn't count on him being her patient. This picture of perfect health probably never got sick.

Carter lifted his Apple Watch and said, "It will take a while for everyone to arrive. If you want you can hang out in the media room downstairs. You'll find a fully stocked refrigerator and snack cabinet. Make yourselves at home."

Since everything was ready to go for our first shoot, we thanked Carter and followed him inside. He greeted the rude couple, who now sat stiffly on the couch. I didn't hear what he said to them, but the couple didn't loosen up much. He pointed to us and said, "This is Ande, our photographer, and her helper, Sarah."

The woman, staring at her phone, didn't even look our way. The man gave a nod and turned his attention to the baby.

Carter walked back to us with a shrug and pointed to the same stairway we had descended earlier. He said softly, "That's my sister-in-law. Debra wants the whole blended family in the photo, so we'll have a large group."

I said, "That's fine. Call us when you're ready."

We left him at the top of the stairs and we went down to chill. The media room brought back memories of a Wilson's leather shop with its strong leather scent. When I saw three rows of reclining leather chairs I knew why. The chairs faced a screen that took up the entire wall. The lights were dim and I didn't want to try to figure out the complicated panel of switches by the door, so we just made our way to the bar area which had ambient lighting.

Sarah whispered, "You were right – Prince Charming has entered his castle! He's gorgeous." She pulled open a drawer. "Look at this!" The drawer was stocked with full-sized candy bars and movie candy, all lined perfectly in rows by type.

I said, "Grab me a Snickers." I'd gotten thirsty being outside and searched for the refrigerator. I pulled on a handle that blended in the mahogany countertop. Bingo. Inside the hidden fridge stood bottles of cold soft drinks, sparkling water, tea, beer, and wine coolers – with multiples of each flavor. "Wow" I took a bottle of green tea and held it up for Sarah to see.

Her eyes widened. "I'll take five of the same, please."

I handed her one. With our snacks in hand, we sat in the cushy recliners and giggled at our good fortune. I said, "This is the life. As much as I want to be on the deck, in the pool, or out on a pontoon boat, I could just stay in this cozy dark room forever."

"Seriously." She closed her eyes and slowly lifted the electric-powered reclining footrest. It made a squeaky sound as the leather chair rubbed its way to a prone position.

We unwrapped our candy, and started to munch when a female voice right outside our open door said, "What a waste of time. Why do we have to be a part of the Fox family photos? I mean, I traveled four hours with a screaming child just to be in a picture? This is not my idea of a productive day."

The woman must be the one we had seen upstairs. Another female said, "I think Deb's losing it. She was so freaked out by his affair she's trying to make sure our families are stuck together for eternity inside a frame."

Carter had an affair? So, that's why Mrs. Fox was so insanely jealous. Sarah's mouth was open and her lips were covered in chocolate from Junior Mints. We couldn't see the women, who must have been wandering around the game room. We sat stone-still in our seats, hoping they wouldn't venture into our theater.

The first one replied, "I sure wish she would tell us who the other woman was."

"Me too. I don't understand why Debra doesn't just let Carter go. It's not like she needs his money."

There was a sharp laugh. "If anything, she would have more without him. He's spending way more than his allotted allowance. Then there's that ridiculous health fair he's sponsoring tomorrow. How much will that cost? I just don't know why she puts up with him... Although he is nice to look at."

When the footsteps drew nearer, we simultaneously sank our heads back further into the leather backrests so as not to be seen. There was a familiar clatter and I pictured one of the women rolling a pool ball across the table.

I was dying to make a comment to Sarah about what they were saying but I was too scared to make a peep. A familiar whiny voice shouted from above. "Dana, Daniella? What are you doing down there? I'm waiting for you."

One of the women said quietly, "Speak of the devil...guess we should go up and pretend to support our perfect sister."

The clicking of their heels ascending the wooden staircase sounded eerily like a typewriter punctuating their line of gossip.

I finally swallowed the bite of chocolate that had been dissolving in my mouth and whispered, "So...Debra's side of the family has all the money."

Sarah stared at me. "And she gives him an allowance?"

I shook my head. "All this time, I assumed Carter was the rich one."

"And he had an affair? Such juicy gossip."

I gulped. "I know! Even though his wife is awful, that surprises me." I thought about it and added, "But he is quite a flirt."

With a slow nod, Sarah said, "Just goes to show you. We don't know anything."

And then without warning, Carter Fox was right in front of us. He posed with jazz hands and said, "Showtime! I'm confident we can wrangle the crowd but please be patient. Some of them are pretty hangry – and I'm not talking about the kids." He gave a wink, warming us up again.

We lowered our footrests and stood. I said, "Thanks for letting us enjoy your amazing media room."

Sarah said, "We didn't need a movie. The snacks kept me entertained."

He gave his winning smile and led us up the stairs, climbing two steps at a time. Sarah's face was comical as she ogled his tight pants from behind.

People of all ages were gathered in the large living room waiting for directions. When had they all arrived? Maybe the movie room was soundproof. Despite their differing hair color, I could tell the two women standing with Debra were her sisters from their matching posture. Debra walked over to Carter and put her hand on his arm in a smug show of ownership before giving me a nasty sneer.

Carter whistled and introduced us to the crowd then motioned for me to take the lead. I started, "As Mr. Fox said, I'm Ande of Picture This on Main. This is my assistant, Sarah."

A few people smiled and nodded. A little girl said, "Where's your bird?"

I looked at the girl and pictured her wearing a brownie uniform from a recent session promoting cookie sales. "Flash had to stay home today, but you can stop by my studio anytime to see him."

I addressed the crowd again. "I'll take photos in a variety of locations, starting with the front steps."

Just as I turned to go, one of the red-headed sisters mumbled, "Great. Now my hair is going to get messed up."

Disheartened by the comment, I wondered if the wind had picked up again. But upon stepping outside, I find a calm, semi-cloudy day, perfect for outdoor photos. I took a deep breath and released it. As the guests filtered through the colossal doorway, I positioned people on the various tiers of the steps grouped by families and height. There was a stylish woman with hair the same color as Carter's who I figured was his sister and a handsome man who just had to be their brother. In fact, most people looked like they just stepped out of a GQ or Vogue magazine. Since everyone except Debra's family was receptive to my directions, I started to gain confidence.

Sarah finished corralling the people while I stood at the bottom of the steps playing with my aperture settings. I scooted back in order to get the full group in the frame.

Once everyone was in place and every face was in focus, Sarah joined me. I said brightly, "Say cheese."

I viewed the image and frowned to see that the Fox twins had apparently been fighting in the picture. When I looked up from the display, Carter was squatting down, reprimanding them while Debra stared at me with disdain.

After a few more tries, I finally got a good shot. It was uncanny how all three sisters scowled while I gave directions, but by the time the photo was taken, they had fake smiles plastered across their faces. Did they learn that kind of thing in finishing school?

As we moved back inside to position people on the double stairway, Sarah whispered in my ear, "I see what you mean about Mrs. Fox. I've never seen anyone so beautiful and sour at the same time. No wonder he had an affair."

I got a few successful shots then led them through the house to the back deck. I surveyed the people as they made their way outside, surprised that I didn't know more of them. Most must be from out of town. One familiar-looking blond college-aged girl stopped to talk to Karen, but I couldn't remember where I'd seen her.

As we set up for the next photo, all three sisters were bunched together. It was bizarre how they all stood the same way with their shoulders thrown back and noses in the air as if they were being directed to pose in that way. As I stood below the group, those three sisters looked down at me both figuratively and literally.

The photos with the lake in the background were my favorites so far. The lighting was perfect and the kids smiled as they watched the gray squirrels jumping on the branches of trees just behind me. I may have to hire a few of them in case Flash needs a break.

Once I'd taken a few pictures in the spot by the gazebo, I motioned Carter over and asked, "Do you want me to take photos of small groupings before we leave?"

He held his hands up. "Oh heck no. Don't go down that road. You would be here all night. I think we're good. My mother will be thrilled with any one of those shots."

"Ok then, you can dismiss the troops. I've got what I need."

He raised his eyebrows at me. "So, will you choose the best photos or do I need to come by?"

A sharp pain went through my calf when Sarah kicked me in a not-so-subtle hint to have him stop by. But as if on cue, Debra Fox glared at me in a warning to stay away.

I said, "I'd feel better if you chose the images you liked the best. Shall I e-mail the proofs to you or would you and Mrs. Fox like to come in?" The second kick was harder and I grunted. I cleared my throat as if I had a frog in it. Sarah must not like my suggestions.

He said, "Would you have them ready by tomorrow? I'm organizing the big health fair at the Rec center. You two gals could drop by and get yourself checked out. It's free. If this becomes an annual thing, I hope our new doctor here will volunteer next year." He winked at Sarah.

She nodded. "Of course. And we'll check it out tomorrow, right, Ande?"

I said, "Sure. I'll stop by with my iPad. The photos won't be edited yet, but you can at least make your choices."

He tilted his head at me. "It's so nice to have such talented people in town." Then his face turned serious and he said, "Have you learned any more about Fiona's death? Such a tragedy for the town of Brookings."

That seemed a bit dramatic since she wasn't a resident in town, but I said, "No. Nothing concrete, but don't worry, I'm actually working on a few leads."

He nodded slowly as he took in the information, then he brightened. "Thanks for coming all the way out here. Ande? Sarah?" He nodded as he said each of our names, then held up a finger. "Oh, you should stay for dinner. We're having a cookout. I make some pretty mean ribs."

Although it was tempting to stay and I figured the food would be delicious, I had no interest in spending more time around Debra, her sisters, or those wild twins. Besides, we had our special dinner plans. "No. We need to be going but thank you." This time I stepped aside quickly to avoid yet another blow to my leg.

"Well then. I'll see you both tomorrow." Carter gave us a wink.

I turned to pick up my tripod. Sarah looked like she was dreaming. I shoved the camera bag in her arms to wake her up from her daze. We made our way around the house to my car. As we walked, Carter announced, "Kids to the playground. Adults inside for cocktails."

Sarah gave me an evil stare and whined, "Why can't we stay?"

I stopped and stared at her. "We have an investigative dinner date tonight. Remember?"

She slumped. "Oh yeah."

"Why did you have to kick me? I'll be bruised for weeks."

She raised her hands in defense, "You kept brushing him off."

"I wasn't brushing him off. I was being professional and besides, you don't know how jealous his wife can be. She's scary."

As we turned the corner to the front of the house, we ran smack into Karen, causing me to gulp in surprise.

"Ladies, did one of you drop this?" She held up the earring I had found. How did she get that? My head swung around to Sarah who gave a guilty shrug.

She took the earring from Karen quickly and said, "Thank you. It must have fallen out of my pocket."

The woman said, "Well, I asked all the other guests and nobody said it was theirs. I wasn't about to show it to Mrs. Fox, for fear it might be owned by the…" She looked around and whispered, "other woman. Oops. Did I say that?"

I blinked at Karen.

"I'm not sure you know, but there has been some drama in the Fox household by way of an…" she held her hand up to her mouth and whispered, "affair. But, I'm glad it's yours, dear. She patted Sarah's hand."

I still wondered if the earring was Fiona's, but when I pictured her as Carter's lover, I nearly laughed out loud. That would be a weird pairing. I said, "Well, thank you so much, Karen. It was so nice to meet you."

Just as we were turning to leave, little Simone ran up to Karen and hugged her legs.

Karen said sweetly, "What's wrong, Punkin?"

The girl pouted. "K.K. are you leaving?"

She knelt down and gave the girl a big bear hug. "No. Sissy, I'm not going anywhere."

After the little one got the snuggles she needed, she ran off to join her brother and cousins.

Karen shrugged at us and said, "Sometimes, they just need a hug." The interesting woman plodded back up the steps as Sarah and I watched.

I shook my head. "Karen is cool. I'm glad those kids have a down-to-earth person in their world."

As we loaded the car. I said, "Whatever possessed you to bring the earring here?"

"I thought we might need to show it to Gary at dinner. It must have fallen out of my pocket when I got my phone out."

"But why did you bring it here?"

She shrugged. "I don't know. I just put it in my pocket."

I shook my head at my goofy friend and started the drive back home. When a deer ran across the road in front of us, I jammed my foot on the brake in time to miss it. The beautiful creature stood still in front of a huge Blue Spruce and posed for us with its big doe eyes. By the time, I got my phone up to take a photo, it had bounded off.

Sarah said, "What is going on with all the wildlife? An owl last night? Then pheasants and a deer today?"

I shrugged and said, "Just lucky to see them and even luckier that we didn't hit that one." I'd had a close encounter with a deer recently when I hit it and the animal flipped over my car. The deer managed to run off unscathed, but my car spent two weeks in the shop getting the dents repaired.

Once I caught my breath again, I said, "Thanks for helping me today. It was sure nice to have you along if for nothing else but to have someone to commiserate with."

"And I got to meet Carter Fox. I can sure see why someone would have an affair with him."

CHAPTER 16

The plan was to meet the boys at Elk Station, one of the nicer restaurants in Brookings. It's not a fancy place, but the food is always great. On the short drive down South Main, I asked Sarah., Do you think I should tell James about the note? I mean, Gary could be dangerous. What if he decided to stop me permanently tonight?"

She shook her head. "Surely he wouldn't attack you in a restaurant. If he was going to kill you, it would be when you're alone, right?"

I shivered at the thought but nodded. "Yeah probably. Then don't leave my side."

We pulled into the parking lot ten minutes early and James stood beside his SUV waiting for us. I had to restrain myself from jumping from Sarah's car and running to meet him.

When I did reach him, he opened his arms and pulled me in for a hug. Sarah's eyebrows raised. "James, this is my best friend, Sarah Anderson. She just got back from a year working with Doctors Without Borders in West Africa. Sarah, this is James White. He's a special ed teacher here in town. His aunt is Marla."

The two shook hands and said typical niceties, but Sarah checked him out a lot more than he did her. I said, "I guess we need to make sure we are on the same page before Gary arrives."

We told him what we knew and James said, "I'll just follow your lead, but if he gets very rude I may have to intervene."

I said, "OK. Oh, James. One more thing you should know; my studio was broken into this morning. I couldn't find anything missing, but the intruder was there looking for something."

His eyes darkened. "Really? I'm sorry, Ande. Well, now I'm worried about your safety."

I waved him off. "My friend, Doc, already installed new locks with a deadbolt. We'll be OK."

When an old red pick-up skidded into the parking lot, Sarah nodded to us and said, "Let's get this party started." We nodded and watched Gary as he stepped out of his truck wearing a blue dress shirt, jeans, and shiny cowboy boots. Sarah walked over and gave him a hug, which had to pain her to do. What a trooper. I was worried about how I could sit at the same table with the jerk without flying off the handle.

He walked in our direction and nodded to both of us. James offered his hand. "Hi Gary, I'm James."

I caught a strong whiff of beer as Gary leaned in to shake hands. We all walked towards the entrance where people stood waiting to be seated. Inside, the hostess, said, "Can I help you?"

I said, "Yes. I'm Ande. I made a reservation for four."

She marked something in the book and giggled. "I was expecting a boy." She grabbed four menus. "Follow me."

I nodded. It wasn't the first time my unisex nickname had been confusing. On my freshman move-in day at SDSU, I was shocked to find that my assigned roommate was a guy. My mother had a field day straightening that one out. But I got a female roommate.

We were led to a table in a dark corner, which made me happy since I didn't want anyone else to hear our conversation. Sarah and I sat across from each other. Soft music played over the speaker. Maybe that would help cover up our voices in the quiet place.

Elk Station, although not fancy, seemed a little too formal for our interrogation, but I started the conversation with an innocent comment. "Sarah helped me with a big photo shoot at Carter

Fox's house today. Do you guys know who he is?" I was certain Gary did but wanted to hear his reply.

James shook his head, no, but Gary rolled his eyes and said, "Oh yeah, the mayor. Thinks he's all that 'cause he's rich."

Sarah said, "Well, his house is amazing and he was kind to us."

Gary scoffed. "It's not even his money - his wife is loaded." He laughed aloud, "But she's cold as ice, so he was probably hitting on you, hoping to get lucky."

At that remark, the three of us buried our heads in the menus. When doing so, I was shocked at how much the meal prices had gone up. I hoped it wouldn't be a problem for anyone.

A pretty young waitress came to take our drink orders. I ordered a glass of Cab Sav and James did the same. Then he said, "You know what? Let's make that a bottle."

Ooooh. Nice. I have never ordered a whole bottle anywhere.

Sarah ordered a mojito and announced, "I haven't had one for a year. Not sure they even have mint in Africa."

Gary ordered a beer and said, "Africa? I'd never go there. Isn't it dirty and hot? And all that poverty." He wrinkled his nose.

That comment had to irk my humanitarian friend, but her response was great. "Oh silly, it's not hot all the time and many parts are beautiful with the ocean and rainforests. I even rode a camel in the Sahara! And the people are so sweet and hard-working."

After a mundane discussion of our local weather, our drinks arrived and we ordered dinner. James turned to Gary and started the real investigation. "I understand you are working on the Main Street reconstruction. How is that going?"

Gary cleared his throat and shrugged. "It's okay. We had to regroup after the boss lady died."

Sarah tried her best to look concerned and put her hand on his. "Oh, that's right. Were you close to the project manager?"

He lifted his shoulders slightly. "No. She was a pain in the ass to work with."

After meeting Fiona, I believed that statement, but still thought it was insensitive.

The appetizers arrived and I asked, "Gary, do you know who will be taking over Fiona's job?"

He twirled an onion ring on his finger as if he was a kid at burger king and said, "I am."

That took me by surprise. Why in the world would Carter Fox choose him? But I smiled to myself. There was the motive—ta-da! Gary wanted to become the project manager and had knocked her off. Sarah must have caught on too because she kicked me lightly under the table.

James said, "Well, looks like congratulations are in order. How about another round of drinks?" He gave us another pour, waved to the server, and pointed to Sarah and Gary's drinks. Maybe he was trying to loosen Gary up. He casually asked another question, "How long did you know Fiona? Did you work together in Rapid?"

Gary yawned as if he would rather be anywhere but with us. "Yeah. Most of our crew worked with her for about three years."

I wanted more information about Fiona but as I framed my question, the drinks came. Gary sucked his new beer down and ordered another before the server even left our table. Woah.

My thoughts were interrupted by the arrival of our food. I tasted my chicken piccata and was happy with my choice, especially since I had gotten a hefty helping of capers.

Sarah swallowed a bite of her steak and pondered, "Even if people didn't like Fiona, it doesn't make sense to kill her."

Gary slurred the next words. "You know how she died?"

Was that a trick question? If he killed her, he obviously knew. If he was innocent, he may not know. Even though it wasn't common knowledge yet, I said, "The police say it was poison."

He chuckled and took a long swig from his bottle then set it down with a clunk. He leaned across the table so far that his shirt dipped in his mashed potatoes. He stared directly into my eyes. With a creepy smirk he said, "Well, you should know. But poison is a little iffy, why didn't you just shoot her?"

I blinked in disbelief. "What?"

I was horrified when he announced in a loud voice, "Story on the street is that you did her in. It was even reported on the news." People at the tables around us turned and stared.

James sat up and said, "No, let's just calm down, Gary."

My body stiffened and I breathed heavily through my nose. Then with clenched teeth, I said, "I didn't do it."

Gary's eyes never left mine as he scoffed, "Whatever. You were in the coffee shop the day she died and I saw you argue with her. Open and shut case." He clapped his hands together.

I'd had it with this jerk. I threw my napkin on the table and stormed off to the bathroom. Why did I let this guy upset me so much? I turned on the faucet, wet a paper towel, and placed it on my hot forehead and then the back of my neck.

Within seconds, Sarah entered. "Are you okay? I'm sorry he's so awful. What in the world did I ever see in that guy?"

"I don't know." I shook my head. Although I had calmed a bit, my reflection still showed a red, agitated face. I said, "Just when I thought he might not be so bad, he had to say that. Why did I think the jerk would tell us something we didn't already know?"

Sarah gave me a hug that calmed me more than the cool water had. "Do you want me to make excuses so we can leave now?"

"No. I'll be OK. I don't even care what he thinks. I'm just humiliated that other people heard him." I wiped my eyes and took a deep breath. "I'll be okay in a minute."

We headed to our table and found Gary's seat empty. When James saw us, he stood. As I sat down I said, "I'm sorry about that. I think I'm really tired and upset. He just got my goat."

He said, "Ande, you don't have to worry about him now."

"What happened?"

Sarah suggested, "Maybe he regretted acting like an ass and decided to leave."

James scrunched up his face. "Not exactly."

I was transfixed. What could have happened to Gary in only a span of six minutes?

He began. "So, when you left, I said, 'Hey, Man. That was pretty rude.' He just shrugged and said something that I'm not even going to repeat. I was defending you when the server walked up. Gary reached out and grabbed her by the waist and said, 'Hey girl. Get me another beer and I'll give you a really good tip.'"

James continued. "I was repulsed and apparently the girl was too because the manager came immediately to our table and asked him to leave. Gary looked around at all the people staring nearby and yelled, 'You all can have your hoity-toity restaurant.' He stood and nodded his head at the bathroom and said to me, 'Tell that killer and Sarah I'm done with them.' Then, he said really loud, 'Adios', and walked out.

I glanced at the other tables, happy that most of the patrons were minding their own business and eating. "Whew! I'm glad I missed that."

Sarah let out a puff of air. "I sure know how to pick 'em, don't I?"

James smiled and said, "Don't beat yourself up. People can be deceiving."

My appetite was gone and not just because my food was cold. I pursed my lips and faced my two remaining dinner dates. "Well, Gary is still my number one suspect. He could easily have poisoned Fiona after I left. I just don't have any proof. You saw how he publicly accused me. He's framing me." I thought for a minute and said, "Besides, I saw him argue with Fiona too."

James put down his fork. "You said you have a suspect list. Who else is on it?"

I said, "Do you know Marla's admirer?"

He lifted an eyebrow.

"Davis. He owns Brookings Flowers. He is obsessed with her."

He nodded. "So that's why she always has fresh flowers on her counter."

"Yep. Well, Davis said he would do anything for Marla, which made me wonder if he would try to get Fiona out of her coffee shop. But, really I can't see him harming anyone. I have heard numerous other people hint they could kill her including Davis, Doc, and even Marla. We were all furious with her."

"Well, I can't see my aunt hurting anyone."

"Right. I still think you know who…" I pointed to his empty seat "had access to Fiona that nobody else did and a good motive to take over the job."

Sarah said, "He could have broken into your studio too!"

I nodded. He could have left me the note if he had access to a printer. I didn't bring that up to James, but the thought of where I'd found the note reminded me of the cookies. I lifted my purse and handed him the baggie. "James, here is your dessert. I almost forgot to give them to you."

"Yum. Thanks."

The astute server brought a box for my full plate of food and handed the check to James amid our protests. James shrugged. "It's not that much. The manager didn't charge for Gary's bill."

In the parking lot, Sarah thanked James and got in her car leaving the two of us standing alone.

I leaned against his door. "Thanks for being our moral support. We don't know much more than we did before, but I got good food and drinks and you got to meet Mustache Man."

He scoffed. "That was a real treat. Let me know if you need more help with your capers."

I lifted my take-home box. "I think I can handle them on my own."

James rolled his eyes at my bad joke. I wanted to reach up and kiss him but standing under the streetlight with Sarah only three feet away, I settled for another hug. I stood on my toes and lifted my arms up. Before I knew it, his warm lips were touching mine. Oh my. Oh my. Oh my. I had to push myself away from him before I got carried away. I blinked, trying to calm myself.

He whispered in my ear, "I hope we can see each other again soon. In the meantime, lock your doors and stay out of trouble."

I could barely speak, but said, "OK. Thanks."

Of course Sarah hadn't missed the amorous exchange and when I entered the passenger door, she sang, "Ande has a boyfriend. Ande has a very cute boyfriend."

Back at home, I unlocked both new locks and said, "I'm glad Doc put these in so fast."

"Yeah. That was nice of him. You're lucky to have him as a friend. Let me guess. He kept a set of keys for himself?"

I nodded. "Yes. I told him to."

Of course, she had to add a conspiracy theory. "Unless he's going to murder us in the night? People can be deceiving."

I couldn't respond with anything but a growl.

After a fitful night's sleep, I awoke Saturday morning to a mockingbird singing outside my window. It was so loud it almost covered up the construction noise. I smiled at the promise of spring until I remembered the break-in and the threatening note. What was the perpetrator trying to find? I searched Amazon for security cameras and studied the specifics to decide which to order. One was similar to the camera Davis had installed last fall. Wait! I'm across the street from the flower shop! He could have caught my intruder on his camera.

I immediately called Davis and said, "Hey Davis. Hope it's not too early to call, but I need a favor from you."

"Sure, Ande. Anything."

"I'm not sure if you heard, but my studio was broken into yesterday morning between 10 and 10:30."

"Oh my gosh! How awful. Did they steal anything?"

"Thankfully no, but the place was a mess. I was wondering if you could check your security camera footage and see if by chance you can see who entered."

I held my breath and waited for him to answer. What if his camera was turned off too? Of course, if he's the person who broke in, he wouldn't want to check. After all, he had seen us leave that morning.

Davis said, "Sure. I'll be glad to. It will have to be in a little while 'cause I'm driving now delivering flowers to the hospital. Not sure if the camera is aimed at your place or not, but maybe?"

I sighed. "Oh, that's fine. Thanks so much. I am just dying to know who did it. Let me know as soon as you find out."

I was so excited at the prospect of learning who the culprit was, that I almost woke Sarah. Instead, I quietly made coffee and returned to bed. I sat with my computer on my lap, and selected the best Fox family portraits so Carter could choose his favorites.

Some of the images were pretty bad even though the lighting and settings were good. Photographing a group that large was always a challenge since someone was invariably making a face or looking another way. In anticipation of that happening, I had taken a boatload of shots in each pose.

It sure would have been easier to e-mail the files to him with a watermark for protection, but Sarah insisted we see him again and check out his health fair.

I went to the kitchen to get more coffee and found Sarah scrolling through her phone on my couch. I asked, "You coming to the health fair with me later?"

"Does it snow in South Dakota?"

"OK. Be ready by eleven. I've got some more culling to do.

Sitting back on my bed I weeded out the bad photos, a job made easier after getting to know the faces. Those sisters were something else. And to think, poor Karen has dealt with them their whole lives. The way little Simone acted towards Karen made me wish the housekeeper was included in the photos as an adopted family member, but that wasn't my business.

I studied the blond girl again but still couldn't place where I had seen her. I should have asked at the shoot because it was going to bug me. After another hour, I had a good selection for Carter to peruse and transferred them to my iPad.

It would be sunny and warm today, which lifted my spirits. I took a shower and chose a springy outfit to match my mood.

As Sarah and I walked a few blocks to the rec center, I checked my phone to see if Davis had written, but found no message. What I did find was that I had forgotten to charge my phone overnight and the battery was at 13%. Darn.

The large gymnasium had been completely transformed into an open space medical center with people lined up at tables waiting for blood pressure checks, vaccinations, and eye exams. As soon as we entered, Sarah said, "I should have volunteered today. Wish I'd known about it earlier."

"As Carter said, there's always next year."

She nodded and headed to a booth where a handsome red-headed guy was taking the blood pressure of an old woman who may have been April. I figured Sarah would keep busy while I scouted for Carter. I scanned the area and spotted my target on the other side of the room talking to a couple with a toddler.

I started that way but was waylaid by two cute little boys in blue uniforms. One said, "You took our pictures at Seth's party."

I wondered how they recognized me without a camera. "I sure did. Good to see you again. What are you doing here today?"

The taller boy said, "We're selling popcorn for cub scouts over there." They pointed to a table near the basketball court.

I smiled. "I'll stop by later and buy some," and walked on.

About the time I reached Carter, the family walked away, leaving me a perfect opportunity to strike.

"Mr. Fox?"

He turned his head and a warm smile spread across his face. "I see you have your trusty iPad."

A girl ran up and told him that one of the tables was wobbly. Carter calmly told her what to do and she ran away. "I think I have a minute to look at the pictures now."

"Great." I turned on my iPad and located the images before handing it to him. "Just scroll to the right. I have a whole lot more if none of these will work."

He smiled while looking through the photos. "These are perfect. I like them all, but I guess I should make a decision."

Even though he studied the photos carefully, his eyes kept darting around the room. His mind was on the health fair. I knew

I should have just e-mailed the prints, but Sarah wanted to see him and she wasn't even around to swoon over him.

Finally, he said, "Can you choose the best ones and order me an 8x10 of each setting? But, for my mother's present, this one will be perfect." He pointed to the photo taken by the gazebo. All the children sat on the dry brown grass, looking far more relaxed and comfortable than when they stood stiffly by their parents. I nodded, agreeing it was a good choice.

He asked, "What is the biggest canvas print size?"

"I'm pretty sure I can get them up to 40 inches by 60 inches but the image quality would be better at a maximum of 30 x 40."

Carter's attention was on the event happening around us, but he was a pretty good multi-tasker and said, "That size will work. Could my relatives order their own or do I need to take orders?"

"I'll e-mail you the images with a watermark for my protection along with an order form. You can forward it out to anyone you want, then they can order directly through me. Or they can stop by to make the orders in person."

I couldn't resist asking him something. "Hey, I have a question; are you the one who hired Gary as the new project manager? If so, how did that come about?"

He focused on me. "Yes. I hired him. Is that a problem?"

I looked around to make sure nobody was nearby. I leaned in. "Actually, I have reason to believe he may have been involved in Fiona's death somehow."

Carter's forehead creased. "Really? What makes you think that? I need to know what you've found out in case I should take him out of the position."

"Well, it's all speculation, but he may have wanted her job bad enough to kill her. It would have been easy for him to poison her since he was always nearby and nobody would notice him going in and out of the coffee shop."

He nodded. "Good for you, detective Ande. I hope you'll keep me informed."

I said, "Well, I'll know soon enough. My studio was broken into yesterday morning and I think he did it. I hope to have proof soon. Davis, of Brookings's Flowers, is emailing his security camera footage today. It might show something and might not."

Carter nodded, then pulled his phone from his pocket and looked at the screen. He held up a finger to me and said, "Excuse me for a sec. I need to take this call. Don't move." He walked away. While he stood underneath the basketball hoop talking into his phone, I looked around. Sarah was still deep in conversation (flirting) with the young man at the Brookings Regional Medical Center booth. I smiled to see her twirl her hair around her finger.

After a few minutes, Carter came back and said, "Sorry about that." He smiled, then reached to his back pocket for his wallet and frowned. "Oh, shoot. I left my wallet in my office and I'd really like to pay you today. Would you mind getting it for me?"

Was he kidding? "Seriously? I stammered, "You don't have to pay me now. I can wait until next week."

"Well, actually I kind of need my wallet anyway to pay the rec center for the use of the building. Any chance you could get it? I'm so dumb for leaving it." He hit his forehead with the palm of his hand. "It's in the top righthand drawer of my desk."

I really didn't have anything else going on today and his office is only a few blocks away. But, according to the clock above the basketball hoop, it was a quarter to twelve. "Doesn't the bank close at noon on Saturdays?"

He said, "Yes. But you should have time to get there before it closes. My office is unlocked."

I shrugged. "Sure. I'll be right back."

I headed over to Sarah and whispered in her ear, "Hey girl, wanna come with me to Carter Fox's office at the bank?"

She looked at me as if I was crazy and whispered back. "Um no. Can't you see I'm busy?" Then she said aloud, "Sam, this is my best friend, Ande. Ande, this is Sam. He works at the medical center and is giving me pointers on setting up shop. We may meet next week to discuss it further." Her eyes glittered.

Glad to see her so happy, I shook the guy's hand and said, "That's cool. Nice to meet you, Sam. Sarah, I'll be right back."

The temperature had warmed up considerably so I tied my jacket around my waist. As I made the brisk walk, I called the photo lab and got the price for a 30x40 canvas print. I just hoped my phone wouldn't die before I could invoice the mayor.

I entered the bank before it closed and without a greeter to greet me I headed down the long dark hall to Carter's office. Why would his door be unlocked when he wasn't there? But, sure enough, the handle turned. As I pulled the heavy floor-to-ceiling door, I was reminded of the last time I was here and Debra had intercepted me. Her accusations about me were wild and unfounded. Hopefully, she wasn't here today, or I'd be in deep trouble. As I thought about Mrs. Fox, I wondered why Carter hadn't called her or even a bank employee to deliver his wallet to him instead of sending me? Whatever. I was here now.

After shutting the door behind me so as not to raise any suspicions from the bank staff, I walked to his massive desk. I sat in his oversized leather chair for a minute, imagining it was my office and desk. I leaned back in his incredibly comfortable seat and marveled at the variety of wood all in one space. Wow. There was mahogany, oak, walnut, and cherry.

I gave up on my fantasy of being a bigwig and opened the top right drawer but there was no wallet. I tried the next drawer to no avail. The bottom drawer was locked so I tried the top center drawer. Still no wallet. I sure didn't want to be blamed for a missing billfold and so was determined to find it.

There was a small key in the top left drawer of his enormous desk but I hesitated to unlock a drawer without permission. Of course, if I had left a wallet in an open office, I would probably want to keep it safe. Maybe he had forgotten to tell me it was in there. The campanile chimed its noon signal and I smiled.

I tried the key in the bottom drawer. Click. It unlocked. I opened the drawer, expecting to find his wallet safe and sound. Instead, there was a lone earring. An earring just like the one I had found the night Fiona was murdered.

CHAPTER 17

I stared. Did the earrings belong to Debra? If so, why was one in Carter's drawer?

Underneath the earring lay a newspaper clipping. I unfolded it and immediately recognized the photo as the same one from the groundbreaking ceremony. The big difference in this copy was that it had a big red heart drawn around Fiona and Carter's heads. Beside the drawn heart, in small neatly written red letters were the words, 'Our love is groundbreaking.'

Oh My Gosh! Fiona was Carter's mistress? I had considered it earlier but found the pairing ridiculous. I shook my head, still finding it hard to believe. They did make a striking couple with their dark hair, but she was uppity and stiff, while he was warm and open. If this was true, could Carter have killed Fiona? Did the earrings belong to Fiona? My breath caught. I remembered him asking me about the one I had lying on my desk. Maybe he broke into my studio in search of the matching earring so it wouldn't incriminate him.

Feeling sick, all I wanted to do was leave his office. I quickly returned the clipping and earring to their place in the drawer and locked it. I wiped my fingerprints off the key with my shirt and returned it to the top middle drawer. I rushed to leave, but when I turned the door knob, but it wouldn't open. I twisted as hard as I could, but the 8-foot door was locked from the outside. Did a bank employee realize it was unlocked and secure the office before closing at noon? I pounded on the door, hoping someone would come, but nobody heard me through the heavy solid wood door in the deserted hallway.

I ran to the desk and picked up the phone to call a teller or bank operator to come let me out, but there was no dial tone. I started punching buttons, but none of them connected me to any live line. My heart thumped as my new suspicions grew.

The good news was that I had my cell phone. The bad news was that my battery was at 3%. I called Sarah first, but my call went straight to voicemail. I tried again. This time when the beep came, I left a message. "Sarah! Help me. I'm locked in Carter Fox's office. Call me right away and please find someone to open the door, but not Carter! He may have been involved in Fiona's death. Please help me NOW!!!"

I hung up and fretted over what to do. I waited to call anyone else in case Sarah called back. In my frantic state, I paced around the large office.

I finally dialed 9-1-1, praying I had enough power to explain my situation. Hopefully, the younger dispatcher would answer the phone instead of Ada.

"9-1-1 What is your emergency?" The voice was old and craggy – definitely Ada's. I said in a loud clear rush, "Ada. It's Ande Nilsen. I need you to listen."

She cut me off. "Andrea, is that you? How are you?"

I started, "I'm locked inside Carter Fox's office at Brookings Bank and Trust. Please send Fred Morris to get me out."

"Today is Fred's day off, but I'll leave him a note."

"It's an emergency."

"Are you in any immediate danger?"

I thought about that. "Maybe. I'm not sure, but the bank is closed and I can't get out."

"We'll send someone by to help you soon, honey."

I started to panic. "And tell Fred I have information for him. It's really urgent...." the phone died, and we were disconnected. I hoped Ada would send someone soon.

My heart raced even faster as I scoured the large office for another way out. I walked past the desk and found a bathroom and splashed water on my face to clear my head. My pulse thumped in my ears and I worried I was having a panic attack. How ironic that the man causing my anxiety was sponsoring a health fair only a few blocks away.

When reaching for a paper towel, I knocked a pill bottle from the sink ledge into the trash. I bent over and read the label. The prescription was made out to Debra Fox – 'To use as needed for sleep.' Why would she need to sleep in his office? Wait. Sleeping pills? Oh my. I used the paper towel to pick up the bottle and stuck it inside my pocket.

I scoured the rest of the room and as expected, the windows couldn't open. I didn't want to break one to escape but kept the idea in the back of my mind if somebody didn't come soon.

Here I was, locked inside Carter's office, knowing he could have killed Fiona. It was all too much for me. I screamed aloud in despair not worrying about what anyone thought. Besides, wasn't that the point? If someone heard me, I might be rescued.

Back at the door, I yelled and pounded as hard as I could. What did that accomplish? Just a hoarse voice and bruised palms. Nobody could hear me.

Just as I'd given up hope and had practically worn a rut in the floor from pacing, the latch clicked. I ran to the door to greet my rescuers, but the person coming through the door was Debra Fox. Oh well. She was better than nobody.

"Oh, Debra! Thank you so much for finding me. I've been stuck in here forever."

I ran to the desk and grabbed my phone and purse to leave. Instead of opening the door wide for me to leave, the woman closed it behind her and said, "You're not going anywhere."

I said, "Wait, don't let that shut behind you, it could lock again." But the look on her face was pure evil. Had she just said I wasn't going anywhere? I was so confused and realized she must be in another jealous mood.

I calmly explained, "I just came to get your husband's wallet. He needed it to pay his vendors and asked me to come, but I couldn't find it. Then when I gave up and tried to leave, the door locked and I've been trapped."

She smirked. "Who do you think locked the door?"

My eyes widened. "You locked me in here? I promise I don't want your husband. He's all yours. I would never...."

She scoffed, "I know that. But I also know you are snooping around where you don't belong. Carter and I will soon take care of you once and for all."

My mouth went dry. I had trouble piecing this together. So, my theory about Carter was right? And now I find that Debra was in on all of it too. Why hadn't I suspected them before?

I took a deep breath and said boldly, "What's next? Are you going to kill me?" I scrambled for a way out. "Listen, I already called the police. And my friend knows everything too. I told her I think Carter was involved in Fiona's murder."

She cackled and said with a superior air, "Oh, your friend won't be causing any problems. Carter has seen to that. And don't worry about the police. Even though I cut the phone lines, I heard your call to the police through the speaker." She pointed to a small round camera on the bookshelf. "I just called that old bat, Ada, and told her I'd gotten you out of the locked office, so the police will not be coming to rescue you. Nobody will."

Although I was upset that the police wouldn't be coming, the statement that hit me the hardest was the one about Sarah. What had Fox done to her? I frantically looked for a way to escape but there was nowhere to go. As I studied the scene, I realized as far as I could see, Debra didn't have a weapon. I had to think of a way to distract her so I could escape.

I made an impromptu plan and moved back a few feet, hoping she would come toward me. She took a step forward, pulling a roll of duct tape from behind her back. She said, "My lord, you are a stupid girl. You might as well give up. This isn't going to end well for you. I'm going to take you on a little ride in my Mercedes."

As soon as she moved one step closer, I dropped my purse and bent down to pick it up. When I did, I pulled on the rug that had slipped last week. I yanked it hard enough to make her slide forward and lose her balance. When she fell to the side I ran past her to the door, but it was locked – this time from the inside.

Behind me, I could hear her scrambling to her feet, but I managed to unlock the door just in time. Once it was open, I rushed into the hallway and took off running at full speed to the Bank's big front door and escaped into the sunlight.

I ran around the building expecting Debra to be right behind me. She appeared, but in her high heels, she was no match for me in my trainers. Where should I go? Sarah! Of course, I had to find her. I raced across Main Street and headed to the rec center.

I entered the same door we had gone in earlier and found that most people were taking down their booths and very few visitors were around. I scanned the room for any sign of Sarah but couldn't see her. I did however spot the guy she had been talking to. I ran towards him and puffed, "Sam, have... you... seen... Sarah?" I leaned over trying to catch my breath, all the while watching behind me for Debra.

He looked at me as if I was speaking another language. And said, "Are you OK? Shall I take your blood pressure?"

I grabbed his shirt and said, "I'm fine. Please tell me where Sarah went."

He furrowed his brow and said, "Well, after you left, this man said he needed to talk to her. She told me she'd just be a minute, but she never came back. I hadn't even gotten her phone number yet. Guess she wasn't that interested."

I didn't have time to argue that. "Which way did they go?"

He pointed to a door. "Over by the basketball end line."

I said, "Thanks, Sam," and ran to the area where he had pointed and hid in the hallway. I peeked around the corner just as Debra entered through the main doors.

I searched the short hallway and found one door on each side. I tried the doors, but both were locked. I yelled, "Sarah?" There was a clunking sound behind one door, so I knocked on it. When I heard a muffled scream, panic set in again. Sarah was locked in there and it sounded like she couldn't speak. I called through the doorjamb – "Sarah, are you OK?"

She mumbled something unrecognizable. Was she gagged and tied? At least she was alive. I said, "I'm going to get help. Stay put!" I figured I'd never hear the end of that comment since it was impossible for her to go anywhere. I just prayed we both lived long enough for her to chide me over it.

I peeked out from the alcove and saw Debra standing beside Carter flailing her hands around as if she was explaining how I'd gotten away. He didn't look pleased, but she was downright furious. Dang. Why hadn't I charged my phone last night? I had to call the police back even if they thought I was a nutcase calling again about yet another locked door.

The couple continued to argue, but when Carter pointed my way, I ducked back, praying he hadn't seen me.

I peeked through the opening. Carter shook his head and took off toward the front door. Debra was busy talking to a vendor. While her back was to me, I tried to get Sam's attention. He was wrapping up cords from his medical equipment and didn't look my way. Just then, the Cub Scouts I'd seen earlier started bouncing a basketball near me.

I said, "Psst. Boys."

One of them turned and stared, then gave a little smile when he recognized me. I motioned for him to come. He got his buddy and they joined me in the small space.

"Boys. I need your help. Do either of you have a cell phone?"

They shook their heads and one boy said, "We're only eight."

I said, "Right. That's OK. Do you see that man over there with red hair? He's standing at a blue booth that says, blood pressure?"

The boys nodded. "Can you go get him for me? Just tell him Sarah needs him right now. It's a big secret from the lady in the green dress." I pointed to Debra. "You'll really be helping your community by doing this. It's super, super important." I reached my hand in my purse and held out a $20. "And this is for popcorn. Just eat it yourselves."

The shorter boy took the money and gave a huge smile. "So it's like a surprise party?"

I said, "Sort of. Sure."

The boys shrugged and walked towards Sam. I crossed my fingers hoping they would follow my directions. Just as they passed Debra, she grabbed one of the boys by the arm hard. I held my breath as the startled boys stared at her. After she spat something at them, they shook their heads and she let go of the boy's arm rather forcefully. Poor kids. I should have known better than to involve innocent children.

I was relieved to see the good little scouts walk straight over to Sam. After they talked to him, he looked my way. Making sure Debra wasn't watching, I motioned for him to come, but held a finger to my lips. I hoped he could tell I wanted him to be quiet. He asked the boys something else and they looked at Debra while they talked. His gaze followed theirs, then he patted them on their heads. When he gave them each something from his table they skipped back to their popcorn booth.

Sam casually lifted a blue plastic tub and headed my way. I watched Debra walk through the booths searching for me.

When Sam got to me, I pulled him through the opening into the hallway and said, "Sarah is locked in this room. I think she's been bound and gagged."

He sputtered, "What?"

I tried to explain without sounding too frenzied. "The woman in the green dress and the man who got Sarah are…well, they're monsters. I can't call the police because my phone is dead. Can you call them and wait here until they get Sarah out?"

"Of course!" He was both unsure and horrified at the same time, but took his phone from his pocket.

Before he dialed, I asked him, "Can I borrow your tub to hide behind so I can escape? I have to stop these killers."

He nodded but wrinkled his nose at the word 'killers' and his fingers hesitated over the dial as if I was cuckoo. But when Sarah made a muffled scream from inside, his eyes widened. He finally realized I was serious and punched in 9-1-1.

I yelled through the crack in the door, "Sarah, Sam is calling the police. I have to go! Listen to my voicemail when you can."

Sam gave the information to the dispatcher as I lifted the big empty bin on my shoulder. I mouthed, "Thank you," to him, entered the gym, and skirted behind the booths to the door. After setting the tub down, I glanced back, thankful to see Debra facing the other way. I left and rushed toward my studio.

I ran the three blocks swiftly, my legs fresh after a short rest. The sweet sound of sirens filled the air and I hoped that meant Sarah would soon be free. I had no idea if the police would apprehend Debra Fox, but my mind was on her husband now.

There was no sign of Carter and my studio looked normal from a distance. But he may have broken in once before and could be lurking somewhere, just waiting to pounce.

As I approached Davis's flower shop, I got a crazy idea and slipped inside. Davis whistled as he worked on an arrangement. He said in surprise, "Hi, Ande. Did you get the video file?"

I said, "No, my phone died." I was getting ready to tell him my plan but had to ask, "Could you see who it was?"

He said, "Well, it was pretty blurry and hard to know for sure, but it almost looked like it was Mayor Fox." Davis shook his head as if that was crazy.

"Davis. It was him! He's dangerous and I need your help."

After I told Davis my plan, I rushed across the street, expertly hopscotching my way, in order to avoid the new craters in the road. I tried to steady my breathing as I got to my studio. The locks were intact and I was able to use my new keys to open the door. Once inside, I plugged in my phone, ran past Flash, and said, "Get ready for a showdown."

I bolted for the stairs taking the steps two at a time and started looking for something weapon-like to distract Carter. Kitchen knives were a possibility, but I wanted more of a bang — not a gun of course, but something with flare. I had an epiphany and ran back downstairs with my find.

I peeked behind my shades to see if Davis was in position across the street. Whew. The lights were off — his cue that all was going according to plan. My nerves quieted a bit knowing I might have backup for my crazy plan if Carter actually showed up.

I unlocked the door and waited beside my desk for the doorknob to turn. I prayed that he wouldn't be packing heat when he arrived, but chances were good he really wanted to get rid of me. The wait was awful. My hand hovered over the phone in anticipation.

Finally, there was a creak and the door opened. My stomach churned as I watched a brown dress shoe emerge. I gulped. Carter was actually coming for me. I quickly tapped record on my voice recorder app then pulled up the home screen so he wouldn't notice he was being recorded.

The next thing I saw was Carter's face, but it wasn't the handsome, friendly one I was used to seeing. His features were contorted in an ugly mixture of anger and hate.

He stepped inside and closed the door behind him. I couldn't see a gun or any other weapon, but this man excelled at concealing the truth, so he could certainly hide other things.

When I spoke, my voice sounded shaky. "I figured you would come. But if you think I'm the only one who can identify you, you're wrong." He took a step toward me. With more controlled force I said, "Your life as you know it is over, Mr. Fox."

He laughed a hideous laugh like a supervillain might, and ran his hand through his thick hair. He took another step. It felt especially eerie because he didn't say a word.

I stood my ground and said, "What? Are you going to try to get rid of me now? I hope you realize the police are arresting Debra as we speak." I didn't know this for a fact but I hoped it was true.

His lip curled up and he finally spoke, "I highly doubt that since she just texted me from the health fair. Your friend, Sarah, may not be found for days."

I nearly fainted at that comment. Had the police not shown up? Had Sarah been taken for a ride in Debra's Mercedes? I studied his face to determine if he was lying, but he looked right into my eyes and didn't blink. His wife was still free? This was awful, but I couldn't risk showing him my fear.

He said calmly, "I need your phone with the video from your flower friend." That didn't make sense to me. Davis would have a copy of it anyway unless Fox had gotten to him first. Although that new thought freaked me out and the man standing in front of me was terrifying, I wasn't about to give up yet. I had to try and get an admission of guilt from him. "Carter, please tell me why you killed Fiona Pratt."

He closed his eyes. "I'm not falling for that. Not confessing anything to you. Give me the phone. Now!...my dear."

This time when he said, 'my dear' my stomach soured. Why had I fallen for his nice guy routine?

I lifted my chin. "Let me guess…Debra found out about your affair with Fiona and was going to cut off your allowance. Then poor Carter would lose his cushy lifestyle. So you got rid of the problem by poisoning Fiona."

He swallowed and shook his head, but something told me his confidence was faltering. When he didn't say anything, I continued guessing. "Maybe you used city money in some sort of kick-back to hire your girlfriend and had to kill her to keep her from telling anyone. Cause then you would be fired."

I waited for him to admit to that one. When he didn't, another idea popped into my head. I tried again. "Or…maybe Fiona broke up with you and you killed her out of spite?"

At that, he broke his silence with a scoff. "She broke up with me?" He chuckled. "I don't think so."

I had hit a nerve even though I had no idea which scenario if any, was right. He took another step toward me and just as I feared, he pulled out a gun from his jacket. My breath caught and chills went down my back as he pointed the gun at me.

He growled, "You should have just stayed out of it and let Fred Morris do his job. He is clueless."

Now that a gun was aimed at me, I changed my approach. "Listen, Carter, you don't have to do this. I was only guessing." I scrambled to think of another scenario that might exonerate him and perhaps calm him down. I considered his wife's deep-seated jealousy. "Wait. Maybe you didn't kill Fiona at all? Did Debra find out about the affair? Did she kill her?"

When he bit the inside of his cheek and blinked, I realized I was on the right track and continued. "Was that Debra's earring I found at the coffee shop? Did you come in here to try to find it? Are you covering up for your wife?"

At my latest theory, Carter's eyes glistened, but his gun remained aimed my way. I went the sympathetic route with as warm a tone as I could muster. "If that's true and you didn't help with the murder, you wouldn't get charged with murder. After all, you were just trying to protect your wife. But even if you wrote me that threatening note, you have to let me go, or things will be much worse for you."

When his gun lowered a tiny bit and his face softened, I was finally able to breathe. Instead of just being quiet, I said, "I still don't understand why you chose me to frame for the murder. I never did anything to you."

His chest rose and fell in one big breath. Why didn't he answer me or put the gun down? Not knowing what else to say, I stammered a question that had nagged at me. "Who was at Spinners last week to hear my conversation about Fiona?"

Finally, he opened his mouth. "You may think you know everyone in town, but I guess you don't."

He continued with a laugh, "And nobody believes you were framed. All evidence points to you and it will stay that way if you do two things: give me the phone and the earring. You can go to prison and get released in no time for good behavior. Your other option lies at the end of this gun."

He clicked the safety off. I closed my eyes and sucked in a breath, readying myself for a real gunshot this time.

I froze, wondering how to get out of the situation, when in a bizarre move, Flash broke the silence by making his obnoxiously loud door buzz sound.

Carter swung around to see who was at the door. While he was distracted, I took the chance and threw a bag of the color-run powder at him, catching him by surprise. As the blue powder exploded on his head, I threw a second bag and a cloud of pink covered him. He waved the gun around, trying to see through the powdery billow.

With my captor thoroughly befuddled, I leaped past him to the door. I turned back and threw the final bag, pelting him on his shoulder. Amid a burst of yellow powder, he pivoted in fury and fired his gun wildly. The bullet missed me but shattered my window. Propelled by fear, I opened the door and ran outside.

I nearly cried to see my plan in full effect. The crowd must have gathered in the last few minutes. All the Main Street business owners stood in a huge circle on the street, some with guns pointed at the door. Davis led the crew holding a pair of floral scissors as his weapon of choice.

Doc and Jon stood beside Mike and Leo, all armed with weapons ranging from handguns to shotguns. Peggy and Marla stood on the outer edge with phone cameras recording the whole scene. I was happy to see James in the group. Even Stan leaned on crutches lending his moral support.

In a surprise addition, rescue dogs were scattered in the mix along with their handlers, one of which was Joy. The most shocking person in attendance was Gary who stood shovel in hand, wearing a menacing expression. This whole thing proves that news travels at the speed of light in a small town and that vigilante justice is alive and well, at least to protect this small-town photographer.

I stood to the side of my door, shaking from the adrenaline rush when Carter Fox exited my studio rubbing his eyes. He looked like a colorful clown with his hair and clothing covered in pink, blue, and yellow.

When the soon-to-be ex-mayor darted to the side to escape, a German Shepherd growled ferociously which caused him to run the other way. Unfortunately for him, a small poodle bit his pant leg which caused the same reaction. Carter finally rubbed his eyes and looked up at the crowd. When he fully registered the scene, he lowered his head and then tossed his gun on the ground, seeing no way out of the situation. Doc and Jon grabbed hold of his arms while Leo took possession of the loose weapon.

The timing couldn't have been better when Fred's police cruiser pulled up. Of course, the extreme rule-follower had to back into a legal parking space, which took a few extra moments. I felt a flood of relief when Sarah hopped from the passenger seat and waved at me. Fred turned to someone sitting behind him. I strained to see who it was when the face turned towards the window. It was Debra Fox. A smug smile crept on my face to see her in custody.

Sarah ran to me and said, "Ande, are you alright?"

"Yes. What about you?" I scanned her but didn't see any obvious injuries.

She said, "Just a few bruises." She held up her hands to show the rope burns on her wrists. She asked, "Did my trick work? I used Debra's phone to text Carter. I didn't want him to know his wife had been arrested."

I nodded. "Oh, yes! You were brilliant! Thank you!" I didn't tell her it had tricked me too and caused me panic. I hugged her and said, "Can you believe we were both locked in rooms today?"

"Yeah. It was terrifying. I got your message, but not until I had been released. I'm sorry I didn't come to save you as you did for me, but my special knife tool and my phone were in my purse across the room so I was stuck with no way out." She pouted.

I squeezed her hand. "It's OK. I'm pretty sure you would have rescued me if you weren't bound and gagged."

"Yeah, and I loved how you told me to stay put!"

I knew she would bring that up and laughed. "Well, I'm still shaking from my own encounter." I pointed to my door.

"Your window is broken! What happened? Where did all these people come from? And why is the mayor so colorful?"

I waved her off and said, "Ahh, nothing much has been happening here. Carter Fox shot at me and hit the window. I doused him with colored powder. Flash saved my life. And these people and dogs contained him. Just normal Saturday stuff."

Her eyes widened with each detail. My blood pressure lowered as I recounted the horrendous event in a lighter tone.

Fred finally exited his vehicle, straightened his hat, patted his gun and walked briskly to Carter. He read the Miranda Warning out loud for everyone to hear, then he handcuffed him in a showy manner. He escorted him to the police car and seated him by Debra. Once they were locked in the car, Fred strutted over to me with more confidence than I had seen since his Pierre counterpart arrived. Where was Joe Cool anyway?

He said, "Miss Nilsen. It looks like you assisted in the apprehension of the real culprits. Thank you for your service to the great city of Brookings."

I shrugged. "I kind of just stumbled into the whole thing."

He straightened and said, "Keep in mind you could have been injured, so next time leave it to the professionals."

I would have rolled my eyes but I was so happy everyone was safe that I let it go.

Fred said, "You should probably thank Ada. She recognized Mrs. Fox's voice when she canceled your plea for help, then alerted me about your problem. By the time I heard about Ms. Anderson being held captive at the rec center, I put two and two together and was on high alert."

Surprised, I joked, "So, Ada actually wore her hearing aids?"

My eyes met Fred's underneath his hat and I thought I caught a slight twinkle at the comment, but it faded fast as he said, "You understand I'll need to get a formal statement from you."

My shoulders slumped in exhaustion and I pleaded. "Do I have to come to the station right now? Any chance I could wait until tomorrow or at least later today?"

He glanced at Carter Fox, who was crying in the back seat of the squad car. "That is acceptable. Meanwhile, I'll work on getting a confession from one, or both of these two. You can give your statement in the morning."

My relief was so great that tears filled my eyes. I said, "Hold on a second. I have something for you." I ran inside the studio and retrieved my evidence and made my way back to the officer.

"Here, take my phone. I recorded my stand-off with Carter. There is also a video from Davis showing him breaking into my studio. Maybe it will give you some proof you need." I pulled the pills from my pocket. "This is a bottle of sleeping pills I found in the mayor's office today." I handed the wrapped bottle to him. "And this is an earring I found outside Viking coffee the night Fiona died. It belongs to Debra Fox. There is matching one locked in Carter Fox's office desk drawer."

He squinted at me. "You withheld evidence?"

Of course, that was what he got from my special display. I shrugged and gave him a half-truth. "At the time, I thought it belonged to Marla."

Fred twisted his mouth in dismay, but he took my stash. "I expect to see you at the station first thing in the morning."

I let out a big sigh and said, "I will be there."

As he started to turn away Sarah lunged forward and gave his arm a hug. He pulled away in surprise and turned to her with his nose scrunched up comically.

She said, "Thank you for rescuing me. You're my hero."

His face turned red. He was rattled and speechless. Finally, he cleared his throat and said, "It is my duty to help those in need."

Before Fred got very far, I said, "Where is the big shot, Detective Jones?"

He turned and his lip curled just a tiny bit before he said, "He is interviewing people at the rec center to see if anyone knows anything." He stood taller and walked away.

Sarah shook her head. "Ande, I wish you had seen him. Fred really took charge. I was impressed with how quickly he took down Debra as she bolted from the rec center. He became a different person. He must work out or something."

I stared at Sarah. "That's incredible. Wait, do you have a crush on Fred Morris?"

"Oh heck no. But I may stop calling him Barney Fife."

We walked to our large group of friends who were still congregated on the street buzzing with excitement. I noticed a new face had joined the group. It was the young doctor, Sam, from the health fair. Sarah gave him a shy wave that he returned.

Questions flew at us, "Did the mayor really pull a gun on you?" "How did you know the murderer was Carter Fox?" "What was that powder?" "Which one of you was locked in a room?" "Did the mayor actually kill Fiona?"

I started to answer, but said, "Thank you all so much for apprehending Carter Fox. I promise we'll get to your questions, but I want something first."

Doc smirked and said, "A beer, right?"

Everyone laughed, but I nodded, "Yes! A beer with friends. And I'm buying. I'll meet you at Spinners."

I watched the group turn to leave and yelled, "Sit outside so the dogs can come too. I'll be down in a few."

Davis led the group down the street. The voices, especially Leo and Mike's, were loud as they talked about the whole ordeal. What a crazy crew.

Besides my immediate circle of friends, two other people hung back. One was the blond girl I couldn't place from the Fox photo shoot. Next to her stood Karen.

I held up a finger to my buddies and walked over to the two. "So Karen, you witnessed the whole thing? I'm sorry your bosses got arrested." I grimaced. "But, it was either them or me."

She shook her head. "It's just terrible, but am not as shocked as you may think. There was another reason the Foxes left The Cities." She took a deep breath. "Debra was so insanely jealous of any woman who gave Carter attention that she actually attacked one of his coworkers who befriended him at his Minneapolis bank. Debra was charged with aggravated assault. Carter thought it might help to be in a smaller town." She hung her head. "I certainly didn't think Debra had it in her to kill though."

I put my hand on Karen's shoulder. "It's just awful. Who do you think will take care of the twins?"

She sighed. "Oh, I will. It's been in the directives since Simon and Simone were born. If anything happens to me, they will go to one of the sisters."

I shook my head just thinking of it all but felt grateful the kids would be raised by this kind, caring woman.

The young girl spoke up timidly. "Hi. I'm Jenny Fox, Carter's niece. I feel just awful. I think I'm to blame for the whole thing." She started to weep and Karen and I stared at her.

She continued. "When Uncle Carter and Aunt Debra moved to town, she took me aside and said if I would be her eyes and ears, she would pay my rent. My own dad said since I didn't work hard enough to get a scholarship, I had to pay my own way. So, I welcomed Aunt Debra's help."

I was stunned. Karen said, "Jenny. Why didn't you tell me?"

The girl shrugged. I sure didn't know about Debra's arrest in Minneapolis and when my aunt started giving me hundreds of dollars a month, I felt obligated to help her. She called me every week to ask what I knew regarding my uncle and any woman."

I felt sick for the poor girl but wanted to know more. I nodded for her to go on.

"So, when I saw Uncle Carter with that Fiona lady, I told my aunt about it. She was obsessed and wanted to know every single thing about Fiona. Then last week when I overheard your group in Spinners talking about her, I listened in." She hung her head.

I instantly pictured the blond girl wearing a Spinner's t-shirt carrying mugs of beer and nodded to myself. So she was the spy.

Jenny continued. "First, the coffee shop lady said Fiona only drank the sassafras tea that was in the refrigerator." She started to cry but continued between sobs. "Then you…" She pointed to me, "…said you were going to take care of the situation."

Jenny put her head in her hands. "I didn't think it was important information but I told Debra everything I heard. I never dreamed she would hurt anyone! Honestly, I didn't."

That answered a lot of my questions. Karen put her arm around the girl. "Jenny, we should go to the police station and give them a statement. And don't worry, I'll take care of you and some of your expenses from now on with no spying required."

I held out my hand to Jenny and said, "Thank you for coming forward and telling me."

I wasn't sure how I felt as I watched the two women walk away. It was all so unbelievable.

My group had been watching the interaction. Once I was alone, they each gave me a hug. First Sarah, then Doc, then Jon, and finally James.

I said, "I need to check on Flash and thank him for his help. I'll fill you in on the latest news in a second. I'll be right back."

This time as I entered my studio, I stopped to breathe and take in the huge mess on my floor. The mix of colors was actually beautiful. I would have to show it to Jon and ask him to replicate my multi-colored mess for a crazy new backdrop. I walked through the powder to get my purse and stopped by the birdcage.

My silly parrot now had some pink and blue added to his green and yellow colors, looking a bit like a cartoon character. While he stood on one leg to preen, I said, "You are the best friend a girl could have. You really nailed the door buzz at just the perfect time." I grabbed my camera and snapped a few pictures of colorful Flash before he could clean off his feathers completely.

I said, "I love you, Flash."

He said, "Say cheese."

I laughed at the goofy bird, but just before I closed the door to meet my friends, Flash sang out, "I love you."

The End

About the Author

Martha Kemm Landes is a native Tulsan and former public school music teacher who wrote numerous musicals and hundreds of songs for her students while teaching music in Oklahoma. She is most known for writing <u>Oklahoma, My Native Land</u>, the state children's song of Oklahoma.

Martha lived in South Dakota for five years where she worked as a community coach. In that position, she traveled the state and met amazing people while soaking up the fascinating culture. She enjoyed capturing the beauty of the lovely state of South Dakota through her photography.

After retiring early, Martha and her screenwriter husband moved to New Mexico. They live with three adopted dogs just outside of Albuquerque and spend time at their log cabin in the nearby Jemez Mountains. Besides writing mystery novels, Martha travels extensively, makes quilts, and volunteers by delivering Meals on Wheels.

Scan for a quick link to the website